*Peace Comes to Honeyfield*

*By Anna Jacobs*

THE HONEYFIELD SERIES

The Honeyfield Bequest

A Stranger in Honeyfield

Peace Comes to Honeyfield

THE PEPPERCORN STREET SERIES

Peppercorn Street

Cinnamon Gardens

Saffron Lane

Bay Tree Cottage

THE HOPE TRILOGY

A Place of Hope

In Search of Hope

A Time for Hope

THE GREYLADIES SERIES

Heir to Greyladies

Mistress of Greyladies

Legacy of Greyladies

THE WILTSHIRE GIRLS SERIES

Cherry Tree Lane

Elm Tree Road

Yew Tree Gardens

Winds of Change

Moving On

# *Peace Comes to Honeyfield*

ANNA JACOBS

Allison & Busby Limited
12 Fitzroy Mews
London W1T 6DW
*allisonandbusby.com*

First published in Great Britain by Allison & Busby in 2018.



A CIP catalogue record for this book is available from the British Library.

First Edition

ISBN 978-0-7490-2045-3

Typeset in 11/16 pt Sabon by
Allison & Busby Ltd.

The paper used for this Allison & Busby publication has been produced from trees that have been legally sourced from well-managed and credibly certified forests.

Printed and bound by
CPI Group (UK) Ltd, Croydon, CR0 4YY

# Chapter One

*London, 11th November 1918*

Georgie Cotterell stole a quick glance at her father's face as she tried to persuade him to change his mind. 'But I only want to go out for a short time to join in the celebrations, and I won't go far, I promise. It's such a special day!'

'No. Definitely not.'

As they stood facing one another, noise from the street echoed into the elegant sitting room: cheers, shouts, laughter, somewhere in the distance a very bad brass band, car horns tooting, every noise you could possibly imagine a crowd of happy people making.

After all the years of war, people were celebrating the Armistice and she wanted desperately to celebrate with them, because like everyone else she was delighted that the war had ended.

His voice softened. 'It won't be safe for you to go out, Georgie. Men can't be trusted to control themselves on such a day, even with respectable young ladies like you.'

The obvious retort escaped her. 'Not so young now, Father. I'm twenty-eight.'

'You've still got time to find a decent chap and get married.'

'I doubt it. How many men have been killed in the war? Hundreds of thousands, you told me once, mostly younger men. So there won't be enough left to go round and they'll be looking for younger, riper fruit than me. I shall be part of a generation of spinsters.'

He sighed and walked across to join her at the window. 'I'm afraid you're right about our losses. The cost of winning has been very high indeed and the pain of recovery will continue for a long time, which is why I continue to be so busy. There are certain people who want the Germans to get off lightly, and others who want to punish them too viciously. I try to put my efforts on the side of fairness and reason.'

She looked at him in surprise. 'You don't often talk about your work.'

'Don't I? Well, the war *is* over now.'

'I'll just go and stand on the doorstep, then,' she pleaded. 'At least I'll feel part of the celebrations if I'm outside.'

'No. I've told you before. Because of my work, I have enemies, and I don't want you lingering on the doorstep even in an exclusive neighbourhood on a day like this. The riff-raff are everywhere and a lot of them will be drunk. The veneer of civilisation can be very thin at such times, I'm afraid.'

'Can't you stay home, then, and we'll celebrate together? I don't know why you have to go to work today.'

'Butterly isn't well. Someone has to be at the helm.'

'Major Butterly seems to be ill rather often lately, and it's always you who has to fill in for him.' She couldn't stand the man. He was not only a fusspot but he made her flesh crawl, for some reason she couldn't work out.

'The man's old. He does his best and he's very good with the paperwork and accounts. Now, I really must get ready to go out, my dear.'

Sure of her obedience, he kissed her forehead and left the room. He would be working in his office till late, even on this special day. He went there most weekends, too.

She'd only come to live here in London with him two years ago and they'd been like two strangers sharing a house, not father and daughter. She'd insisted she wanted to do war work, and not just rolling bandages with a group of gossipy ladies. She wasn't trained as a nurse, but hoped she might be accepted as a driver in the Voluntary Aid Detachment. Her friend Bella had driven ambulances.

But no. Her father said if she became a VAD, she could be sent anywhere in the country at a minute's notice and that wouldn't be safe. Doing *something* to help the war effort had been one of the few times she'd held firm against him, though as usual her father had discovered a way of reaching a compromise. He'd obtained an informal job for her as one of a group of ladies organised by Lady Berrens, a close friend of his, telling her she'd be making a difference without having to leave home.

And indeed, it had been very worthwhile to help ferry wounded officers around London, taking them to hospitals, to see specialist doctors, to visit relatives, whatever was needed to help them in their convalescence. She loved anything connected with motor cars and intended to buy one of her own as soon as vehicles were being produced again for civilians, but hadn't told her father that. She had her own money, after all, and if he objected, she'd just do it.

The main thing that had tempted her to join Lady Berrens' group had been that she'd have to learn how to drive. Her father had been surprisingly helpful about that, even taking her to the Post Office himself to obtain her driving licence and as he paid the five shillings it cost, he joked about how expensive she was.

Then, as she put the licence carefully away in her leather shoulder bag, he had grimaced and spoilt the mood of the day.

'Why do you insist on carrying that huge thing around with you, Georgie? It makes you look like a suffragette. A small, plain handbag would be much more ladylike.'

He wasn't exactly against women getting the vote, she'd give him that, and indeed, he was fairly modern in his attitude towards women, but he disapproved strongly of everything remotely connected with suffragettes, and it was they who had started the fashion for larger handbags.

'A small handbag isn't practical, as I've told you before, Father, and it wouldn't hold even half the things I need for my war work.' Not just her purse, handkerchief and notebook, but a brush, comb and spare hairpins, because her long curly hair would come tumbling down at the slightest provocation. She'd have had it cut short but her father had objected vehemently to that, saying it was her crowning glory.

When he'd added without thinking, 'As it was your mother's,' with a dreamy look in his eyes, Georgie had given in. She knew so little about her real mother, she'd treasured even that small piece of information. She'd pleaded several times for more details of the mother she had never known, who had died after a difficult birth with twins, but he'd stubbornly shaken his head.

It had only taken a few trips to show her how genuinely useful her work was, not just because wounded men needed this sort of help but also because they usually perked up when they were chatting to a young woman who could make them smile. She carried Fry's chocolate cream bars in the handbag her father despised, when she could get them, because they were such a convenient size. She'd never met a soldier who didn't welcome a sweet treat.

She was still staring enviously out at the celebrating crowds, when her father came downstairs again. As she turned round, he stopped in the hall and raised his hand in farewell. She waved back, admiring his trim, upright bearing. He was still a fine figure of a man, even though he was past sixty. He looked younger now she'd persuaded him to stop wearing formal morning clothes and a high, starched wing collar. He was carrying a briefcase as usual, even today, and wearing his 'uniform' of neat, navy-blue suit and felt homburg.

She sat down again, losing herself in thought. Her father had been a distant figure for most of her life and she'd wondered why he stayed away from them. She'd only found out a couple of years ago that she and her twin brother were the offspring of his mistress who'd died in childbirth, not his wife whom they'd thought to be their mother. He must have loved their real mother so deeply, he couldn't bear to talk about her. What else could explain the way he refused even to tell her the name of her mother?

He'd bribed his wife to pass them off as her own and then kept his distance. Georgie now knew that it had been one of his wife's conditions for doing it, that he stay away. A way of punishing him, probably. But he'd wanted to avoid the stain of bastardy for them, because people would ostracise those not born in wedlock.

Life in the country hadn't been too bad when Georgie had her twin to love, but poor Philip had been killed in France and after that she'd felt desperately alone in the world. She was glad when she found out *that woman* wasn't her mother because she'd come to hate her father's wife, who had even tried to trick Georgie out of an inheritance and into a marriage with a scoundrel, wanting the money for her own invalid son.

It had been a relief when Georgie's father rescued her, told her the truth and brought her to live with him in London. Her father's wife was becoming increasingly strange and was now living in a secluded house in the countryside with a stern housekeeper to keep an eye on what she did.

Why did her father continue to refuse to tell her more about her mother, though? It didn't make sense. Well, there must be *some* relatives on her real mother's side who could tell her more and one day she'd find them – she was just as determined about that as he was to keep them secret.

The word 'peace' echoing from the street brought Georgie back to the present. The Armistice, official end of the horrors of war, was to be declared at the eleventh hour of the eleventh day of the eleventh month. She glanced at the clock. When it struck eleven in half an hour's time, she wanted to be with other people, not on her own in this too-quiet house.

She went to the window, looking longingly at the crowds outside. No, she wasn't going to obey her father's ban on joining the celebrations. This was such a special day. It would be something to tell her children about – if she ever had any.

She went back out into the hall, unbolted the front door quietly, so as not to alert Mathers to what she was doing, because he had been manservant to her father for so long, he'd know what his master wanted and try to stop her going out. She stood for a few moments taking it all in. She'd never seen such crowds or felt such happiness. It seemed to surge around her in waves.

Surely she couldn't be in danger in a street as respectable as this? It was daylight, there were people all around and if she wore her VAD raincoat, which was one of her plainer outer garments, and her small felt cloche hat, she'd look like a maidservant on her day off. She could see several young women similarly dressed in the street now, arms linked, cheering and bobbing to and fro in clumsy dances.

Oh, she couldn't bear to be kept out of it, just could not stand it!

Promising herself not to go beyond the end of the street, she put on the raincoat, tightened the belt and left the house, cramming the hat on anyhow, then closing the door quietly behind her.

As she stood at the top of the four steps that led up to the front door a car drove slowly past, loaded with cheering passengers, some sitting on the bonnet or standing on the running boards, where they clung to the edges of the open side windows.

One man held out his hand to her, a mute invitation to join them, but she ignored it. She might be willing to disobey her father occasionally but she wasn't stupid enough to go off with a complete stranger.

He shrugged and gestured to another woman further on, who did jump on to the running board beside him.

After a few moments Georgie ventured down the stone steps. As she stood at the bottom, three young women walked past – or rather danced past – with their arms linked and the one nearest grabbed her hand and dragged her into their line.

At first she allowed it, skipping along with them, but when they reached the end of the street, she decided she'd gone far enough and tugged her arm away. Reluctantly she turned to make her way back to the house. She could still stand outside near her home and watch the merrymakers, after all. Still cheer with them, too.

She didn't know what made her look down the narrow alley at her side of the street, but what she saw had her running down it, yelling for help at the top of her voice.

Patrick Farrell limped along the street, doing his best to avoid being knocked over by the merrymakers who filled it. He was tired and his leg was hurting. Mostly he could manage without that damned walking stick, but he should have brought it with him today.

Sometimes he could ignore the pain, unlike earlier when it had dominated his life and he could only lie in the hospital bed and wait for it to stop throbbing. He shouldn't have come so far, though, and needed to find somewhere to sit down and rest for a few minutes. He doubted he'd be allowed to sit on the steps in front of any of these elegant houses, even on a day like this.

Ah, well, he could manage. The leg was a lot better, though it would never be as good as it had been when he was a lad, running wild. The doctors said he was lucky not to have lost it. He felt lucky even to be alive, given what he'd experienced and seen during the war. Why had he made it through battle after weary battle – Arras, Ypres, Passchendaele – when so many others had died?

Most of the time, he hadn't been able to see what benefit had been gained by spending so many lives on moving a few yards this way, followed by a few yards that way. But then, he wasn't an officer, had only been an acting sergeant, so what did he know about strategy?

A bitter huff of laughter escaped him. Only what he saw with his own eyes, that's what, and no one had ever reckoned he was blind or stupid.

He'd copped a Blighty at the battle of Amiens, and been so weary of killing that he'd been *glad* the leg wound was bad enough for him to be sent home to Britain and discharged from the Army. He'd done his bit for his country, nothing to be ashamed of there. Who cared if he had to limp for the rest of his life? He'd survived, hadn't he?

He pulled out his pocket watch, a bit battered but still a good timekeeper. The war was about to end and he'd been discharged only a few days ago, so he'd not have to wait around for demobilisation like so many others.

Luckily the Army had paid for him to stay in a hostel for a few weeks. He needed that respite to build up his strength.

He raised his hand in response to an older woman with a smiling face sitting in a car waving at everyone, then nodded a greeting to a couple of soldiers in shabby uniforms passing by.

They glanced at his lapel before they smiled back. He fingered the silver war badge he always wore there. He'd been told by the discharge committee to wear it proudly. He didn't know about 'proudly' but he'd damned well earned it, hadn't he? And at the very least it had stopped people looking at him as if he was malingering and ought to be in uniform.

Eh, what was he going to do with himself after he left the hostel? He hadn't worked that out yet. His poor old mam had died last year, so he'd no home to go back to. He doubted he even had any possessions, either. Not if his younger brother had anything to do with it. Hagan had failed the medical and been jealous when Patrick passed it and went off to war. Fancy being jealous of that!

Patrick sighed. He had some money saved, because he wasn't stupid enough to drink all his wages. But there wasn't nearly enough for what he really wanted to do.

Realising he was standing still again and people were having to edge round him, he decided to move a few paces further up the street to where there seemed to be an alley. It'd surely have a wall he could lean against, or even a dustbin or box he could sit on to rest his leg.

That's when he heard the screaming – a woman's voice and it wasn't screaming in pleasure, but in terror. The sound was drowned out by the hubbub in the street, but you couldn't mistake it once you moved out of the melee.

He jerked forward, forgetting his gammy leg and nearly

falling over as it gave way. Steadying himself against the wall, he looked down the alley and saw two women struggling with a big fellow. One of them had her clothing torn and there could be only one reason for that.

Yelling, 'Hoy! Stop it!' at the top of his voice, he set off running, a lopsided gallop, but it still covered the ground.

To his dismay the attacker shoved the women aside and turned towards him, raised fists clenched. Oh, hell! He could hardly stand upright let alone fight his way out of trouble.

But the taller of the two women must have noticed his limp because she came after her attacker rather than picking up her hat or helping her companion, who was desperately scrabbling to set her clothes straight.

The man laughed as he knocked Patrick over then kicked him in the ribs. He raised his foot to kick again, but the woman surprised him by clouting his head from behind with a big handbag and knocking him off balance. Then she picked up a chunk of stone and waved it threateningly.

Patrick tried to get up and someone leant out of a window and yelled that the police were on their way. It couldn't have been true on a day like today, but it did the trick. The attacker cursed and ran off. At the end of the alley, he shoved his way into the crowd and disappeared without any of the joy-makers turning to look what he was running from.

Whoever had yelled closed the window again.

The woman who'd helped Patrick got down on her hands and knees beside him. 'Are you all right? Did he hurt you?'

He forgot himself for a moment as he took in the glory

of hair that had cascaded down when her hat was knocked off. It was beautiful, just beautiful, that dark, gleaming hair was. Then he realised she was waiting for an answer and pulled himself together. 'Yes, I'm fine, thank you.'

She dropped the stone and helped him up.

He tried to joke about it. Sometimes it was joke or weep. 'Fine rescuer I am, eh? I can hardly walk, let alone fight.'

'You still tried and you distracted him. I'm grateful for that. I think you made the difference just by being here.'

He caught sight of the other woman, who was weeping and trying to hold her torn clothes around her upper body. 'I think your friend is more in need of help than me.'

'She's not my friend. I don't know who she is. When I saw her being attacked, I went to help. I thought the man would go away if I ran towards them screaming, but he didn't.' She shuddered. 'He laughed as he grabbed me and said he'd have us both. And he was so strong I couldn't get free. I'd better go and see to her. Don't go away.'

As if he could! His leg and ribs were throbbing and he felt sick with the jabbing pain. He prayed that brute hadn't made his leg worse. He'd had more than enough of doctors and hospitals.

She went back to the other woman, pulled off her own coat and wrapped it round her, then picked up her fallen hat and crammed it on her head anyhow. It was crooked and the hair was still loose about her shoulders.

She guided the weeping stranger back to where Patrick was standing and gave her a little shake. 'Now, calm down. You're all right now. We'll look after you.'

It sounded a bit harsh, but if she hadn't spoken sharply, the other woman might have had full-blown hysterics.

'I'm Georgie Cotterell.' She looked at him, waiting.

'Patrick Farrell.'

They both turned to the other woman, who was still mopping her eyes.

'Rosie Baggett.' She looked down at herself and began sobbing again.

'You're all right now! Do try to stop crying or everyone will stare at us.'

'But he's torn my clothes. They'll go mad at me for that when I get back. I come out without permission, too. I'll lose my place for sure.'

'You're a maid?'

'No, miss. I'm a machinist in a workshop.'

He couldn't help smiling. She'd addressed Georgie as '*miss*' automatically, clearly recognising the voice of authority. He'd lost the habit of kowtowing to anyone. When you fought alongside a man, you didn't care whether he had been a gentleman or a coal heaver in civilian life; you only cared whether he'd hold fast. What had mattered most of all out there had been helping one another stay alive.

Patrick hadn't even wanted to kill the enemy, just to stop them killing him. He reckoned they were probably conscripts, like him, and wishing themselves out of the carnage.

'Where were you going when you came to help us, Mr Farrell?' Georgie asked, keeping an eye on the other woman and patting her back gently a couple of times.

'Nowhere in particular. They turn us out of the hostel during the day if it's fine. I wanted to join in the celebrations, like everyone else. Only I walked a bit too far.' He grimaced and rubbed his leg. It wasn't throbbing as badly now but it still hurt, dammit.

'You're recovering from a wound?'

'Yes. It got me out of the Army as well as bringing me back to England. I've three more weeks in the hostel, then I have to find a job and somewhere else to live.'

'What did you do in the Army?'

'Transport. Mechanic and driver, whichever was needed. Acting sergeant at the end.'

She smiled, such a lovely smile, it made something in him jerk to attention, something that had been quiescent for a good while. A woman like her was way beyond his reach but he could admire her, couldn't he?

'I've been driving too, Mr Farrell, taking wounded men here, there and everywhere in London for the past eighteen months.'

'Wounded officers, no doubt?' No one like her had ever driven him around, that was sure. He'd been crammed into ambulances or into the backs of lorries most of the time.

'Yes. Not other ranks, unfortunately, though they deserved it just as much. Look, we can't stay here. My home is just along the street. If we go there, we can all have a cup of tea. I'll find you something to wear, Rosie, and you can rest that leg, Mr Farrell.'

He hesitated. 'Won't your parents object?'

'No. There's just my father and he works for the government. He's at the bureau even today, though he did leave a little later than usual.' For the first time she wondered why. He was usually so punctual, leaving the house at eight o'clock sharp, much earlier than most people in his position. But she'd heard him using the telephone and talking to Mathers in that quiet voice he used when he didn't want to be overheard.

'Must be an important job.'

'I suppose it is. He never talks about his work, even to me, but it's behind-the-scenes war work.'

'Well, good luck to him. It takes all sorts to win a war. If we hadn't had backup and supplies, we'd have got nowhere.'

Georgie looked at Mr Farrell, really looked this time. He was gaunt and strained, like many of those who'd been in the thick of the fighting and come home injured. But he'd probably be quite good-looking if he were fit and put on a bit of weight. He was tall, with brownish hair of an indeterminate shade that was neither brown nor auburn – rather a nice colour. His eyes were brown, too, and he had a firm, well-shaped nose. He didn't have an educated accent but he wasn't at all servile towards her and she liked that.

It didn't seem right that on a day like this someone who'd been wounded for his country should just be turned out on the streets, so she added, 'We'll have something to eat while we're at it.'

'Thank you, miss. That's very kind,' Rosie looked down at herself. 'This blouse will be good only for the ragbag now, that's for sure.'

Everyone started cheering just then and Georgie glanced at her fob watch. 'Eleven o'clock. The war is officially over.'

A man passing by gave her a quick twirl round, cheered and walked on. He had such a happy smile she didn't feel at all threatened by him.

Two women – one young, one old – stopped to kiss Mr

Farrell's cheek and the older one glanced at his badge and added a thank you for serving his country. Lots of people were embracing one another, strangers or not. That felt odd, but nice.

Georgie didn't know what made her do it, but Mr Farrell looked so haunted that she gave him a hug and kissed his cheek in her turn.

He stared down at her with a slow smile. 'Thank you.' Then he returned her kiss.

He wasn't aiming for her lips but she moved her head and his mouth lay on hers for just a few seconds. She felt hot with embarrassment that he might think she'd done that on purpose.

He pulled back and sucked in a quick breath. 'Sorry. I meant that for your cheek.' He turned and gave Rosie a gentle hug. 'Peace at last, eh?'

She nodded and blew her nose.

Georgie wanted to touch her lips because his had been so warm that she still seemed to feel them on hers. How strange! When her former fiancé, now dead thank goodness, had kissed her, she'd hated it. She would never have got engaged to him if her father's wife hadn't nagged her so unremittingly that it had seemed as if anything would be better than continuing to live with *her*.

'I don't need to trouble you and your family. I can manage to get back to the hostel,' Mr Farrell said.

'The streets are so crowded, you won't find it easy to get anywhere at the moment, and I can see that your leg is still hurting. Much better for us all to go back to my house until things calm down. You must be getting hungry and I know I am.'

He gave a slight shrug, accepting the truth of what she said. 'That's very generous of you, Miss Cotterell. I'd be grateful for a bite, I must say.'

Their eyes met and his were serious, thoughtful, as if he was trying to understand her and her motives. Then he glanced at her lips and gave her another of those faint, apologetic smiles.

She wasn't sure she understood why she was doing this, only that she wanted to help him. Him and all like him who'd put their lives on the line to defend their country, she added hastily in her mind.

# *Chapter Two*

When he left his house, Gerald Cotterell got into the front of the car next to the chauffeur from the bureau. 'Everything all right, Saunders?'

'I'm not sure, sir.'

'Better stop and tell me about it.'

The car slowed down and turned into a quiet side street where there were no revellers and few windows overlooking the street.

'I was told to leave you at the side door to the bureau today, sir. Is that right?'

'Oh? I don't usually go in that way.'

'I know, sir.'

'No other instructions?'

'Not to me. But I lingered a little and heard the major make a phone call. He was very guarded, didn't name any names, but it sounded as if some sort of ambush was being arranged.'

'*Butterly* was arranging that?'

'Yes, sir. Quite surprised me, too. He only usually deals with paperwork. But he was very fidgety all the time you were out yesterday.'

'And there aren't many people around at the bureau today,' Gerald said thoughtfully.

There was a long silence, then Gerald opened the car door. 'I've not stayed alive by taking chances. Tell them you dropped me near the park and I gave you no explanation.'

'You'll be on your own then, sir. Wouldn't you be safer going home?'

'Not this time. I think being among strangers and celebrating the Armistice may be safer today.' He straightened up and closed the car door, raising one hand and walking off briskly, turning into a narrow ginnel between the backs of houses partway along.

The chauffeur sat for a moment, surprised, then set off again. He'd seen some strange things at the bureau, but this was one of the most puzzling.

It took them a few minutes to make their way slowly through the jubilant people to the other end of the street. Georgie kept an eye on Rosie, who might have stopped weeping now but who was shivering from time to time and looking behind her, as if afraid of being attacked again.

She watched Mr Farrell, too. His injured leg was obviously hurting badly but he said nothing, only gritted his teeth and put one foot in front of the other.

When she tried to open the front door, she was surprised to find it locked, so rang the doorbell.

Mathers came to open it. 'I'm sorry if I locked you

out, miss. I thought you were resting in your room.'

'I went outside to share in the celebrations, just in our own street, of course.'

He turned his head, looking down his nose at her companions, so she explained quickly what had happened. But he still didn't step aside.

'You'll need to move to let me bring my friends in.' Mathers could be overprotective of her, encouraged in that by her father, no doubt. He stepped back, thank goodness! She wouldn't have known what to do if he hadn't.

She led the way into the hall and after hesitating, he closed the front door and locked it again, moving quickly to bar the group's way once more.

'I'll take your, um, visitors down to the basement and find them something to eat in the kitchen, shall I, miss?'

'No, thank you, Mathers. I'd rather you brought some food up to the morning room so that the three of us can eat together. Something simple will do. Sandwiches and cake, perhaps?'

She didn't hesitate to offer hospitality because her father seemed to have fewer difficulties in obtaining food for his household than most other families. There were a lot of complaints about the wartime shortages reported in the newspapers. Presumably he got this preferential treatment because of his job and because he sometimes entertained visitors in his study late at night. He had told her to leave these people to him as they were there on bureau business.

As Mathers was still hesitating, she said firmly, 'Mr Farrell put himself in some danger to come to the rescue of Rosie and me, and he's hurt his injured leg as a consequence. Shall we say food in half an hour?'

For a moment she thought Mathers was going to refuse, then he nodded.

'Will you show Mr Farrell into the morning room to wait for me, please, Mathers?' she said crisply. 'I'll take Rosie upstairs and find her something to wear. The scoundrel who attacked her tried to rip her clothes off.'

Mathers flushed. 'Oh. I'll, um, send Nora to help you.'

'No need. I know we're still short-staffed and Nora will have enough to do getting our food ready. I know my way around my own bedroom. I won't be long, Mr Farrell. Don't go away.'

He looked at her and winked, clearly understanding the message that he was to put up with no nonsense from Mathers.

'Thank you, Miss Cotterell. I'm much obliged. It'll be good to rest this leg before I start back.'

Patrick looked round the house appreciatively as he was shown into a room at the back, which contained a table and six chairs near the window, with two easy chairs near the fire. It was, he guessed, a small room to people like these, but it was bigger than the whole of the ground floor had been in his mam's house.

And there was a fire lit here even though no one was using the room at the moment. Miss Cotterell's father definitely wasn't short of money. He limped across and held his hands out to the flames, appreciating the warmth.

Mathers stayed where he was, studying Patrick's silver pin.

'Served in France, did you, Mr Farrell?'

'Yes. I copped one at Amiens. It's taking my leg a while to get better.'

'What rank were you?'

'Acting sergeant.'

The older man nodded and seemed to thaw a little. 'I'll fetch you a cup of tea while you're waiting for Miss Cotterell, if you like.'

'I can wait till the food's served. I don't want to trouble you.'

'No trouble. Nora and I had just brewed ourselves a pot when the doorbell rang.'

He was back within a couple of minutes, by which time Patrick had been unable to resist giving the fire a bit of a poke then sitting in the armchair set temptingly near it.

When Mathers put the cup of tea down on a small table near the armchair, Patrick said, 'Thanks. Much appreciated.'

The older man nodded and vanished again, coming back a few minutes later with a tray of cutlery, small plates and teacups, which he set out on the table.

That amused Patrick, though he hoped he'd hidden it. Doing the meal in style, were they? Was this to overawe him or to show up his table manners? It'd overawe that poor young lass, he was sure. What was she called? Rosie. She was rather scraggy, with a look some people had if they'd never eaten well.

'I brought you another cup of tea, Mr Farrell. These cups don't hold much for a thirsty man.' Mathers deposited it nearby and took the empty cup away as he left.

That surprised Patrick.

He was finishing this second cup – and damned good tea it was, too – when the women came back to join him, with Rosie looking neat and tidy again.

'Oh, good!' Miss Cotterell said. 'Mathers brought you something to drink.'

He couldn't keep the mockery from his voice. 'I think I passed some sort of test by having been wounded in the service of my country. This is my *second* cup.'

She caught the humour at once and gave him a quick grin. 'Very big honour from Mathers. But we all respect what our fighting men have done for us.'

Rosie had said nothing and was still standing by the table. Miss Cotterell turned to her. 'Do come and sit down near the fire.'

'I'd be better in the kitchen like Mr Mathers said, miss, really I would.'

'I prefer you to stay here, if you don't mind.'

Rosie plonked herself down bolt upright on the edge of one of the chairs from the table, leaving the armchairs for the other two.

Patrick turned his head as a maid brought in a tray of sandwiches and little cakes. She looked at Miss Cotterell disapprovingly.

'We can manage now, thank you, Nora. I know how busy you are since Jane left. Did you get a chance to go out and see the celebrations?'

'I didn't want to, miss. I don't need that sort of thing to remember my William.' She turned and spoke directly to Patrick, indicating the food. 'I'm sorry we can't do better for you than this.'

The poor woman looked as if she'd been doing a lot of crying, he thought. 'This will be fine. Did you lose someone close to you in the war?'

'Yes. My fiancé.'

'I'm sorry for that. I lost a lot of good friends.'

Miss Cotterell looked a bit surprised at this frank exchange and when the maid had left, she said, 'I think you've passed some sort of test with Nora as well as with Mathers, Mr Farrell. She doesn't usually talk about her fiancé.'

'I think it's this thing.' He touched the silver badge. 'It comes in useful, can build a bridge between strangers.'

'You earned it, I'm sure. Now, do come and sit at the table.'

He waited till she and Rosie had sat down then did so himself and took a sandwich from the big plate she was offering. He hadn't realised how hungry he was and when she put another sandwich on his plate without asking whether he wanted it, he nodded his thanks.

Even Rosie forgot to be overawed and tucked into the food. It surprised him that their hostess didn't nibble her sandwiches in a ladylike manner but took proper bites. Strange group they were, he thought, as he accepted a third sandwich. Nice of her – Georgie – to bring them here and feed them, though.

Strange, too, that he couldn't think of her as Miss Cotterell, but kept using her first name in his mind. It suited her. A tomboy's name. Her hair had been pinned neatly back again while she was finding a blouse for Rosie, but tendrils were escaping already. He'd love to tug out the hairpins and let it tumble over her shoulders once more.

Oh, hell, he shouldn't be thinking about her like that. She was way out of his reach. What on earth had got into him today? It was a good while since he'd had feelings like that about a woman.

* * *

Once they'd finished eating, Patrick decided it was time he left. His leg was still aching, but he didn't want to impose, so he pushed his chair back and stood up. 'I'd better leave you to get on with your day now, Miss Cotterell.' He hoped she hadn't seen him wince as he put his weight on the leg.

'I'd better go too.' Rosie bounced to her feet.

But Georgie wasn't having that. 'No, please don't leave yet, either of you.'

'Are you sure?' he asked.

'Very sure. Sit down on one of the easy chairs again and have a rest, Mr Farrell. I can see how painful your leg is. It'll still be crowded and noisy out there in the streets, and you don't want to get bumped about.'

He gave in to temptation and eased himself down in the wonderfully comfortable armchair again. 'Well – just for a little while longer.' When Georgie found a footstool for him, he couldn't hold back a sigh of relief as he put his bad leg up on it. It wasn't usually this bad, but that sod had kicked it.

Rosie didn't sit down but began stacking the dirty crockery on the tray Nora had left on a small table near the door.

Georgie let her do it and waited till she'd finished. 'Thank you. Now, come and sit by the fire, Rosie. I want to ask you something.'

'Ooh, miss, I don't want to seem ungrateful but I really should be getting back.' She shot a worried glance at the clock on the mantelpiece. 'They'll have noticed I'm not there by now.'

'You said they'd dismiss you for sneaking out.'

'They probably will, but I'll soon find another job.'

'You're looking shaken up still.'

'I'll be all right, miss. I'm feeling a lot better for having something to eat, thank you very much. It's just . . . well, I panicked when I couldn't stop that horrible man. My family may be poor, but we're respectable and no man has ever . . . you know, grabbed me like that, let alone seen my underwear.' Her face was scarlet by now.

'What does your father do?'

'He works for a carter. He's good with horses, but there isn't always work for him these days because a lot of horses were taken off to war, poor things, and anyway, he says more people are using motor cars. We manage, though, because Mam takes in washing and I give them my wages, and my younger brother brings in some money running errands.'

'What exactly is your job?'

'I've been doing sewing in a workshop, on a machine, but it isn't a nice place to work and we girls have to live in. They treat us like slaves. The workshop had to close today because of the celebrations and the man from the council came round to check that it had, but they still didn't allow us to go out. Mean, I call it unfair too, when everyone else is taking a holiday. I was that mad about it, I climbed out of the back window and on to the outhouse roof.'

Georgie studied her. 'Do you really think they'll sack you?'

Rosie hesitated, then sighed. 'Sure to, miss. I'll be all right, though. Mam will let me sleep on the sofa till I find another job. I just hope Mrs Dashton doesn't keep my spare clothes and things, or I don't know how I'll manage.'

'Who's she?'

'Matron of the workshop. She keeps an eye on the girls and the dormitory.'

'Why would she keep your things?'

'She did that when they sacked another girl. Compensation, she called it, for all they'd taught her.'

'Then I'd better come back with you to get yours and make sure they don't steal them as well.'

Rosie gaped at her. 'You'd do that, miss?'

'Yes. And if you're looking for work, perhaps we can find you a job here. Would you be interested? We're a maid short.'

'Oooh, I'd love it. Only, will your housekeeper agree, miss? I'm not trained as a maid. All I know is sewing and helping Mam with the washing.'

Rosie was proving she wasn't stupid by asking this question, Patrick thought, listening to the conversation with great interest. Georgie had a nice way with her, didn't talk arrogantly to those poorer than her. He'd had officers like that, too. One had been the son of a lord but had spoken to the men beneath him as nice as you like.

'We don't have a housekeeper, Rosie. I manage the house and look after my bedroom myself, because we're short-staffed. We have a daily cleaner and a washerwoman. Mathers and Nora share the other jobs. When Mathers isn't out with my father, that is.'

'Then it'll be your father who has to agree to me working for you? Will he do it?'

'He doesn't usually concern himself with the servants. It'll be all right for me to make the arrangements, I promise you.' She stood up. 'I'll just carry this tray downstairs to the basement and have a word with Mathers and Nora about you. Please don't go, Mr Farrell. I want to ask you something as well.'

As she moved towards the table, Rosie came forward. 'I can take that, miss. I'm feeling a lot better now. You can't beat good food for putting heart into you. And if I'm with you, Mr Mathers and Nora can ask me questions. They'll want to know what I'm like.'

That lass still didn't quite believe she'd get a job here, Patrick guessed.

As the door closed behind them, he leant his head back against the chair and closed his eyes. Just for a few moments.

In the kitchen Georgie explained the situation and both servants studied Rosie, who had stood to one side after she deposited the tray on the side table Nora pointed to.

Rosie studied the two servants just as closely and when Georgie had finished, said, 'I'm a hard worker and I learn quickly. Miss Cotterell won't regret taking me on, I promise you.'

After exchanging glances with Nora, Mathers said, 'We can give it a try, then. You might not like the work, though. Some don't.'

She couldn't hide her amusement. 'I'll like any honest work that pays regular wages, Mr Mathers. Me and my family need to eat.' She hesitated. 'Only, I'd need paying weekly, because otherwise they'll go short.'

'That's perfectly understandable,' Georgie said. 'I'll come with you to pick up your things from the workshop.'

Mathers cleared his throat. 'It'd be better if I went with Rosie, miss. I'll make sure they don't try to cheat her out of her belongings, I promise you. You should stay indoors now. They're still making a racket out there and it'll get worse as the daylight fades. If you don't need me, now would be a good time to go. Shall I show Mr Farrell out first?'

'No, thank you. I want to speak to him about something else.'

He looked doubtful, so she said, 'I'm sure I'll be perfectly safe with him. *He* isn't likely to attack me.'

'I could come and sit with you,' Nora offered.

'Thank you, but there really isn't any need.'

Well, that had gone well, Georgie thought as she went back up to the morning room. Mathers was willing to give Rosie a chance, and from her expression so was Nora. They could definitely do with extra help around the house and the girl had a nice, open look to her face.

But they weren't nearly as sure what to think about Mr Farrell.

She wasn't either. She trusted him instinctively, but he didn't seem to fall neatly into any category of society, which was unusual. He had more of an air of command about him than of servility, for all the way he spoke.

Before Mathers could do anything about Rosie the telephone rang. Mathers went into what had once been the butler's room to answer it, closing the door.

His master's voice said, 'Shhh!' so he cleared his throat. These were signals at both ends that this phone call was not to be discussed with anyone else and voices were to be kept low.

'I've had to leave town suddenly. I can't tell you when I'll be back.'

'Could you give me a hint?'

'*Siebenzeit* are causing trouble again and they seem to

have acquired an unexpected ally. I fear I'm the target of his attention.'

'Oh?'

'Took me by surprise. You know how to contact me, but only if it's desperate. Keep an eye on Georgie. Bring in help if necessary. I may be away a few days.'

'Yes. Right.'

The phone went dead and Mathers hung the earpiece up on the holder, staring at it for a minute or two. This news had come as a shock to him. Not many people knew about this secret pro-German organisation that worked behind the scenes in Britain, but it was part of his master's work at the bureau to keep an eye on them. Surely even these people would now accept that the war was over?

He went back into the kitchen and his worries must have shown on his face, because Nora asked, 'Bad news, Mr Mathers?'

'Yes. Um, a friend has been killed in the very last minutes of the war.'

'Oh, I am sorry.'

'Yes. So am I. Rotten luck, eh?'

He turned to Rosie. 'Well, let's get going.'

# *Chapter Three*

When Georgie got back to the morning room she found Mr Farrell asleep, his exhaustion showing clearly on his face. He wasn't sleeping peacefully, though, but was twitching and restless, as if having bad dreams.

She tried to close the door quietly, but it made a small clicking sound and he jerked awake, fumbling for an imaginary gun.

She saw anxiety flicker briefly in his eyes and said quickly, 'It's only me. Don't get up. I'll join you by the fire.'

By the time she sat down, his expression was calm again. She couldn't help thinking how cosy it would be to sit here with someone and chat quietly. She spent far too much time on her own when she wasn't working, because her father was out a lot, and though she met people when she worked, the women were mostly older and none of them had become close friends.

'How did it go with Rosie?' Patrick asked after a while.

'She must have made a good first impression on Mathers, because he's taking her to where she worked to get her things in case they try to keep them. They sound to be dreadful people.'

'There are plenty like them around, ready to take the last farthing from those weaker than themselves.'

'I was wondering what *you* were intending to do now, what sort of job you were looking for, I mean. Perhaps my father or I could help you?'

'Kind of you to offer. Do you have a job for a mechanic with a gimpy leg?'

'Is that what you want to do, work as a mechanic?'

He shrugged. 'Sort of.'

She leant forward, curious about the expression of longing on his face. 'Do tell me what you'd really like to do?'

'It's not possible.'

'Tell me anyway.'

'Well, all right. I have it all planned in my head. I used to dream about it in the trenches. It helped keep me going.' He looked at her uncertainly.

'Go on.'

'I'd like to have my own workshop, where I could repair cars and motor bikes, sell motor spirit and other bits and pieces.' He smiled. 'The Americans I met call it gasoline and some people in both countries call it petrol, but I prefer "motor spirit".'

'How interesting. Do go on.'

'I'd take on an apprentice, train him to become a mechanic. I did that in the Army, train lads, I mean, and I was good at it. I reckon there's going to be a bright future working with cars for those who can get a start now. Rosie told us her father can't find enough work with horses, and things will only get worse in that area.'

'I agree with you.'

'We're only just getting started with road transport, but it'll be like the railways, change people's lives, and far more than most folk realise. With trains you're tied to the rails; with cars you can go nearly anywhere, and on your own, not in groups.'

'I know. That's one of the reasons why I love driving.'

'You do? There aren't a lot of women who'd say that.'

'I've been driving all over London doing war work, as I told you, but that'll soon be over, I suppose. When things settle down, I'm going to buy my own car and then I'll be free to go where *I* want.'

'That's an unusual ambition for a woman.'

She shrugged. 'I think I must be an unusual woman, because I don't want to spend my life looking after a house, let alone stay indoors most of the time. My father allowed me to join a group of ladies doing war work, but I think that was to keep me from joining the VADs. I'm sure he'll want me to settle down to a quieter life once the war is over.'

Patrick nodded and fell silent. She stole another glimpse at him. For a few moments, as he spoke about his dreams, his eyes had been brighter, and she could understand that. She sat thinking about the picture he'd painted. What he'd said made sense to her and sounded not only interesting but promising as a new type of job. Only it'd probably cost too much for him to set up a workshop from scratch.

'Do you have any money at all, Mr Farrell, if you don't mind me asking?'

'Only what I've saved. And they didn't pay us big wages in the Army, I can tell you. If I start at all, I'll have to start in a small way.'

'I have some money. It's lying idle in a bank but I want to use it to do something interesting. And it's one thing my father can't control.'

He looked at her in puzzlement. 'Your own money? What does that mean? The only money I have is what I've earned, but from what you've said you've never worked for wages.'

'No, I haven't. My grandmother left me an annuity, a sum of money which is invested and pays me interest every quarter. I gained control of it once I passed twenty-five. Before that, it was paid into a bank account in my name, so it mounted up over the years. It's still lying there idle, because it doesn't cost me anything to live with my father. As it's not likely I'll get married, I may use it to travel once the world settles down again.' She added quietly, 'But that's a useless sort of life, isn't it?'

The words escaped Patrick before he could consider what he was saying. 'Why do you think you won't get married? You're a fine-looking woman and not stupid. A man would be lucky to have a wife like you.'

She could feel herself flushing. 'Oh. Well, um, thank you. But consider the effects of the war on women like me. There won't be enough husbands after so many have been killed. I'm not only getting on towards thirty, I'm too opinionated for most people's taste. And I won't play the meek wife, not for anything.'

He managed not to smile. He couldn't imagine her being meek. She was too vivid.

The front door knocker suddenly sounded loudly, as if someone was impatient to get in.

She jumped to her feet. 'What on earth—?'

He got to his feet more slowly. 'Did you say Mathers had gone out?'

'Yes. So I'd better answer the door.'

'I'll come with you. There are a lot of drunks hanging around in the street from the sound of it.'

Before Georgie got to the door, the knocker sounded again.

She saw Mr Farrell pick up a walking stick from the hallstand, clasping it below the curved handle, so that he could use it as a weapon if necessary. Taking a deep breath she unlocked the door, surprised to see Captain Jordan, who worked with her father, accompanied by a soldier.

'Better let us in quickly,' the captain said, interposing his body between her and the street. 'You should stay well back from the door and windows from now on, Miss Cotterell.'

'Why?' Had her father sent him? What on earth was going on? How could she be in danger?

Mr Farrell touched her arm to indicate she should move backwards.

To her surprise the two soldiers followed her inside and the captain locked the front door without asking her permission.

She indicated the morning room down the hall. 'You'd better come and sit down, Captain.'

He turned to the soldier. 'Stay on watch near the front door.'

He came into the room and closed the door but made no attempt to take a seat. 'I've just come from the bureau. We're here about your father, Miss Cotterell.'

She felt her heart lurch with fear. 'What's happened to him?'

'We don't know. He vanished on his way to work, told his driver there was something he had to do and got out of the car. He didn't let anyone know where he was going. Major Butterly is worried about him.'

He walked across to the window. 'Good. You've got wooden internal shutters.' He pulled the shutters across, giving a strange half-light to the room.

She exchanged amazed glances with Mr Farrell. 'What on earth is this about, Captain?'

'Before I say anything else, I'd like to know who your visitor is.'

'A former Army sergeant, who's recovering from an injury.'

'Known him for long, have you?'

She hesitated. 'Well, no. But he saved me and another woman from trouble today, at some risk to himself.'

'What regiment?' the captain asked.

When Patrick told him, he asked about the regiment and his military service in general. He relaxed visibly at Patrick's answers.

She was utterly bewildered by now.

The captain turned back to her. 'Perhaps it would be better if you and Mr Farrell sat down, Miss Cotterell. I need to sort a few things out with you.'

She waited, bracing herself to hear bad news, she didn't know why.

'There was an important meeting this morning, which your father would never have missed voluntarily.'

'Has the driver no idea where Father went?'

'No. He was more than just a driver, of course, but a bodyguard too, as you're no doubt aware.'

She opened her mouth to speak but he held up one hand to stop her.

'An hour ago we received a message from your father, sent anonymously, given to a lad in the street to deliver for sixpence. The lad said a lady gave it to him, but he couldn't describe her very clearly. Your father said he would need to go into hiding as something had cropped up.

'We fear for your father because he's co-ordinating the gathering of some information which will be very useful in the coming peace talks.'

'But the war's over now. Why would my father need to go into hiding?'

'The open war is over, yes. However, there will be skirmishing behind the scenes for years to come, and not just about the peace negotiations. There have been various groups working in secrecy all through the war. Major Butterly thought someone should be assigned to protect you, because they might use you to get at your father, hence my presence here until someone can be assigned.'

She felt a surge of relief that her father was safe.

'Your father might prefer you to go down to Westcott House with men to guard you,' the captain suggested.

'I'll help you work out the best way of getting there. Unfortunately, on a day like today it's not easy to get hold of suitable men to guard you, and I have other pressing duties I can't neglect. You have Mathers here, though, who can definitely be trusted and who is very capable with a gun. Could he be fetched, please, so that I can brief him?'

'He's out of the house at the moment.'

'What? Where has he gone?'

She explained.

The captain scowled. 'Let's hope he gets back soon, then. We won't leave you until he returns.' He studied Patrick as he said that, frowning in thought.

She felt as if the ground was shaking under her feet. How could all this be possible? And was her father really in constant danger? She'd just thought he was being . . . well, fussy and overprotective of her, as fathers of unmarried young women often were.

The silence went on for a long time, then the captain turned to Patrick. 'I wonder if it would be possible for you to stay here until Mathers returns, Farrell? And even afterwards, perhaps. You might be limping but that won't prevent you from firing a revolver. They must have thought well of you to make you up to sergeant.'

'If I can help Miss Cotterell in any way, I shall be glad to do so. And I'm a pretty decent shot, actually. Or I would be if I still had a revolver.'

'Good.'

The captain sounded so relieved at this response that Georgie couldn't help staring.

He turned to her again. 'Do you know where your father keeps his weapons? I'd prefer Mr Farrell to be armed.'

Georgie wasn't going to let them talk about her as if she was so feeble she was unable to help herself. 'I can use a gun, too, Captain. My father made sure of that.'

'Excellent. Perhaps you'd kindly show me what weapons you have in the house? And then carry one with you everywhere you go. You too, Farrell.'

'I can't show you anything. My father wouldn't want any outsider knowing how to get into his gun cabinet let alone what it holds. But I can go into his study and get some weapons out for Mr Farrell and myself.'

The captain looked unhappy with this but nodded and moved back to join his companion in the hall.

Farrell winked at her and followed him into the hall. Somehow *he* gave her more confidence than Jordan, who seemed very much on edge today.

She took out two revolvers and ammunition, then locked the cabinet and secured it again, putting the guns beside her on a small table.

What next? she wondered, staring down at them. Did she trust Jordan? Well, he must be all right if he worked for her father, but you were never quite sure what he was feeling.

For some reason she trusted Patrick absolutely. He had looked so alert from the minute she'd found she might be in danger, almost like a man reborn. That was because he now had a purpose, she guessed. It must be hard for a man to be busy fighting for years and then suddenly have nothing to do with his time.

She loaded her own revolver and tucked it in her belt before calling the men to come in. She gave one to Farrell, who checked it in a way that said he was well aware of how to use it. Then she waited, gun in hand, to find out what the captain thought she should do next.

She wasn't doing anything until Mathers came back and gave his opinion, though. He worked directly for her father, not the bureau, and the two men had been together for a long time. His loyalty was beyond question.

She looked at Jordan and frowned. Mathers was the only man she could say that about. She didn't know anyone from the bureau well enough to pass judgement on them.

She looked across the room at Farrell. He had made a good first impression on her. But she'd still keep her eye on him till she was sure.

Gordon Mathers walked along beside Rosie Baggett, who was still wearing Miss Cotterell's raincoat and a rather squashed old hat of her own. It took them over half an hour to make their way through the crowds to the workshop in a poorer area where Rosie had been employed.

As she indicated that this building was it, she looked apprehensive. 'We girls have to go in the back way.' Even her voice sounded wobbly.

He took one look at the side alley and sighed. Definitely not the sort of place he usually visited. Someone could have swept away the dirt and debris, surely? And those were definitely rat droppings.

Rosie rapped on the back door and the voices inside fell silent. A woman came to see who it was, her cheeks flushed and a smell of port wine wafting from her.

She scowled at Rosie. 'So you've come back, have you? Well, you're not staying. You're fired.'

'I've only come to collect my things. I don't want to stay on here.'

'The cheek of it. After all we've taught you. Couldn't sew a straight seam when you came to us, you couldn't. Well, Miss Impudence, we're keeping them things of yours as compensation for having to train up a new girl.'

Mathers intervened. 'If you don't give Miss Baggett her possessions back, my employer, who will be this young woman's employer from now on, will call in the police and ask them to look into your theft. And since he's a well-respected gentleman who works *with* the police regularly, I rather think they'll take his word against yours that it is a theft.'

A man who hadn't shaved that morning lurched to his feet and came across to join them at the door. 'He's bluffing, Flo.'

Rosie edged closer to Mathers, looking terrified.

The woman looked uneasily from one to the other, then said coaxingly, 'Not worth the trouble of finding out, Skeet. Her things won't bring that much anyway.'

For a moment there was a stand-off, then the man shrugged. 'Do as you please, Flo. But *he* can stay outside while she fetches them.'

His eyes raked Rosie's body so rudely that she whispered to Mathers, 'I'm not going up to the dormitory with Skeet. She makes him stay away from us when we work here, but she'll not help me against him now.'

'It's a good thing Miss Cotterell didn't come back with you. Let's sort this out quickly.'

Skeet stepped forward. 'Come on, Rosie. I'll take you upstairs.' As he reached out for her she let out a shriek.

There was a sudden blur of movement and for all he was the bigger of the two men, Skeet went spinning across the room.

Mrs Dashton backed away from Mathers, who had snatched up a large kitchen knife in the confusion. 'Go and get your things, Rosie. Quick as you can. And you two stay here.'

Rosie ran through a door at the back of the room and Mathers smiled grimly as he stared at Skeet, slapping the blade of the knife against his palm. 'I should think I'm a better fighter than you, especially since you're half-drunk.'

With a growl, Skeet lurched to his feet, but Mrs Dashton rushed across to push him back. 'We don't want no trouble with the police, Skeet. Our master wouldn't like it and that Rosie isn't worth it.'

For a moment all hung in the balance, then Skeet shook his head and sat down again. 'Pity. I'd a fancy to try her out.'

Before Mathers could say or do anything else, the two of them began arguing about his womanising at the tops of their voices.

He was glad when Rosie appeared at the back of the room. She darted across to his side before the other two saw her.

'Got everything, lass?'

'Yes. They'd been through my stuff, but I found my best blouse in her room an' took it back.'

'That's *my* blouse,' Mrs Dashton said at once. 'You're nothing but a thief.'

Mathers raised his voice. 'If you keep insisting it's stolen property, I'll ask my employer to have a word with the police tomorrow. They can be brought in to decide who's the thief.' He stared at her. 'I should think it'll be easy enough to do that, though, because you're twice her size at the top and that blouse won't fit you.'

The matron breathed deeply but she didn't reply, turning instead to start arguing with Skeet again.

'Thank you, Mr Mathers,' Rosie said gratefully. When he gestured to the door, she was out of it like a shot.

'No need to run!' he chided as he followed her. 'They won't come after you once we're away from here because they won't know where to find you.'

She brushed away a tear from her cheek. 'You don't know Skeet. He'll have me followed by one of his lads and then come after me another time. I'd better not go home for a while, either, because I bet he'll send someone to threaten Mam as well.'

'Why would he do all that now you've stopped working there?'

'To keep people frightened of him. Everyone is round here.'

'I'm not.'

But Mathers decided to make sure they weren't being followed, because Mr Cotterell wouldn't want rough folk like Skeet and Mrs Dashton poking their noses into his affairs, especially now.

Once they were a few streets away, he took Rosie into a house on a side street. It was neither big nor small, not remarkable in any way, and the door was in need of painting.

'We'll take a little detour, go in here one way and out another.'

Rosie looked at him anxiously and he smiled. 'It's all right, lass. You don't have to be frightened of me.'

There was a man outside keeping the revellers off the steps. He nodded to Mathers, who stopped to say, 'Little detour needed, Pete, in case we're being followed.'

'Better use the cellar today, sir. There are too many nosey people about, looking for places to burgle.'

'All right. Look snappy, lass. We need to get straight back to Miss Cotterell. And I'll carry that bag for you from now on.'

He led her down some stone steps that took them from the hall to the cellar and the man on duty down there opened a door that led to a passageway under the ground.

The passage was lit by large electric bulbs hanging from the ceiling here and there.

Rosie stared up at them in amazement. 'Fancy using electric lights in a cellar! Must have cost them a fortune.'

'Worth it. Mr Cotterell has electric lights in every room at his London house, yes, and electric table lamps too, but electricity isn't available in the country so he has to use oil lamps there.'

'Fancy. Um – how did you manage to toss Skeet across the room like that, Mr Mathers, if you don't mind me asking? He's a big man.'

'It's a way of fighting I learnt from a good friend. They do it that way in the Orient.'

'I wish I could toss men who annoy me across the room,' she said feelingly. 'I'd have done it a good few times, I can tell you.'

'You're too little to deal with big chaps that way. I'll teach you a few tricks for protecting yourself, though, once things settle down. Now let's save our breath for walking and get back quick as we can.'

# *Chapter Four*

Nora came rushing up to the sitting room door to announce breathlessly, 'I just saw Mathers coming down the back alley with Rosie, miss.'

The captain said curtly, 'I'll go and have a word with him.' He followed Nora down to the basement.

Georgie didn't follow him immediately because she wanted a quick word with Patrick. 'Look, are you sure you don't mind staying with me?'

'Happy to. I'll need to fetch my things from the hostel, though. If I leave them there overnight, they might get stolen. I hope you'll trust me to do my best to protect you, if necessary.'

'I trust you absolutely.' She realised abruptly that she did trust him.

He looked surprised. 'Why?'

'I don't know. I just do.'

'I'll do my very best to deserve your trust. Eh, it's good to feel useful again.'

She nodded. She'd guessed right, then. Fellow feeling. She'd had a taste of feeling truly useful in the last two years and didn't want to give up that sense of satisfaction.

Patrick was still looking at her with a quiet, serious expression on his face. 'Are you all right, Miss Cotterell?'

'A bit bewildered and not sure what's happening, but don't worry. I'm not the sort to panic.'

'No. I saw that when you helped me chase away the fellow who was attacking Rosie.'

Voices floated up from the servants' quarters in the basement and she said suddenly, 'I want to hear what's happened to Rosie. Let's join them.'

She ran lightly down the stairs to the kitchen and Patrick limped after her as quickly as he could. When she turned at the bottom of the stairs to grin at him, he couldn't hold back a chuckle. Eh, she was a lively one. Not the sort to accept being bossed around, from what he'd seen.

Most men wouldn't like that, but he did. He'd seen his mother act as a doormat to the men of her family for years and had often wished she'd damned well stand up for herself.

Georgie reached the kitchen just as Mathers was locking the back door. Rosie was waiting to one side of it, looking anxious.

The captain, who was standing by the back window, asked, 'Are you sure you weren't followed, Mathers?'

'I don't think so, sir. We had a little trouble retrieving Rosie's things, so on the way back, I took one of the official diversions Mr Cotterell uses sometimes. You'll know about those.'

'Yes, of course.' He studied Rosie, seeming mildly surprised by her appearance.

Georgie moved forward. 'This is our new maid. Welcome to our home, Rosie. Nora will find you a bedroom, and start teaching you your duties.'

When the two women had gone upstairs to the attics, the captain turned his attention back to Georgie. 'As I said before, I think your father would want you to go to Westcott, where you can hire people you're sure about to guard you. We need to make plans to get you there.'

'I'll still be needed to drive wounded officers round London for some time yet. I'm not going to neglect my duty.'

'Ah. Well. I had your name taken off the roster of drivers before I came here.'

'*You did what?*'

'You'd be too much at risk, driving round. If they captured you, they could use you to get at your father.'

'I'm still finding it hard to believe all this,' she said quietly. 'And I do not wish to go back to Westcott House. It's been shut up for over a year. It won't be ready for anyone to stay there.'

His voice was soothing, as if he was dealing with a stupid child. 'I'm sure you'll be able to find staff in the village and get the place running again, Miss Cotterell, people you know and trust. That'll pass the time nicely and will be useful to your father.'

'No.'

Patrick was hard put not to smile at how quietly emphatic her voice was and how astounded the captain appeared at this blunt response.

'Miss Cotterell, you do not have a choice,' the captain said earnestly. 'You'll be safer in the country, believe me.'

'Well, I intend to make my own decisions, the first of which is to stay here for a while and see what happens. For all we know, my father may return home tomorrow.'

'You don't have enough staff here to keep you *safe*. And certain people know where you live.'

'Who are they?'

He hesitated, then said, 'I think this may be the work of an organisation called *Siebenzeit*. They have been . . . a nuisance, lately. We're not sure they even recognise that the war has ended, and perhaps for them it never will.'

'Then perhaps I can hire one or two more people to help keep watch here in case of an all-out attack on this house,' she said flippantly.

The captain lost patience at this. 'How would you know they'd be loyal? You might be hiring men who intend to kill your father and yourself, if he won't do as they wish, for all you'd know about them.'

Patrick had a sudden idea and cleared his throat to get their attention. 'Maybe I can help you there. I know one or two chaps at the hostel who're well enough now to help guard Miss Cotterell.'

'Look—' the captain began.

Georgie interrupted. 'Could they be reached by telephone? Perhaps a couple of them could join us here?'

'There is a telephone at the hostel, so some could be reached. I'm not sure exactly who'll be there, mind. Most of the chaps went out celebrating, but like me they'll have found it tiring so they may be back by now. A few didn't feel like celebrating, so even if the porter's out, there will definitely be someone available to take a message.'

'Oh, really, this is ridiculous!' the captain exclaimed.

'You need *able* men to guard you, Miss Cotterell.'

'I need people like Mr Farrell, who was *able* enough to rescue me today,' she snapped. 'Phone your friends, Mr Farrell. I'll pay them whatever you think reasonable for doing this job – and you, too, of course.'

'Thank you. May I use your telephone?'

'Of course. This way.' She took him into her father's study and shut the door on the captain. 'I'd better wait with you in case they have any questions.'

'You're sure about this?' he asked in a low voice.

'I'm sure I trust you. I'm not sure I trust Jordan. I've never liked him.'

'I think liking often has a connection with trust,' he said in his quiet way. 'Though not always. I suggest you suspend judgement on Captain Jordan.'

'And on you?'

'On me, too. Always keep something in reserve.'

Which only made her trust him more, for some strange reason.

Patrick unhooked the earpiece from the holder and waited for the operator to speak. That happened more quickly than he'd expected on a day like this, maybe a benefit of calling from Mr Cotterell's house.

He waited for the operator to put the call through to the hostel. He'd be interested to meet Georgie's father, who sounded to be a remarkable man. Most chaps seemed to be nervous when dealing with important people, but they died as easily as unimportant ones in his experience and after what he'd been through, well, he doubted he'd ever be in much awe of anyone. Maybe only the King and Queen. And he'd not be likely to meet them!

'Barford Hostel.'

He recognised the voice. 'Oh, hello, Thomas. Patrick Farrell here. Is Dennis back yet? . . . Oh, good. Can I speak to him please? I'm sorry to disturb you on such a day but it's very important indeed. There's a chance of a temporary job for him, you see.'

'That'd be good. Hold on a minute, lad.'

He smiled as he waited. The porter at the hostel was a tiny man, shrivelled by his many years. He called all the men staying there 'lad' and did everything he could to help them, winning their respect in many ways, because he was a practical, knowledgeable chap as well as kind.

A breathless younger voice came on the line. 'Dennis here.'

Patrick explained. 'It's just a short job, few days probably, but they'll pay well and maybe have enough influence to help you get a permanent job afterwards, or at least give you references that people will value.'

'I'm in.'

'What about Martin? Do you know where he is? Can you get hold of him and bring him to this address? You should both pack your clothes and leave any other stuff with the porter if you have too much to carry. And could you bring my things too?'

He knew that like him, his friends had lost a lot of their possessions when injured, and didn't own more than would fit into a small bag, but was trying not to embarrass them.

Georgie had a thought and tugged at his sleeve. 'Tell them to get a cab here. I'll pay.'

'Just a minute! If you can find a cab, grab it. Miss Cotterell will pay for it this end. She wants you here quickly. And remember this number. Telephone me here if anything goes wrong.'

Dennis was not noted for lengthy speeches. 'Must be urgent. All right. We'll be as quick as we can.'

Patrick placed the earpiece back on its hook and watched it swing gently to and fro for a few seconds before turning to Georgie. 'They're good lads, those two. Just so you're not shocked: Martin had the side of his face blown away, so he's badly scarred and one ear's mostly missing. It's a wonder he can still hear, but he can. His eyesight is still all right, too.'

'It won't worry me what he looks like.'

'Good. And Dennis has some fingers missing on his right hand as well as a big scar across the side of his forehead. The hand doesn't stop him firing a revolver accurately, but they decided he wasn't fit to be trench fodder any longer and he didn't complain.'

'You've been pals for a while?'

'Not that long. We met at the hostel, but I'd stake my life on them being trustworthy. It forms a bond, being in hospital does, then the hostel, especially for those of us without families. Who else is there to turn to but each other? You'll be well protected with me and them, I promise you. They've got their wits about them, those two have, even though they do look a bit odd.'

'I'm sure I've seen worse when driving men round London. That sort of thing happens to officers too.'

'Yes, of course you will have. That's all right, then. Um, I hope you don't mind me asking, but would you have anything for them to eat when they get here? The food at the hostel isn't up to much.'

'Of course. I'll go and check what's available with Nora. She manages the provisions.'

'I'll come with you. And you've still got your revolver, haven't you?'

'Oh, yes.'

'Better safe than sorry at the moment, eh?'

'Much better.'

The captain was in the kitchen, discussing the state of the nearby streets with Mathers, but there was no sign of Nora.

Georgie turned to Patrick. 'I won't wait for the maid to return. I'm quite capable of making sandwiches.' She went to inspect the pantry and got out some things for making sandwiches, brandishing a tin at him.

'Thank goodness for tins of corned beef!' she said to Patrick as she hunted out a bread knife.

'You slice the loaf, I'll butter it,' he said.

They began working together so efficiently it felt as if they'd done it before. This was yet another thing about her which took him by surprise, how she mucked in. Ladies from her background didn't usually, not the officers' wives he'd met, anyway.

It was an effort not to let his eyes linger on her beautiful hair and soft womanly curves as they worked. He wouldn't insult any woman by staring rudely at her body, but this one was a tidy piece, she was indeed.

When Nora and Rosie came back to join them and offered to take over the food preparation, they went back to the sitting room.

Georgie was annoyed by the way the captain looked down his nose at Patrick and offered only a patronising remark. She turned her back on him and talked directly to Patrick.

'Should we prepare beds for your friends, do you think?'

'Are we staying here?'

'It's what I'd prefer. Even if we do leave, which I'm not sure about yet, we won't be able to go tonight. From the sounds of it, the streets are still full of people.'

The captain joined in. 'My instructions are very clear: you are to be taken to a place of safety as soon as possible. You really should leave this evening.'

She pressed her lips together for a moment or two to stop herself from snapping at him. 'Well, it'll soon be dark and there are still crowds in the streets. Also, we'll need to prepare the car and keep an eye on it overnight.'

'I'll send a mechanic to look it over.'

'Mr Farrell *is* a trained mechanic,' she reminded him.

'I'd rather my chap checks the vehicle and you don't leave till he's done that.'

'It's *not* necessary and I'm not letting anyone near my father's car unless I'm sure of them.' She rang the bell to signify an end to this conversation.

There was a tap on the sitting room door and Nora came in.

'Did you want something, miss?'

'Yes. We have two guards arriving shortly. Which rooms should we prepare?'

'There's only one spare bedroom in the servants' quarters now, miss.'

'At least one of us will need to be in the same part of the house as you,' Patrick pointed out. 'As close to your room as possible.'

'We'll look at the bedrooms on my floor, then. Come on. I'll show you round and you can work out who will go where, since you're in charge of security, Patrick.'

The captain hesitated, then waved them away as if giving them permission to do that.

'That man gets on my nerves,' Georgie muttered as they reached the first floor.

'He hasn't won my liking, either. Enjoys ordering people round too much for my taste.'

She began to fling open doors. 'This is my room, my father's room, and there are two guest rooms on this floor. It's not a big house.'

'Seems big to me.'

She didn't comment on that remark. 'Which room do you want?'

'I'll take the one right next to yours, if that's all right. I'll ask Dennis to sleep near the car and Martin to sleep in the ground floor hall. I noticed a sofa there. We'll all wake at the slightest noise, I promise you.'

'Dennis could sleep *in* the car. He'd be more comfortable.'

'You won't mind?'

'Of course not.'

She took him up to the attic and showed him where the servants slept.

'Rosie will probably think she's in heaven with a room of her own,' he murmured. 'It was kind of you to give her a job.'

'We need her help.' She paused by the biggest bedroom in the attic. 'I think Mathers might want to share the watch-keeping with you. He can be responsible for this top floor, perhaps. I know he has a revolver.'

'Be better if you suggest that to him than me.'

She didn't pretend not to understand why he said that. 'I suppose so. I'm not looking forward to going back to everyone keeping to their own class as the war effort winds down. I've met so many interesting people during the last two years of the war.'

He couldn't hide his surprise at that. 'I don't think everyone will go back to the old ways.'

She chuckled. 'I can't see *you* kowtowing to anyone, for a start.'

'I might have to, to get a job.'

'Well, don't kowtow to me. I can't stand it.'

His scowl vanished and a smile took its place. 'I can't imagine bowing and scraping to you . . . miss.'

'See that you don't . . . Mr—oh, it's no good. I can't think of you as Mr Farrell.'

'Patrick?' he offered.

'Yes. And I'm Georgie.'

'You're sure? Then it's agreed. Friendships can spark to life very quickly in troublesome times, I've found.'

'If you're lucky enough to find a new friend.'

He nodded, then Mathers came to join them and they went back to discussing the arrangements for keeping watch after the captain and his soldier left.

Mathers was another one who didn't look down his nose at people, once they'd passed his scrutiny. He seemed a steady, quiet chap if Patrick was any judge, but not one to be made a fool of.

When Jordan got back to the bureau, he was called in to Butterly's office.

'What's the news on Cotterell?'

'We've not seen or heard from him.'

'Damnation, the man has a whole set of security records

on key personnel that we can't lay our fingers on. Bad enough that he got permission to do that, even worse that he's now gone missing. Have you no idea what he's done with them?'

'I'm afraid not, sir.'

'Well, when he comes back things are going to change, whoever I have to see to get official permission. What about the daughter? Where have you placed her?'

Jordan sighed. 'I've not placed her anywhere. She's insisting on staying at home, so I've hired some ex-soldiers to guard her. She'll be all right there and—'

'I'm not sure I like that.'

'It's done now, sir.'

'We'll replace them with some of our own men as soon as things settle down tomorrow. Probably by mid-morning. Write down these men's names in your notes.' He waved one hand in dismissal.

Jordan didn't allow himself to frown until he was out of sight. Butterly didn't like to be contradicted in any way and was a stickler for details, but he was in a strange mood today. Better not mention to him that Georgie Cotterell was going down to Westcott. It'd only send the major off into another tirade. The man liked to keep everything under his control, which was why he had trouble with Cotterell, who was only loosely attached to the bureau.

Unfortunately, Jordan didn't know the names of the two men who were coming to help Farrell. Oh well, he'd get them tomorrow. It might be rather later than mid-morning before he could find anyone to replace them with.

## *Chapter Five*

The night passed peacefully, and though Georgie was woken a couple of times by noises outside, when she listened carefully, it turned out to be merely revellers passing the house. There seemed to be nothing disturbing the silence inside the house.

The following morning, however, just as it was starting to get light, there was a tap on her bedroom door and it opened without whoever it was waiting to be invited to come in. She jerked upright in bed, reaching for the gun, but even before he spoke, she realised from the silhouette that it was Patrick.

'It's only me, Georgie. Can you come quickly and look at something?'

'What's wrong?'

'I think there's someone keeping watch on this house at the back. You can't see him from here because your bedroom's at the front, but you can see him from the window of the room I slept in. A few minutes ago, as it started to get light, Dennis looked out from the window of the former stables and saw a man hanging around in the back laneway. He nipped into the house to let Martin know and *he* came up to tell me.'

Georgie was out of bed in an instant, slipping into her dressing gown and ignoring a slight feeling of embarrassment because this was so important. She didn't wait for her slippers but remembered to pick up her revolver before following Patrick into the next room.

They each stood behind the edge of a curtain, peering down at the back lane and yes, there was a man there, mostly hidden in a nearby gateway, but fidgeting so that not only did his shadow move but he showed parts of his body now and then.

'Do you recognise that man? I don't know how long he's been hanging around, but I should guess he'll have been there all night.'

She squinted but couldn't see clearly enough at that distance. 'I think there are some binoculars in Father's study.'

'Can you fetch them? I'll stay on watch here.'

'Yes.' She ran down the stairs, waving one hand to Martin in the hall. 'Just getting something for Patrick.'

The binoculars were where she'd remembered, so she snatched them and hurried back upstairs to her place near the window.

It took her only seconds to adjust the focus on to the figure huddled in a gateway just along from where her father now parked a car rather than horses. She studied the man's face carefully as he stared along at their stables. 'I feel I've seen that man before, but I'm not sure where – maybe driving

Father to work one day. No, not that. But where?'

She shook her head. 'Mathers is the one you should ask. He goes to the office with Father far more often than I do and would know all the people there. I usually wait for Father in the reception area. You haven't heard Mathers go downstairs yet, have you?'

'No. I'll fetch him. You keep watching.'

When he'd left, Georgie caught sight of herself in the wardrobe mirror and blushed to realise that her dressing gown had fallen open showing the lacy neckline of her nightgown, which was too low to be considered even vaguely respectable. She pulled it up and cinched the belt of the dressing gown more tightly, but didn't take the time to get dressed yet; it was much more important to keep an eye on the watcher.

Mathers arrived, also in a dressing gown, and while Patrick was showing him the man in the back alley, she rushed into her bathroom and flung on the clothes she'd worn the day before.

When she rejoined Patrick, Mathers was still studying the figure at the rear of the house.

'Do you recognise him?'

'Sort of. One of the clerks from your father's office, perhaps, or . . . No! I've got it.' He snapped his fingers. 'It's the son of the caretaker there. He assists his father now and then, cleaning the floors and emptying the rubbish. We didn't feel the need to check him out beyond making sure he was who he claimed, because that caretaker's been with us for years and has been nothing but trustworthy.'

'Is there any reason you can think of for the son to be watching this house?'

'Of course not.'

'Could he be a traitor?'

'I doubt it. He can't possibly have access to important information and he's only at the bureau occasionally. But why is he keeping watch here? It doesn't make sense.'

'Who could have told him to do this?' she wondered aloud. 'And why?'

'Money, I suppose, miss,' Mathers said.

Patrick continued to stare out of the window, thinking aloud. 'They'll continue to watch this place and if her father doesn't return soon, Captain Jordan may come back and insist on taking Miss Cotterell away, claiming it to be "somewhere safe".'

'We need to get her away quickly without them noticing,' Mathers said. 'But how do we do that?'

Farrell seemed to Georgie to stand taller, straighter, and his voice became crisper, more authoritative. 'We'll work something out, but first, let's call Martin and Dennis upstairs to look at that chap through the binoculars so they'll be able to recognise him again.'

Mathers seemed a lot more accepting of Patrick and his friends than the captain had been, Georgie thought, and she'd trust his judgement. 'I think the maids should take a good look at him too. When you're not around, Nora has to answer the door.'

'I'll tell her not to do that on her own from now on,' Mathers said at once.

After the maids had seen the watcher, they got dressed and went to the kitchen to put the kettle on and start breakfast.

Rosie came upstairs again a short time later, breathless

and seeming excited. 'There's a pot of tea brewing in the kitchen, miss. Nora wants to know if you're coming down as usual or whether I should bring up a tray.'

'We'll take it in turns to come down to save you the trouble,' Georgie said.

'If you can wait a minute or two,' Mathers said, 'I'll get dressed then take over the watching here, while you two get something to eat.'

He was frowning and she was sure there was something else on his mind, but what? Did he know where her father was? If anyone did, it'd be him.

Patrick was left on his own with Georgie. 'I meant what I said: you can't stay here. I doubt these people will stop watching this place, even if we chase this chap away, because it's their main link to your father.'

'I agree. But if they see us leave they'll follow us to Westcott. They must know where our country house is.'

'We might be able to trick them into *thinking* they see you leave the house, so they'll follow, then we could perhaps go to Westcott and spend a short time there before moving on somewhere else.'

He stood back to study her. 'If we make you look different, you and I can slip out openly. The trouble is, your clothes are all very expensive and that shows. And your hair's rather distinctive, too. Men will notice it.'

'I think that's a compliment.'

'Definitely.'

Georgie looked at him speculatively. 'Actually, I own a pair of trousers, which I bought when I was going to join the VADs.' She went to fetch them and held them against herself to show him. 'Father threw a fit when I showed them to him, but if I wore them and pinned my hair up under one of his country hats, people might not even realise I'm a woman.' She waited for his answer.

She was rewarded with a quick, speculative glance at her body and a chuckle. 'Good idea. Though you'd only fool people at a distance. You're very . . . um, feminine in shape.'

Mathers came back just then so she hoped her blushes hadn't shown.

Patrick explained their idea to him and she showed him the trousers.

'Your father won't like it, miss. He asked Nora to sneak those trousers out of your room so that he could get rid of them, but she couldn't find them. You must have hidden them well.'

She'd only put them on top of the wardrobe and Nora must have seen them, but Georgie didn't say that. 'I'd just have bought another pair if those had vanished. I've tried wearing them around the house and I must say they're very comfortable to move about in. You men are so lucky.'

Mathers gave the offending garment a disgusted glance. Clearly he shared her father's views on women wearing trousers. 'Hmm. Well, as it happens those things might come in useful today.'

After a moment's thought, he added, 'Perhaps we should let the captain know what we're doing?'

'I'm not giving that man a chance to stop us leaving. I don't intend to spend days, maybe even weeks, shut up in this house or shut up somewhere else he wants to put me. Not only would I go mad from boredom but I'd be a sitting target and eventually these villains would find a way to get at me, I'm sure.'

She picked up the trousers and went next door to her room to put them on. She couldn't help feeling a bit shy as she came back and the two men studied her. It was one thing to consider yourself a modern woman, quite another to wear trousers for the first time in public without a long tunic over them like young women working on the railways and doing other manual jobs wore.

'You might get away with it at a distance,' Patrick said.

Mathers grimaced. 'Yes. You might. And I'm afraid you may be right about the need for a disguise. But I still don't like you going out in public dressed like that.'

'Miss Cotterell's safety must come first,' Patrick said diplomatically. 'We need to work out how to trick anyone watching into thinking they've seen her leave the house and let them follow that person. One of the maids, perhaps?'

'I could ask Rosie to wear your clothes and escort her out of the house myself. If you wouldn't mind lending her some of your older garments, that is, miss?'

'It won't work. I'm much taller than she is.'

'Just try it, miss. You might have something that will fit her.'

Nora was sent for to help Rosie don the disguise and the three women went into Georgie's room.

'What's it like to wear trousers, miss?' Rosie asked.

'It feels a bit strange but they're very comfortable. Never mind that, let's try these on you.' She handed over one of the new shorter skirts, which she hadn't dared wear in front of her father yet, and a blouse which had shrunk in the wash.

Rosie blushed as she shed her own clothes and exposed ragged underwear.

Georgie stood back to look at her. 'You're much shorter than me and so thin that even my smallest skirt nearly drowns you.'

The other two nodded.

'They might fit Nora, though.' Rosie studied the older maid. 'Why don't you try them on?'

Nora did this and Georgie gave her a hat with a wider brim, which partly concealed her face. Then she found an old jacket and a country hat in her father's room to complete her own disguise.

They went to show the men, who all nodded approval of the effectiveness of their changed appearance.

'Since Miss Cotterell looks like a man,' Patrick suggested, 'she and I could simply walk out of the house. Pity we can't go in the car.'

'Why can't we?' Georgie asked. 'We'd be a lot safer if we could get away without using trains or buses, and I'm sure Father would agree about that, at least. He has other cars at his disposal.'

'And if you do that, you'll be able to take one of your friends with you, Mr Farrell,' Mathers said. 'If it comes to trouble, you won't be able to protect her on your own.'

'If we look like a group, won't they simply follow us?' Georgie worried. 'No, surely two people would look more natural than three?'

Patrick grinned. 'Martin can crouch down in the back of the car and I can make it seem as if there's something wrong with the car engine. I can talk loudly about having it repaired as we're getting it out of the stables.'

Georgie noticed that Mathers was looking at him with increasing respect. She too was impressed by the way Patrick kept offering practical solutions to problems.

'If we want to keep all three bodyguards with Miss Farrell, we could arrange to meet Dennis somewhere as well,' Patrick went on. 'He could leave the house first, with Rosie and a shopping basket, and give anyone following him the slip at the shops.'

Everyone fell silent, considering this, then Mathers said reluctantly, 'It might just work. You could arrange to meet him *and* Rosie somewhere, Mr Farrell. I can give the two of them directions to one of the diversions your father uses sometimes – no one will know where they go after they leave here.'

'Why put poor Rosie in danger?' Georgie protested.

'I'm sure your father would prefer you to be accompanied by another woman.'

She opened her mouth to question this then shut it again. He was right. But she only intended to spend a couple of nights in her father's country house while making better plans for finding a long-term refuge. Unless her father reappeared in the meantime, of course.

Where on earth was he? Was he safe?

Dennis and Rosie left first, with him carrying a big, covered shopping basket. They visited the nearby grocer's to place an order, then walked along to an address Mathers had given them.

Inside the house they were questioned carefully, but they'd been given a special password and it was accepted. One of the men on guard there took them down to the cellars.

'I went through a place like this with Mr Mathers,'

Rosie whispered. 'Who'd have thought these passages were hidden here under London?'

They were taken quite a distance underground then up some stairs where their guide unlocked a heavy iron door that led into a scullery. After checking that all was clear in the narrow street outside, he wished them well and went back down to the cellar.

They'd left the basket behind, Rosie had changed her hat and added a different scarf to her outfit and she now took Dennis's arm, as if they were a courting couple.

'We'll go and wait in the park, as agreed.' He glanced up at the sky. 'I hope the rain holds off.'

'It'd be worth a wetting to get Miss Cotterell away safely,' Rosie said. 'She's been that kind to me.'

'Yes. Patrick's the same. Help anyone, he would. Just a friendly word from someone who doesn't look at you as if you're a scary monster helps sometimes.'

She patted his arm. 'You'll look better in a year or two. My cousin got scalded and that's what happened to her. The scars fade, but only slowly.'

'Do you really think so?'

'I know so, saw it happening with my own eyes.'

'Well, thank you for that, lass. It cheers me up. It can be . . . difficult, facing people who stare.'

'Any decent person would be grateful for what you've done for your country.'

Dennis gave her hand a squeeze. 'You're a real tonic, you are, Rosie.'

Once Martin had curled up on the floor in the back of the large car, covered by a blanket, Patrick went to fetch Georgie.

'I've got my things and I've packed Rosie's too.' She'd added some of her own underwear to the bundle because Rosie had so little.

'Good thinking. Can you crank the car engine?' he asked. 'I know a few tricks to make it seem as if the engine isn't going properly, but I need to be at the wheel to do that.'

'Yes, of course I can crank the engine. My job was driving around London, don't forget.'

'There's no "of course" about it. Most women haven't got the necessary strength.'

'I had to be able to start a car to do that sort of war work. There were no weaklings among us.'

'All right. We'll open the doors of the stables and—'

'If you're the driver, it's up to me to open the doors.'

As she was doing that, she caught sight of a man's shadow on the ground stretching out from the place where the watcher was hiding. He wasn't very good at this. Not giving any sign that she'd noticed it, she swung the cranked handle a few times and got the engine started. Then she waited for Patrick, who drove the car out in fits and starts.

As she closed the garage doors, she heard someone inside bolt them: Mathers no doubt.

'This car's still not firing properly,' Patrick called out to her as agreed. 'We need to get that mechanic to check it as quickly as he can in case it's needed. Hurry up, damn you!'

She got inside and they drove off down the back laneway.

'Sorry about the language.'

'I've heard worse.'

No one tried to bar their way as they left the lane. No other vehicles were in sight in the street, either.

Indeed, it was early enough for most residents and their servants in this suburb to be having breakfast still.

The watcher hesitated but two men, clearly servants of some sort, weren't what he'd been told to look for, so he had a quick pee behind a nearby dustbin and settled down again to keep watch.

He didn't like the idea of them going after Cotterell's daughter, but he had no choice. He had to do as he was told. He owed too much money.

Mathers went back into the house and hurried upstairs to join Nora in the room where Patrick had slept.

'They've driven down the lane and that man is still there. Dirty devil he is, went and relieved himself against the wall.'

'Well, he can hardly go and do it somewhere proper if he's been told to keep watch here.'

Nora looked at herself in the mirror again. 'What do you think?'

'I think you look ready to go shopping, *Miss Cotterell*.'

She smiled at being addressed by her mistress's name, studied herself in the dressing-table mirror and pulled her hat lower down. 'Must be nice to wear clothes like this all the time.'

Mathers went to hail a taxi, then ushered the 'young lady' into it and locked the front door, before joining her.

As they pulled away from the house another car fell into place behind them and stayed behind them all the way to Lady Berrens' house.

The front door opened without them needing to knock

and a burly man came out to open the car door for 'Miss Cotterell'. A man who'd slipped out of the rear seat of the vehicle following them got hastily back into it again.

'I reckon they were going to snatch her off the street!' Mathers exclaimed as he hustled Nora inside quickly. 'That must mean you fooled them. I hope she and Patrick stay safe.'

'There's nothing you can do to help her now, Mr Mathers, except pray,' Nora said.

Lady Berrens came to the doorway of a room at the back of the house and beckoned to them. 'Come and tell me what's going on. Why did you phone for someone to be waiting to let you in quickly, Mathers?'

She listened in shock. 'I do hope those men can keep poor Georgie safe. Where can Gerald Cotterell be?'

'He knows enough to look after himself,' Mathers said grimly. 'He usually takes me with him on his little trips.'

She frowned. 'They must want to get at him through her in the chaos following the Armistice and then use him to influence negotiations.'

'That's what I thought, my lady.'

'I'm sure he'll have a good reason for not taking you with him this time. Will it be safe for you to go back to his house or do you want me to find somewhere else for you two to stay?'

'Nora and I will go back and I'll bring in someone I know to help guard the place. We can't leave it unoccupied. We ought to stay here for a little while as if it's Miss Cotterell making a normal visit, though. Would that be all right, my lady?'

'Of course. But if Nora is supposed to be Georgie, you

can't go to the servants' hall, so you'd better come and join me in the morning room. I have another visitor there, my friend Mrs Tesworth. She's used to helping people in trouble, because she works for the Greyladies Trust, so she won't blink an eye at having you there.'

He saw Nora look uneasy as her ladyship said that. He felt uneasy himself to be sitting down with a titled lady, not to mention her friend. These were strange times. Well, he'd had a strange war. Some would think he hadn't been in danger, but they'd be wrong. He had seen some of what Mr Cotterell had done in the service of his country and admired his employer for that, been proud to help out.

Whoever these traitors were, they were going to a lot of trouble to try to get hold of Mr Cotterell. Did the secret machinations of the various nations involved in making peace ever cease? he wondered. Vicious, some of them could be.

# Chapter Six

Patrick drove slowly and carefully, not wanting to attract anyone's attention. 'Martin, are you all right staying hidden in the back of the car for a while?'

'Hell, yes. I've crouched in far worse places than this in the trenches.'

How often they all still referred to those dreadful days! Patrick thought. Would the memories ever fade? Not completely. Some things were etched in your very soul. 'Good lad. I told Dennis to wait in that park we've sat in on fine days. He and Rosie can stay out of sight among the trees at the back.'

'Good choice.'

Once he felt to be beyond any watchers who might be lurking near Mr Cotterell's house, Patrick told Martin he could get up from the floor.

'Where exactly are we going?' Georgie asked.

'I'm taking us to the workshop of an old friend, who'll help me out with whatever I need.'

'What do we need? Is there something wrong with the car?' Georgie asked anxiously.

'Nothing wrong at all and you may think I'm being too cautious, but I'm going to borrow Chad's van to pick up the others. That means the whole operation will take us a bit longer, but the most important thing of all while we're still in London is to keep this big car out of sight.'

'I should think the watcher will still be expecting you to bring it back after it's been repaired. He won't be suspicious for quite a while.'

'We'll be well out of London by the time he starts to worry. Once we've got my friend's van, you can stay here with Chad while I make my way to the back entrance of the park and pick up the others.'

'I think we should all drive there together,' Georgie said. 'After you've parked your friend's van, Martin and I can stay in it and keep the doors locked.'

'It's too dangerous for you to stay in full view of people passing, Georgie. You don't look like a chap from close up.' A quick glance sideways showed him that the stubborn look had returned to her face, not to mention that stubborn tilt to her chin, so her next words didn't surprise him at all.

'It'll be much safer to leave someone in the van, you know it will, Patrick.' Their gazes clashed and she added, 'Let's get one thing clear: I spent most of my life letting other people tell me what to do, the more fool me. Nowadays I make my own decisions, or at least I join in any discussion about what's best for me to do.'

As they stopped to let a lady with a small child cross

the road, she fell silent but not before he'd seen anger flash in her eyes. It didn't seem to be aimed at him because she was staring straight ahead now. Perhaps it was anger at something that had happened in the past. Most folk had regrets about something or other, when you really got talking.

He stopped arguing. No use beating your head against a brick wall.

When they set off in the van, Martin said suddenly, 'I think Georgie's right. It's safer for us to stay together and have someone in the van. If there's any trouble, I can hold my own in a fight as well as you, though I doubt anyone will come after us in this. Maybe you're being a bit too cautious, my old lad. They don't even know we've got Georgie out of the house yet, and we're in a different vehicle with three people who look like men in it.'

'I suppose I am being cautious, but there's a lot at stake. Nonetheless, keep your revolver to hand every minute I'm gone, Georgie.'

'You think they'll come after us with guns? In the centre of London?'

'Who knows? I'm not prepared to take any risks. There are plenty of former soldiers who've smuggled guns home with them. They claim to have lost them in the mud or else they really do find guns in the mud.'

A short time later he added, 'From the way Captain Jordan spoke of him, your father must be a very important person behind the scenes.'

'Yes. But Father won't do the enemy's bidding, whatever they threaten. He's a patriot first and foremost.'

'I hope we all are.'

'I doubt they'll catch him, anyway. I've only lived with him a couple of years, but he's cunning. Anyway, we're wasting time arguing. I'm *not* going to be left behind, and that's that.'

Martin was still grinning when they reached the park.

'Look after her,' Patrick said as he got out of the van. 'I'm leaving the engine running in case we need to get away quickly.'

He was about to suggest Martin take over the driving seat, but Georgie slid across into it before he could speak.

'Martin and I will look after one another.' She patted the gun concealed on her lap now under her scarf.

What a woman! he thought as he strode along to the back gate of the park. What an absolutely magnificent woman! Not a sign of fear.

It was something of an anticlimax to find Dennis and Rosie waiting, as arranged. The three of them were back at the van within two or three minutes from him leaving it. The others crammed into the back and he got into the front, not protesting when Georgie drove them back to his friend's workshop. He wanted to see how good a driver she was, and presumably she wanted to show him.

It was no surprise that she proved to be very capable.

He jumped out and opened the gates of the workshop's backyard for her to drive the van in.

When she got out of it, he gave her a mock salute and she inclined her head in response, understanding his hidden message of approval.

The big car was parked inside the workshop and they got everyone into it quickly.

Patrick thanked his friend and said to Georgie, 'If you don't mind, I'll drive now.'

Chad went to open the gates and shut them immediately they drove off.

Patrick was grateful there was an Angus dash mirror installed so that he could see what was happening behind them. In his opinion, all official motor vehicles should have one of those. He made sure to glance into it at regular intervals.

'There doesn't seem to be any sign of pursuit,' he said after a while. 'How long does it take to get to Westcott House by road, Georgie?'

'Three or four hours, depending on traffic and whether we break down or not. But I've been thinking, and I definitely don't believe we should stay there for more than a day or so. And as for hiring people to help protect me, that'd just tell the people in the village that I was there.'

'I agree. They're bound to look for you at Westcott once they realise you've left the London house.'

'If Nora managed to fool them today when she impersonated me, she may have bought us time.'

'We can telephone Mathers tonight to find out.'

'And have the operator listening in and telling everyone who wants to phone me that I'm away from London? I think not.'

'I was intending to make the phone call and pretend to be Mathers' cousin.'

'We'll discuss it when we get to Westcott.' She gave him a confident smile. 'Anyway, I might know a better place for us to take refuge.'

'Might you, indeed?'

The disadvantage of the dash mirror, he found, was that he could see the grins on his two friends' faces in the back, and the way Rosie was smiling. Was it so obvious he was attracted to Georgie?

He didn't continue the conversation, just made occasional comments on the scenery or the idiotic things some other drivers did. Drivers ought to be *taught* to drive safely, in his opinion and have to pass some sort of test before they were let loose on the roads. He'd been well taught in the Army, and was grateful for it.

But whenever he said that, people got angry at the mere thought of such an inconvenience. Those rich enough to buy a car wanted to hop in it and drive off straight away – or get their chauffeur to do that.

Only there were a lot of people hurt or killed on the roads, according to the newspapers, especially pedestrians who weren't used to how fast motor vehicles could move.

When he realised Georgie hadn't tried to chat, he kept his eyes on her. But she seemed all right. Just rather quiet. Well, she had a lot to think about. Her cosy world had just been turned upside down.

Once they arrived at Westcott, Georgie directed him round to the back of the house and suggested he leave the car under the open end of the stables, where it'd have some shelter from the weather as well as being out of sight from anyone passing by, though there ought not to be people passing by.

Two vehicles, which belonged to her father, were already standing there and once Patrick got closer, he could see the outline of a third car inside the former stables.

He got out but left the engine running. He walked along the back of the roofed area and Georgie followed him.

'Do you recognise the other car, the one inside the stables?'

She frowned. 'No. I wonder who it belongs to?'

He turned at the end. 'I think we need to find out whose car it is, then. Do you think someone else is staying here? If so, we should leave at once.'

'I agree. Look, our caretakers should be around somewhere. We can trust them, I promise you. They may know what's going on. Father does sometimes invite people down here occasionally. I'll go and find them.'

As she turned to leave, Patrick grabbed her arm and pulled her back. 'You're not going anywhere alone. You and I will go inside together and Martin can sit in the driving seat with the motor still running in case we have to make a quick escape.'

'Surely no one will be expecting us to come here so soon?'

Even as she spoke, a door at the rear of the house opened and an elderly man peered out.

'Who's that?' Patrick's voice was sharp and his hand stayed clamped tightly round her arm.

'Cecil. Our caretaker.'

The old man smiled at the sight of Georgie and waved to them.

'He doesn't look upset in any way.' She waved back and as Patrick let go of her arm, she hurried across to the house.

'Mr Cotterell didn't say you were coming down, miss.'

'It was a sudden decision. I recognise Dad's Humber and the Talbot, but who does that other car belong to?'

'Your father sent the one in the stables down, said to keep it out of direct sight. He said you might want to use it if you came down here.'

'He hasn't said anything about that to me.'

'You know Mr Cotterell, always thinking ahead, doesn't tell you anything till you need to know. Perhaps he was going to give it to you as a present when the war ended – well, that's what my Marge thinks. He told us what a good driver you are.'

'He did? Goodness. Wonders will never cease. Anyway, let me bring my friends in and we can explain why we're here. Can you ask Marge to make us all a cup of tea?'

When Cecil had disappeared inside, Patrick said thoughtfully, 'Do you think it'd be all right with your father to take one of those cars and leave this one here? I'll check them all out and make sure they're in good working order.'

'I'm sure Father would approve, given the circumstances.'

But she was rarely sure of anything where her father was concerned, except that he'd try to protect her. That, she knew for certain.

Once they were inside the house, they questioned Cecil, who assured them that he hadn't seen any strangers around the house or village and that of course he and Marge wouldn't tell anyone they were here.

'One night here, at least, don't you think, Patrick?' Georgie asked.

The others looked at him, waiting for him to make the decision.

'Yes. Maybe even two if we find out that Nora and Mathers fooled them about you still being in London.'

He was a born leader, Georgie thought. Had the war done that to him or had he always been like that?

Marge made them a scratch meal of bread and cheese, with some of this year's apples brought down from the attic for a dessert, and they all ate together in the kitchen.

When told their visitors intended to stay for a night or two, both caretakers seemed overwhelmed.

'You won't have to look after us,' Georgie told them gently, knowing they were rather frail. 'We don't need fussing over. I know when Father comes down he brings more staff to help look after him, doesn't he?'

'He's very thoughtful that way,' Marge agreed.

'And don't you usually hire Mrs Dobson from the village to help you? If she's free, get her in full-time for a few days. I'll pay.'

Patrick said quickly, 'No, don't do that! Miss Cotterell is forgetting that we don't want anyone else to know we're here.'

'Yes, of course. Foolish of me.' Georgie sighed.

'The trouble is, miss, the master hasn't been down here for a few months so we haven't got a lot of food in.'

Georgie hoped she'd hidden her surprise at that. 'Well, it's really important to keep our visit secret. Is there some way you can obtain food locally from people who won't give us away?'

'Oh yes, miss. Sometimes your father sends injured men here to recover and asks us to keep it secret. We know who can be relied on.'

'Do you need extra money to feed us?'

'No, miss. Your father always leaves us plenty. He trusts us not to waste it.'

'I'm sure he does. That's all right, then.'

'I can help Marge round the house while we're here, miss,' Rosie offered.

'So can we all, whether it's with inside or outside jobs,' Dennis offered.

'There you are. We'll all muck in. So that's settled, Marge.'

But what wasn't settled, in Georgie's own mind at least, was the puzzle of what had been going on for a while. Her father had definitely told her he was going to Westcott two or three times in the past few months, and he'd been away for several days on each occasion. And he hadn't mentioned sending people to stay there without him, either.

She'd been too busy both times he'd visited to accompany him and it occurred to her now that he might have arranged for his friend Lady Berrens to give her a fuller than usual workload around then.

She looked up as she heard her name.

'I need to have a private word with Miss Cotterell about our future arrangements,' Patrick said. 'So if you've finished eating, Georgie, can you please spare me a few moments?'

'Yes, of course.'

What now? she wondered.

# *Chapter Seven*

Georgie led the way along to a small sitting room at one side of the front part of the house and gestured to Patrick to sit down. It didn't have a fire lit and was cold, but that was the least of her worries.

'Let's look at our situation as if we're comrades-in-arms, which we are, actually,' he said quietly. 'You and I need to be more open with one another. We should be working as a team, not each trying to get our own way.'

That was the last thing she'd expected to hear. But it hit home. Oh, it did. 'You're right. We're facing a sort of small war together.'

His expression was so kind, she didn't hesitate to confide in him. 'No man except my brother has ever spoken to me so fairly and openly in my whole life as you have.'

He took her hand and she grasped his tightly. So few people had actually touched her, too.

'You must have met some unpleasant people, lass.'

'Yes. Lived with them, actually. The woman I thought was my mother and the man she tricked me into getting engaged to. Not to mention my older half-brother, who was never well and made up for it by being nasty to everyone else. He died a couple of years ago. So did my fiancé.'

'Killed in the war like your twin?'

'No. My brother just died. Weak heart. My fiancé was killed. He turned out to be rather violent, so good riddance.'

'But you still have your father, surely?'

'He's not exactly loving, and anyway, I've only really known him for the past two years. He rarely came here to Westcott and I rarely left it, apart from going to school. I think he locked away his emotions when my real mother died. He must have loved her greatly, more than he's ever loved anyone else. Though I do know he cares about my welfare. But things have to be done his way.'

'My mother always hugged me when I needed comforting. I think you need that now.' Patrick pulled Georgie into his arms and gave her a close hug.

She stiffened against him, then suddenly gave in to temptation and hugged him back, because there was nothing horrible about the way he touched her, nothing at all like her former fiancé's attempts to maul her body. Laying her head on Patrick's shoulder she sighed, feeling wonderfully safe with this kind man.

He held her until she stirred and didn't attempt to stop her moving away from him, which she also appreciated.

'Come and sit down on the sofa with me, Georgie, and tell me more about where you think we could take refuge without them guessing how to find us.'

She didn't attempt to reply for a moment because she had to ask him, 'Why did you do that?'

'Do what?'

'Hold me. Hug me.'

'I've been wanting to do it for a while, but a man of my station in life doesn't usually attempt it with a lady like yourself. But you looked so sad, I couldn't help myself.'

'Oh. Well, even a lady of my station might welcome it – from the right man and for the right reasons. If someone really cared, it would be good to be hugged more often.'

'Cared about you?' His voice was harsh. 'That would be easy to do, Georgie. But I'm in no position to support a wife, let alone a lady like you, so I daren't do anything about my feelings.'

'I have enough money to support *myself*, thank you very much. I told you that already.'

'And what sort of man would that make me, living off his wife's money?'

His wife! she thought in wonder. He'd said the word 'wife'! Did he mean that his feelings were already strong enough to contemplate that sort of future? She knew she was developing feelings for him. It had happened so quickly, she'd felt as if she'd been struck by lightning. 'The last thing I care about is our social differences, Patrick.'

'One of us has to care, because the rest of the world will.'

She chose her words carefully, trying not to frighten him away, and yet not make him feel obligated to her if that wasn't what he truly wanted. 'It's the person who matters to me, Patrick, not how much money he has or who his parents are. And whether a man is supporting his wife or the other way round would be no one else's business.'

'Ah, Georgie, Georgie . . .'

He studied her as if he was trying to see into her soul, then said quietly, 'Look, we'll see how things go between us then, eh? Not rush into anything.'

She gathered her courage together to offer him one final encouragement, 'But not rush away from it, either?'

He reached out to caress her cheek. 'Definitely not, my lovely lass. As long as you're sure, we can't help but get to know one another better at the moment.'

'I'm very sure.'

'Then if that's agreed – and it pleases me greatly, I promise you – let's concentrate on the safety of our group now. Where is this place we might be able to hide?'

'There's a village in Wiltshire called Honeyfield, about an hour's drive from here, give or take, and the big house is used to house women who've been ill-treated. The people who run it are lovely and I'm sure they'd not turn us away for a night or two, though I don't think we should stay there for longer. And I have a friend in the village itself as well, Bella, who used to be engaged to my twin.'

She paused to get her emotions under control. Sometimes it was agony to talk about Philip. 'Bella's married to someone else now and she and Tez have a small child. He's my twin's child but her husband doesn't mind that. I like Tez very much and my brother would have approved of him and Bella marrying, I'm sure.' She looked at him ruefully. 'What a tangle my family's relationships are in!'

'All families have their tangles. You think we can stay with Bella and Tez?'

'No. Their house isn't big enough, so we'd have to stay at Honeyfield House.'

'Who exactly owns this big house?'

'The Greyladies Trust. It was set up many years ago to help women in trouble and Tez's mother is on the committee. So Bella can keep in touch with Lady Berrens for us, as well as with her mother-in-law. I'm sure one of those two will know when matters are resolved with my father, because they've been involved in war work with him.'

'Did you tell Mathers where you were thinking of going after Westcott?'

'No. The fewer people who know, the better, don't you agree? Though he may guess.'

'And you didn't mention it to Captain Jordan?'

'No. I don't really know him, you see.'

'Quite right. Go on.'

'When there's news of my father, we can come out of hiding and . . . and build new lives, as everyone else will be trying to do now the war is over.'

He frowned and flushed slightly, before adding, 'But what are we going to live on while we're at Honeyfield House? There will be five of us to feed, and neither the lads nor I have a lot of money, nor does Rosie. I've some money in the Post Office Savings Bank, if I can get to it.'

'We'll take some of my father's money from here. I'm sure he won't mind. But I don't think it would matter if we had nothing. The trust provides food and sees to other expenses, and they're quite used to helping fugitives.'

She paused for a moment, still thinking it through. 'It's women they usually help: women who're running away from husbands or from people in their family who treat them cruelly – or from men who've attacked them and left them with a child.'

'I wish my mam had found someone like that to help her when she found she was carrying me after her employer had forced himself on her. He turned her out and denied everything. She managed, but she worked hard all her life, so very hard.'

'She loved you, though, and you loved her. I can hear it in your voice. You must have been a big comfort to her.'

'I like to think so. She married a kind man later, but he wasn't very clever with money, so she was still struggling to put food on the table. I have a younger half-brother. But I don't know what he's doing now Mam's dead. We don't get on all that well.'

She patted his arm. 'And I don't even know my real mother's name, so there we both are – bastards.'

He looked at her in shock. 'I don't like to hear you use that word about yourself.'

'It's the truth.'

'Well, perhaps when things settle down, you can persuade your father to tell you more about your mother.'

'He's refused several times already. He always says to let her rest in peace and not upset her family. I doubt I'll ever persuade him to change his mind about that, though I get the impression he loved her dearly.' She wiped a tear away with one fingertip.

Patrick put his arm round her shoulders and gave her a quick squeeze and again she felt comforted by his touch. But they couldn't stay there for too long, so she pulled herself away reluctantly.

'If that's all you need to discuss, Patrick, let's rejoin the others and I'll sort out with Marge where we're all going to sleep.

* * *

Westcott amazed Patrick in many ways as he was shown round the old house, but unfortunately its size only emphasised the differences between him and Georgie.

He'd been billeted in big houses a few times, but they'd been full of men, with beds crammed into the big rooms, so that you didn't get this sense of spaciousness and elegance. And there had been people coming and going all the time as well as patients: nurses, doctors, orderlies, visitors.

This house was full of shadows, silence, well-loved old furniture and a myriad possessions. There was even a room Georgie called the 'library', saying the word casually. To him it was a treasure house with walls full of books, enough of them to provide a lifetime's reading. How he envied Mr Cotterell and Georgie that, far more than the size of their house!

'You'll want your old room, Miss Georgie?' the old housekeeper asked after she'd panted her way to the top of the stairs.

'Yes, of course. But I need to have my friends sleeping nearby, in case there's trouble. And if there is, you and Cecil are to go and hide in the cellar, as my father ordered.'

'Yes, we know, miss. We're too old to be anything but a hindrance if there's any unpleasantness. But the door to the little side cellar is sticking, so we can't open it easily, or close it fully, come to that. We'll have to get someone in to look at it. It's probably feeling its age, like me and Cecil are.'

'One of us can have a look at it for you tomorrow morning,' Patrick offered. 'Us lads are all good with our hands.'

'That'd be a big help, sir. Thank you.'

In the end, Georgie arranged for Rosie to sleep on a

truckle bed in her dressing room, which would placate her father's sense of propriety, and for the three men to share a bedroom across the landing.

'This used to be my father's wife's room.' Georgie scowled round it.

'All her clothes have been cleared out, though, miss,' Marge said. 'The master saw to it himself, wouldn't let her do any of her own packing. I helped him and we crammed everything into trunks to send to her new home. She was very angry and—'

Georgie finished the tale for her. 'And she probably threw a fit of screeching hysterics.'

'Yes, miss. She did that a lot towards the end. I've heard she doesn't do it much these days. Getting very forgetful, they say.'

Patrick saw Georgie scowl at the doorway as if she hated even the room Mrs Cotterell had occupied. Only it was the closest to hers, so it made sense for them to use it.

'One of us should stay on watch at all times,' he reminded the others.

Georgie looked as if she was going to insist on doing her share of that, but a huge yawn caught her unawares and he said quickly, 'Leave it to us three men. We're more used to staying awake than you ladies are.'

'All right. Just this once, mind. And only because I'm too tired to keep watch properly.'

He didn't answer, because he'd just noticed a low bookcase stuffed full of well-worn books in a corner of the bedroom. He pointed to it. 'All right if I have a look through these?'

'Yes, of course. Read any you want.'

Dennis yawned. 'I'm going straight to sleep.'

Patrick tilted his head to read some of the book titles. 'I'll have a quick look at these before I turn in. Sometimes I have trouble dropping off and if I read for a few minutes, it helps.'

He looked at the two men. 'I know you're tired, but before any of us go to sleep, lads, we need to be sure of where all the entrances are. And I want to double-check that every single one is locked and bolted for the night.'

He got Cecil to show them round the ground floor again, after which he and Dennis went back upstairs and left Martin on watch patrolling the interior of the house.

As he got into bed, Dennis teased his companion for being a bookworm, but within two minutes he was breathing slowly and deeply.

Tired as he was, Patrick couldn't resist having a quick look at the book titles. When he saw one on the bottom shelf that he'd long wanted to read, he pulled it out. Other books tumbled out with it, and behind them he saw a mess of papers.

'What on earth—?' He bent to gather them up and realised they were letters. He didn't mean to read them but when he saw the first paragraph of the top piece of paper, he stiffened and brought his oil lamp closer.

He read the first two letters, whistling softly in surprise because he was so deeply touched by the tender love they showed between Georgie's father and the woman he couldn't marry but clearly loved desperately. What did the Frenchies call it when love struck like that? *Un coup de foudre*. He'd had many a chat with his allies, ranging over everything you could think of and some phrases had stuck in his mind.

It just went to show that making a match of convenience wasn't always the best thing to do, even for people he considered rich. Money hadn't brought Gerald Cotterell happiness, whereas Patrick had seen at first-hand how happy and loving his mother and stepfather had been together, and they'd always been a bit short of money.

He didn't read any more of the letters, feeling as if he was intruding on their privacy, but gathered up the rest carefully and put them in his bag underneath his clean underwear. These were not for his two friends to read.

He put the book into his bag with them almost as an afterthought, not attempting to read it now, because he had too much to think about, the main thing being should he show Georgie what he'd found or not? Or would it only make her sad?

He was still worrying about that when he fell asleep.

The first thing that came into his mind when Dennis woke him to take his turn at patrolling the house was the papers and how Georgie would feel about their contents.

That didn't stop him keeping careful watch.

# *Chapter Eight*

When the group gathered for breakfast in the morning, Georgie noticed that the men had found time to shave and make themselves as smart as possible. A lot of soldiers had picked up that habit in the Army, she'd noticed, and still kept it after they'd been demobbed. Some of them even walked more briskly down the street as if they were ready to start marching at any second.

'Did you read yourself to sleep?' she asked Patrick.

'I didn't read anything but I chose a book and I've put it in my bag. I'll give it back to you after I've finished reading it, if that's all right.'

'Keep it. We have plenty of books here and those looked well worn.'

'It doesn't matter to me if a book is worn. We used to pass them round in France and read them to pieces in the quiet times. I taught a few of my chaps to read better from tattered old books.'

'I'd like to read better,' Rosie said wistfully, then clapped one hand across her mouth as if she was afraid she'd offended them.

'Once this is over, I'll see you get the chance,' Georgie offered. 'I bet you missed a lot of school helping your mother with the younger children.'

'How did you know?'

'I've met others with the same problem. It's easily fixed.'

'Ooh, thank you, miss.' She jumped up after she'd finished eating and without being told, went to help Marge clear up and wash the dishes, while the men asked Cecil what they could do to help.

He wasn't much use, but kept looking at Patrick for guidance.

'One of you can repair that cellar door for a start, then see if there's anything else needs mending. I need to speak to Miss Cotterell again. But see you stay indoors, whatever you find to do. And keep away from the windows.'

Patrick turned to Georgie. It had seemed so obvious when he woke that she had a right to know. 'Do you have a few minutes?'

They went back into the small sitting room and she took a seat on the sofa, clasping her hands together in her lap as she waited for him to speak. When the seconds ticked past and he said nothing, he watched her puzzlement grow, but he was having trouble working out how best to tell her.

In the end he said it bluntly. 'Last night when I was choosing a book, I found some papers hidden at the back of the bookcase in my bedroom.'

'Papers? What sort of papers?'

He went to sit down beside her on the sofa, taking her hand. 'They're letters. I'd not normally read another person's private letters, but they were crammed behind the books any old how, so when a few fell out, I had to pick them up. I couldn't help seeing the top one.'

Another pause while he studied her hand and searched for more words. 'They're love letters from your real mother and father to one another.'

She gasped. 'My *real* mother?'

'Yes. At least, that's what it seems like to me.' He let go of her hand to fumble in his pocket and pull out some pieces of paper. 'There are quite a few others. The rest are in my bag, hidden among my clothes.'

'What are they doing in his wife's bedroom, then?'

He handed the pieces of paper to her. 'Perhaps she found them and crumpled them up. I didn't do that to them. She might have been intending to destroy them then changed her mind.'

Georgie took them from him with a hand that trembled and stared down at the top sheet, reading it slowly, then rereading it. 'Mary Jane. So my mother was called Mary Jane. Only she doesn't sign her surname.'

Tears welled in her eyes as she read a couple more letters. 'Oh, how they loved one another! I'm glad he had that for a while, because *that woman* was one of the nastiest people you could meet. I wonder where this Mary Jane lived, whether she has any family left there.'

'If I bring the other letters, we could see if there are any envelopes among them. The address will tell you her surname and where she came from.'

'Yes. Please do. I'll wait here.'

While she waited she stared at the pieces of paper, trying to smooth them out. Her father would never have screwed up letters from the woman he loved, even if he wasn't pernickety about keeping things neat. So Adeline Cotterell must have got hold of them and hidden them in her bookcase.

Was there no end to that woman's spite? Couldn't she even have left her estranged husband his letters from a dead woman who could no longer be a rival? Clearly not.

The minutes seemed to pass very slowly as Georgie waited. A couple of times she mouthed the words 'Mary Jane'. Such a pretty name.

Patrick pounded up the stairs to his bedroom. The papers were an untidy mess and he had nothing to put them in, so he clutched them against his chest and ran down again, nearly bumping into Dennis in the hall.

'Everything all right, Patrick, lad?'

'Yes. Fine. I'm helping Miss Cotterell with something. You keeping busy?'

'Yes, I'm working on that cellar door with Cecil. I'll come and fetch you if we need help fixing it, but it seems straightforward enough. Martin will keep watch on the house while I'm down there.'

'Fine. Right.'

He knew Dennis was surprised by the abrupt way he'd responded, but he'd seen Georgie's face when she found out her mother's name and he knew she was close to tears. She needed a friend beside her as she did this.

If there was anything he could do to help her, he would.

Some things were important, whoever you were, however much money you had. And hurtful.

Georgie was still sitting on the small sofa with the first few letters in her lap. He saw that her eyelashes were wet and when he got closer, he noticed an ink smear on the handwriting of the top letter. The smear hadn't been there before, so a tear must have fallen on it.

He wanted to pull her into his arms, but didn't allow it, just held out the rest of the letters and said gently, 'Here you are. Do you want me to stay with you while you read them, or leave you alone?'

'Please stay.'

He sat down beside her and watched her hands tremble as she tried to sort out the other papers. When she dropped a couple, he picked them up. 'Want me to help with that?'

She nodded, holding them out to him, saying in a low voice, 'I'm not as strong inside myself as I thought. Only . . . I've been wanting to find out about my real mother ever since I discovered two years ago that Father's wife wasn't related to me. I've wanted to know so desperately, Patrick, and he wouldn't tell me a thing.'

He made a soothing noise.

'Even to know my mother's Christian name is wonderful.' A sob escaped her and she clapped one hand across her mouth.

How could he help it? He took her hand and pulled her into his arms – only for a moment, just to offer comfort. She seemed so alone in the world, except for her father, and he rarely spent time with her.

'Let's sit at the table together, Georgie, lass. It'll be easier to see what's what if we spread these out.'

When they were seated shoulder to shoulder, she hesitated so long he began to go through the papers. More letters, some from Mary Jane, some from her 'loving Gerald'. But no envelopes. It was as if someone had destroyed them on purpose to remove the address.

But just as he was about to give up hope, an envelope came to light near the bottom of the pile, caught between the two pages of the same letter. He recognised the handwriting at once: Georgie's father's.

'I reckon this is what you're looking for.'

She took it from him, managed to hold it steady enough to read the address, and said in a hoarse whisper, 'Mary Jane *Baxter*. Her surname was Baxter.'

She took a few deep breaths as she read on. 'And she lived in Swindon.'

'Do you want me to make a note of the address?'

She gave a hiccup of laughter that was almost a sob. 'No need. I couldn't forget it if I tried.' She clutched his arm. 'Patrick, will you take me to Swindon? Now, at once. If we find this address, there may be some Baxters still living there. I may have . . . family.'

'It's a long time since she died, Georgie.'

'I know. Over twenty-eight years. But even if her family has moved, there's got to be someone in the street who knows where the Baxters are now, there *has* to be! Please will you take me to Swindon? It's not far away. I *have to* find out.'

And heaven help him, he said yes, only keeping enough control to add, 'But we have to make escape plans first, plans for all of us to get away from here quickly if need be. We can't leave the others here like sitting ducks.'

'Yes. Yes, of course.'

Her eyes were bright with unshed tears, such beautiful eyes. Oh, he'd kill dragons for this woman!

'And Patrick, thank you. You don't know how much this means to me.'

He had a very fair idea, just from the expression on her face. He was learning to read her feelings. This was a calculated risk, he knew, but he thought they had time to do it.

Patrick gave Georgie a few moments to pull herself together, then got to work. He'd always been good at planning operations, had helped his captain with them regularly. 'We might as well go this morning if Swindon is only an hour or so away. But first, will your friend in Honeyfield be on the phone? We need to let her know you'll be coming, and bringing four friends with you.'

She looked startled. 'Of course she is! Why didn't I think of that before? Oh, I'm being so stupid. Shall I go and telephone her now?'

He grabbed her arm. 'No. Not yet. Let's go and look at the other cars, see what condition they're in. We'd be better taking one of those, if you're sure your father wouldn't mind.'

They went out through the kitchen, stopping at the door as they noticed that light rain was now falling.

'How stupid. I didn't even notice that it had started raining,' she said.

'Here. We'll take this.' He grabbed one of the umbrellas from the battered hallstand nearby and held it over himself and Georgie as they picked their way across the muddy yard. He nearly fell once on the slippery ground, thanks to that damned limp, and she had to hold him steady for a few moments.

Kill dragons for her! he thought bitterly. He couldn't even walk properly.

The car they'd used to get here was standing where they'd left it next to the Humber and the equally large Talbot. Cotterell must have plenty of money to buy four motor cars, three of them just to keep in the country – or did the government pay for the latter?

The car Patrick was interested in was the one in the stable itself, dimly visible through a dusty window, and there wasn't even a padlock on the big double doors. Anyone could have driven off in it.

He left the umbrella by the door and led the way inside. 'Ah! It is a Swift light car. I thought I recognised the outline. Pity this one hasn't got a solid roof. Open cars are a bit chilly at this time of year – they're draughty even with the hood up. Help me raise the hood to check it out. Let's hope the motor is working properly.'

She went round to the other side of the vehicle and he didn't need to tell her what to do, as he would another woman. Together they pulled the hood up. It was in excellent condition, moving smoothly as they clipped it into position.

He walked round examining the vehicle. 'Nearly new tyres. Good. I've never driven one of these before. I wonder why the makers put this bulb horn on at such an awkward angle? Ah, good! There's an acetylene generator for the lamps in case we have to drive at night.'

She was studying it too. 'It's a neat little car, isn't it?

I haven't driven one before either. I usually drive bigger vehicles in London. This one would be easier to handle in busy city traffic, but of course we have to have enough room in our cars to accommodate injured men and often their nurses or orderlies as well.'

She stepped back and frowned at it. 'Are you sure this one will suit our purpose, though? Some of the country roads round here have appalling potholes and bumps. Even father, who rarely criticises the government, thinks they should do more about making road surfaces fit to travel on.'

'I'll drive carefully, I promise you. This car will serve our purpose better because there are more smaller cars around.'

'It is small, isn't it? Only a two-seater. My father rarely travels anywhere without a couple of other men in attendance, so he always uses big cars.'

'They'll be looking for a big car. If we drive it to Swindon and ferret around, we can perhaps find out about your mother.'

'Yes, of course.'

'The others could wait for us here at Westcott. I think we dare allow ourselves one day's grace before we have to take into account the likelihood that our London watchers will have found out you're no longer there. But just in case, we'll tell the others where to meet us if we don't return.'

'Why should we not return?'

'This is a car we don't know. It hasn't been used much, so might have engine problems that delay us, however well maintained. Cars do, you know. Rather often, too.'

They both smiled wryly at that. It was all too common

to come across a car that had broken down, especially on country roads. People usually took that possibility into account when driving somewhere, and also when expecting a visitor coming by road, unlike one coming by a train which ran to schedule.

'Or what we find out might delay us, in which case we'll phone and tell them to make their own way to Honeyfield. Or we may even decide to go somewhere else while tracing your family. I always like to allow for the unexpected when making plans.'

She looked at him expectantly. 'So we're going?'

'Yes. It'll be better than hanging around with nothing to keep us occupied, and you need to know. I'll have a quick look at the engine while you pack your clothes in case we don't get back tonight.'

He staggered backwards, laughing, as she flung herself at him, hugging him and even planting kisses on his cheek.

'Thank you! Thank you so much, Patrick.'

He gave her a kiss back, enjoying a moment's happiness amid the worries for her safety. 'Now look, when it comes to phoning your friend in Honeyfield, I think we should do that from a public phone, not from here. We're bound to find one in Swindon.'

Her exhilaration faded. 'You really think those men will follow us down to Westcott, don't you?'

'Yes. But I can't see them doing it immediately. Go on. Tell the others what we're doing and then pack your bag. I'll see if I can find a spare can of motor spirit to take with us, then I'll have a word with Dennis. It won't take me a minute to pack my things.'

* * *

As he watched her cross the yard, he touched his cheek where she'd kissed him and smiled. The kisses had been nothing more than a friend's salute, but they had been sweet nonetheless.

Oh dear, he was heading for heartbreak. Her father would never allow him to court her, even if he could afford to keep a wife. His dear old mam would have said the same thing: she'd firmly believed it was tempting providence to step out of your place in the world.

Only, the war had thrown so many of them out of their places, and how would they ever go back to the old ways? It wasn't possible, it'd be like crawling back into a narrow box and staying there. He wasn't the only one to reckon that if you were good enough to give your life for your country, you were good enough for anyone to associate with after the war ended.

He'd had a lot of thinking time in the trenches. He'd come to the conclusion that everything you did in life changed you. There was even a good side to the war for him, because it had not only given him a trade, but introduced him to so many different people and ways of life. Why, he could even speak a little French and German. Once he heard a foreign word, it seemed to stick in his mind.

The last captain he'd served under had told him he had an excellent brain and to be sure to make use of it after the war. Patrick had valued that compliment greatly from a man he respected more than anyone else he'd served under.

And what was he doing standing here like an idiot gawping at a fair when there was so much to be done? He pushed away his memories and got on with preparations for the journey.

He patted the car when it was ready. It was a little beauty and seemed to be in excellent working order. He finished by fetching one of the big, square cans from the pile that now occupied one of the horse stalls and strapped it into place on the rear luggage rack of the car next to the tool kit. You couldn't rely on finding a shop selling cans of motor spirit. This wasn't theft; it was part of looking after Mr Cotterell's daughter.

Georgie came out to join him more quickly than he'd expected, so he ran indoors to get his own things. As he was coming downstairs, he found Dennis waiting for him in the hall, which saved him the trouble of searching for his friend.

Dennis was blunt. 'Are you sure you know what you're doing, lad?'

'Not sure at all. But she needs quite desperately to find out about her mother's family and I think we'll have a day or two's leeway before our pursuers look for us here. The other thing is, these Baxters might take her in and then she'd be safe, because no one from *Siebenzeit* can possibly know about that side of her family.'

'Aye. I suppose you have a point there.'

'It was the deciding factor for taking this risk. Look – if we don't get back tomorrow or the day after, you drive the others to Honeyfield and we'll meet you there. Use whichever of the other cars you prefer. Her father won't mind. You've still got the address?'

'Of course. We all wrote it down. But I thought she was going to phone them first? She hasn't been near the phone.'

'We'll do that from a public phone while we're out, so no operator can listen in and gossip.'

Dennis clapped Patrick on the back. 'Good luck, then. I hope things work out for her.'

'You're to take charge if we get delayed or if the three of you have to run for it. I trust your judgement on when to leave. Make sure the car you choose can start at a moment's notice. You're all right with driving now, fully recovered in that sense?'

'Oh, yes.'

'Then you're definitely the best one to take charge. Do you remember what Cecil told us about the back road into the estate?'

Dennis nodded. 'Yes. Actually, I've been wondering whether we should leave one of the cars there in case we have to make a quick getaway.'

'Good idea. You do that, lad. There are some spare cans of motor spirit in the old stables. Take one of them. I reckon we'll keep the car out in that lane even after Georgie and I get back.'

He went back to join her in the stable yard, getting out the starting handle for the little Swift. It started first time, which seemed a good omen, but he had to ask again, 'Are you still sure about doing this, lass?'

'Yes, of course. Why, they might even have a photo of her.'

Oh, the longing in her voice. 'Off we go, then.'

They left the grounds by the rear road. He hoped they'd be successful. It wouldn't be his fault if they failed to find any Baxters.

He didn't try to make conversation as he drove. His senses were all on the alert, as they'd always been on operations, keeping watch for the slightest sign of trouble.

But the further away from Westcott they got, the more

he regretted his offer to take her to Swindon. It was risky and he didn't usually take risks.

Only the possibility of her family letting her stay with them kept him going – and the happy anticipation on her face.

# *Chapter Nine*

Dennis took Martin and Rosie into the small sitting room to explain what was going on. He didn't want the caretakers to know anything about it. When he'd finished, he added, 'I don't understand why Patrick is taking this risk; all I know is, I don't like it.'

Martin nodded. 'I don't like the sound of it, either.'

'It must be very important to Miss Cotterell,' Rosie said. 'But they'll be back tonight, won't they? And we'll be safe enough here in the meantime.'

'We hope so. Unless those people have found out more quickly than expected that Georgie isn't in the town house. Since this house is too big to protect, I'm going to take precautions of my own.' He explained about Patrick's suggestion and the other two nodded.

'I'll take the Humber out for a spin into the village first, though, because I think that'll be the best one to take. I'll try to find another way to get back here.'

He looked from one to the other and said slowly and emphatically, 'Make sure you both know where the lane is. If there's any trouble and we get separated, we'll rendezvous at the car.'

Rosie looked at him in dismay. 'Well then, I'm taking a poker to bed with me. It's what my mum does if there's trouble in our street and Dad's not at home. She's only had to use it once, on a drunk who was trying to break in and grab some food. After that folk stayed away from our house.'

He nodded approval. 'Good for your mother! Anyway, think on: if you hear anything suspicious at any time, day or night, stop what you're doing and be ready to run, even if you have to leave your things behind. If necessary, get out of the house on your own and make your way to the car as quietly as you can.'

She nodded but she looked so small compared to him and Martin that Dennis hesitated for a moment, worrying about her. But what could he do? He and Martin couldn't defend a huge house, two elderly people and a slip of a lass like Rosie if they were outnumbered. All they could do in such circumstances was flee and let the caretakers hide in the side cellar now its door was mended.

It was bad enough fighting a war in another country, far worse when you had to deal with it in your own country *after* peace had been declared. That was so wrong it made him furiously angry. Why could these people not accept that they had been defeated?

How long would it take for things to settle down again in Britain, he wondered, really settle down? Or was this secret stuff going on all the time?

Not only was the country in a mess after the years of fighting, but people were in a mess too. They didn't need more problems. He felt most sorry of all for the poor wretches who were suffering from shell shock. He still had nightmares about what he'd seen and done in the war, and probably always would, but they seemed to live in one continuous nightmare.

He looked down at his hand. Ah, he was one of the lucky ones, only missing two fingers. And Rosie didn't seem to mind his injuries at all.

Patrick drove towards Swindon, which he'd visited once or twice when training in the Army. He stopped near the centre when he saw a wooden construction that might be one of the newer telephone kiosks. You couldn't always tell. Some looked like fancy garden sheds and he'd even seen one with a thatched roof, and damned silly that had looked to him. He preferred to use a kiosk, though, rather than paying for access to a public phone in a shop, where anyone could overhear what you said.

He sagged in relief when he got close enough to see the sign on top of the wooden structure indicating that phone calls could be made from there. This one was a Post Office kiosk, with white lettering on a blue background, and a penny in the slot mechanism on the door. Some kiosks had attendants and then they'd be able to listen in to what you were saying.

At the moment he didn't want anyone to be able to overhear their plans, because he didn't know who to trust. Why, even that uppity captain who'd come to tell Georgie about her father could be a traitor, for all they knew. He certainly hadn't been a friendly chap. A snob, the chaps in the Army would have called him.

'We can both cram into the kiosk,' Georgie said.

When they'd done that, he tried to ignore her warm, firm body, but of course no red-blooded man could help noticing that a pretty lass's soft curves were pressed closely against him.

They had to get the help of the operator, of course, but they'd planned what to say so as not to give anything specific away. Unfortunately, there was no answer from her friend Bella at the other end.

'Thank you. We'll try again later,' Georgie told the operator and put the phone down.

'Pity,' he said.

'Can't be helped.'

They had to stop a couple of times to ask directions, because it wasn't easy to find the way round the town centre, so it wasn't till mid-afternoon that they found the address on the envelope. Simpton Street turned out to be a row of smallish houses in the old town, part of an area where the Great Western Railway employees were housed.

Number 17 boasted a tiny oblong of neat garden in front and windows so clean they sparkled even in the weak winter sunlight.

Georgie made no move to get out of the car and looked at him as she had before, pleading silently for his help.

'Do you want to do this alone or shall I come with you?' he offered when she didn't speak.

'Would you mind coming with me, Patrick?'

'Of course not.' He got out of the car but she was out of

the passenger seat before he could help her and leading the way towards the front door.

The woman who opened it was young – far too young, he'd have thought, to be closely related to Georgie's mother – and she had a small child behind her, clinging to her skirt.

'I'm looking for relatives of Mary Jane Baxter,' Georgie began.

The woman stiffened. 'Why? She's been dead for nearly thirty years. Surely you knew that?'

'Um, yes. Sort of. I mean, I knew she was dead, but I didn't know her name or where she came from until recently.'

'Why are you looking for her relatives, then?'

'Because she was my mother. My name's Georgie Cotterell and I grew up not knowing about my real mother or her family. I've only just found out her name, you see. I'd like very much to find her family, talk to the Baxters about her, perhaps get to know them. My twin brother was killed in the war, you see, so I have no one else.'

The woman's tense expression softened for a moment. 'Oh dear. I'm sorry, I really am, but they won't want to speak to anyone connected to her. I'm not a Baxter myself. I married your mother's nephew by her sister and our name's Grant. His mother won't even have her sister's name spoken, flies into a rage if anyone mentions her.'

Georgie looked so shocked, Patrick was wondering what to do when the young woman studied her more closely and said, 'Now I come to think of it, you look like your mother. My husband has some family photos and she's in some of the groups as a young woman. His mother tried to throw them all away, but her mother saved them from the dustbin because her other children were in them. His grandma gave them to my Wally before she died.'

'You have photos of her? Oh, please, do you think I could—?'

The woman didn't let Georgie finish.

'I really am sorry, but there's nothing I can do to help you. I can't go against my Wally's mother, it wouldn't be right.' She started to close the door.

Patrick put his hand out to stop her. 'Surely you could ask them if they'd meet Miss Cotterell? It doesn't seem fair to carry on the feud to her daughter, whatever their opinion of this Mary Jane?'

'My mother-in-law isn't well so I definitely can't upset the family at the moment. They're really worried about her. They thought she'd recovered from that Spanish flu, but she can't seem to pull herself together and the doctor says she's got pneumonia now.'

'Will you at least let us give you an address to contact if your husband changes his mind once his mother's better?' Georgie pleaded.

'Well, that wouldn't do any harm, I suppose. As long as you wait to hear from us. I'm not promising anything. And please don't come knocking on my door again if you don't hear, because once my Wally decides something, he won't change his mind.'

'Have you got a piece of paper I can write our address on?'

'I'll fetch one.' She closed the door and they heard footsteps going away from it.

Patrick put one arm round Georgie. 'I'm so sorry.'

She said in a whisper, her voice wobbling slightly, 'It

never even occurred to me that they'd have disowned her so completely they even destroyed most of the photos of her.'

The young woman opened the door again and held out a piece of cheap pad and a stump of a pencil. 'This is all I've got, I'm afraid.'

'It'll do.' He turned to Georgie. 'Shall I use your London address?'

'No. My friend's address in Honeyfield might be better. Let me do it.' She wrote her name, then under it 'care of Mrs Bella Tesworth' and her friend's address and telephone number. As she handed the paper back to the young woman, she said wistfully, 'Your husband is my first cousin, then.'

'Yes. His name's Wallace Grant, only everyone calls him Wally. He's not in the Army because he works on the railways and is needed there.'

'Thank you for your help.' Georgie held out her hand but the woman didn't shake it.

'That man wrote to tell the family when Mary Jane died – the man who ruined her wrote, I mean – but he can't have said anything about twins or even Ma would have told us. Wally's dad remembers his wife burning your father's letter. He said he'd never seen her so angry.'

She took a step backwards. 'I shouldn't even be talking to you without my husband knowing. I'll tell Wally about you tonight and if he wants to get in touch, we know how.'

As Georgie opened her mouth to ask if she could just have a look at a photo of her mother, another child cried out from inside the house. The woman said, 'Sorry!' and closed the door in their faces.

'At least she didn't slam the door,' Georgie said as they

walked back to the car. She stood next to it as if she didn't know what to do.

In the end, Patrick opened the passenger door and said gently, 'Get in, lass. We can't stay here.'

She did that like someone sleepwalking.

He drove away, not trying to speak because she was weeping, tears running down her cheeks, tears she made no attempt to wipe away.

It hurt him not to be able to comfort her, so he took the first turn that seemed to lead out of town and once they were past the houses, he stopped the car in a gateway by the side of a narrow road. There were no habitations in sight and they were next to a bare ploughed field, so they were as private as they were likely to be today.

Only after he'd checked their surroundings did he switch off the engine, take her in his arms and let her sob against him. Her father was wrong not to have told her anything about her mother. Very wrong.

# *Chapter Ten*

When Georgie had stopped crying and calmed down, Patrick said quietly, 'We'd better set off again. It'll be dark soon and I think we should go straight to Honeyfield. If the sky would only clear, I could guarantee to point us in roughly the right direction by the stars.'

'You don't think we should go back to Westcott, then?'

'No. Apart from you wanting to meet them, I thought you might be able to take refuge with your mother's family if anything went wrong, because I doubt whoever's trying to get to you will know about them. Only, since that's not possible, I'm taking you to the safest place we can think of because your safety is my first consideration.'

She shook her head as if bewildered.

'You're certain this Bella will help you?' he asked.

'Absolutely certain. But what about the others? They'll be waiting for us at Westcott.'

'I've already told Dennis to join us in Honeyfield if we don't return tonight, remember, and that they're to set off first thing in the morning.'

'I'll never forgive myself if they get hurt because of me.'

'We've tried to plan for all eventualities, Georgie. No one can know exactly what's going to happen.'

'You're a clever man.'

'Tell me I'm clever after we've arrived safely at your friend's.' He got out of the car and tried to crank up the engine, but all it did was cough a couple of times, then fall silent.

His second attempt didn't even make the motor cough.

'Oh hell, that's all we need. The carburettor's probably blocked.'

'Can you fix it? I'm afraid I know very little about repairing car engines. We volunteer drivers were told to send for help if our vehicle broke down. You could do that in London, but there isn't even a house in sight here.'

'I'll be able to sort the carburettor out if it's something straightforward. Let's see what they've got in the tool kit to help me take it to pieces.' He went round to the rear of the car and found only strapping where the tool kit had been attached, with two frayed pieces of woven canvas strap still attached to the metal grille.

He thumped one fist against the other. 'How did I miss seeing that the straps were worn? Those bumpy roads must have jerked the box around and given the straps the final death blow. I checked that there was a tool kit, but I didn't think to inspect the straps that attached it to the luggage grille. Georgie, I'm so sorry. This is all my fault.'

'Of course it isn't. It's simply bad luck. Could have

happened to anyone. I daresay we can find someone to help.

'I'll go and look for—no, I'm not leaving you on your own. Are your shoes all right to walk along rough country lanes?'

'Yes, of course.' She held out one neatly shod foot and there was enough daylight left for him to see what she was getting at.

'Those look to be good, solid shoes.'

'Don't tell anyone, but they're men's Oxfords. They're made of strong leather and far more comfortable to walk in than ladies' lace-up shoes, which usually have narrow heels.'

'I've never understood why women want to balance on those spindly little heels.'

'I don't do it very well, I must admit, and women's shoes aren't as good to wear when you're working. I always wore these when I was driving people around London and I had to help some of the men into and out of buildings, especially when there were steps. I thought these shoes would be better for our journey.'

'Good girl. Very sensible.'

She flushed slightly as she added, 'I've got rather large feet for a woman, anyway, I'm afraid.'

'All the better to walk on.'

'My father's wife always mocked me whenever I needed new shoes.'

'Even when you were a child?'

She nodded.

'Then she's a cruel woman. You're tall, so you'd look silly balancing on small feet. Why do women worry about such things, anyway? Men don't stare at women's *feet*, believe me.'

She smiled. 'I'm well aware of what they mainly stare

.t, thank you very much. Anyway, you can be sure I won't slow us down and these shoes will keep the mud out better than most.'

'Thank heavens for a sensible woman! I think we'd better take our bags with us so that we don't leave a trace of who we are in the car. You never know who'll happen by and poke around in it.'

'We'll need the bags, anyway, if we have to spend the night somewhere.'

He didn't stop walking but fell silent for a few moments, then said, 'Georgie, it'll look bad us turning up together at this hour, not married and so far from home. People won't treat you with respect, and if they think the worst, they may even refuse to take us in.'

After a few more yards, he put out one hand to stop her walking. 'Look, if we have to seek shelter for the night, how about we pretend we're married?'

'They'd soon realise we're not.' She held out her left hand and waggled her fingers at him. 'I haven't got a wedding ring, or even a mark where one might have been.'

'Actually, I have one.' He fumbled at his neck and produced a cord with his ID tags on it, a hexagonal tag on the main cord, and a smaller red one attached to that cord by another shorter loop. 'I suppose I should stop wearing these tags now, but they've been through a lot with me. And besides, I keep this gold ring on the cord as well. It was my grandmother's wedding ring and my mother insisted it would be lucky for me to have it with me.'

'She must have worried about you.'

'Yes. I think it comforted her that I had the ring and it

felt good to hold it in my hand sometimes. Comforting, part of home, you know?'

'Yes. I can understand that. And I'd be honoured to wear your grandmother's ring.'

'Who'd have thought it would actually come in useful? Still, we'll only do this if you truly believe it's a good idea.'

She didn't hesitate. 'I've just had a short, sharp lesson in what happens to young women who don't obey society's rules: their families cast them off like the Baxters did my real mother. Here, I'd better put the ring on now in case we meet someone.' She held out her left hand.

It took him a minute or two to get the ring off the cord, then he slid it on her finger and they both stayed close together looking down at it.

'How lucky. It fits perfectly.'

'So it does.' She waved that hand about, but the ring stayed snugly in place.

He was having trouble fastening the cord round his neck again, so she took the ends from him. 'Let me do that.'

He smiled at her as she finished knotting it. 'Don't forget to introduce yourself as Mrs Farrell. And, um, in case you're worrying, I promise I won't – well, try to take advantage of you.'

'I've already told you that I trust you absolutely, Patrick. That hasn't changed.'

He stared at her, so touched by this he couldn't think what to say.

'And if I do forget to use my new name, I'll look shy and confess that we're newly-weds.'

He took her left hand, raised it to his lips and kissed it. 'I'd be very proud to call you my wife. Any man would. I wish . . .'

He didn't finish what he'd been going to say. Things were happening too quickly between them. Until he met her, he hadn't believed it was possible to feel that way about someone at first sight. 'Here, give me your bag, Georgie.'

'I'm fine. It's not heavy. You carry yours and I'll carry mine. We don't want you stumbling under the extra weight.'

That broke his bubble of happiness. 'Damned leg!' he muttered, feeling ashamed.

As they walked along, she said suddenly, 'Do you mind me asking: is your limp permanent?'

'I don't mind you asking anything. I think I'll always have a limp, but one doctor said I might be able to walk more normally if I got a special shoe made for that foot. Only there was so much red tape to be got through for them to provide one, I couldn't even get it started before they turfed me out of the hospital. There hasn't been time to sort it out since. As I could manage to get around without help, I was sent into the hostel and given a month there to find a job and get on with my life. But there aren't many jobs for men who can't walk properly.'

'Will it cost much for such a shoe?'

'More than I want to spend at the moment, even if I can find a cobbler who knows what he's doing. I daren't spend my discharge money and savings on paying for a special shoe until I've got a job, you see.'

'Your limp might give us away now if anyone asks after us. People remember details like that.'

'Well, I don't have any choice about whether I limp or not.'

'A good cobbler might be able to make a temporary insole to help till you can get a special shoe made. That wouldn't cost as much. I could lend you the money.'

'No need for that.' He realised his voice had been rather sharp. 'I'm sorry to snap your head off. I'm still not used to it, you see, not really – limping, I mean. Sometimes I set off walking without thinking and nearly fall over when that leg doesn't do as I expect.'

'That's all right. It'll sound as if we really are married if we quarrel.'

That surprised him and he couldn't resist asking, 'Is that what you think marriage is about, quarrelling?'

'It's what I saw in my father's case. On the rare occasions they were together, he and his wife argued all the time, with her shouting like a fishwife and him turning icy cold and walking out of the room. She doted on our elder brother, but she hated me and Philip. We could never understand why. Luckily she mostly left us alone, so it wasn't too bad. We always had each other, you see, and a very loving nanny.'

'Well, just to set the record straight, Georgie, quarrelling isn't the main thing I've experienced with the married people I've known. Our nearest neighbours were fond of one another, though they might have an occasional shout, and my mother and stepfather didn't quarrel at all. He might not have been much good as a provider but he was a kind chap, and always treated her with respect, and me like his real son. I was truly sorry when he died.'

'You were lucky, then.'

Patrick fell silent and when Georgie looked at him, wondering why he wasn't speaking, he put one finger to his lips to tell her to keep quiet. She looked round and saw they were approaching a junction where the lane met a lighter wider road. He always seemed to be more alert to their surroundings than she was.

She was spending too much time watching him, not what was going on around them.

They both looked up and down the road, which was clearly not a main one, because it was far too narrow. A signpost on the opposite side pointed to two places in opposite directions, each of them apparently two miles away.

Patrick squinted across at it in the rapidly failing light. 'I don't recognise the place names. Do you?'

Georgie shook her head. 'No. They must be small villages, given how narrow this road is.'

'Are you all right to continue walking for another couple of miles?'

She was, but she was worried about him because his limp seemed to have got worse. But they didn't have much choice. 'Yes, of course. Which way do you think we should go?'

'Who knows? Country roads can twist and turn as if people have all day to go somewhere, so it's anyone's guess which direction will get us to a village more quickly. Let's turn left.'

'Fine by me.'

By the time they'd walked a couple of hundred yards, she could see he was in considerable pain, so put one hand on his arm to stop him. 'Your leg's hurting badly now, isn't it, Patrick? Let's have a rest.'

'Just for a minute or two. It's a while since I've walked so far, especially on rough roads, but we've no choice.'

Suddenly they heard voices and footsteps coming towards them. 'Be ready to run,' he whispered. 'Don't wait for me.'

'I'm not leaving you.'

Before he could say anything else, the owners of the voices came into view, two women warmly wrapped against the cold evening and with arms linked. They stopped at the sight of Patrick and Georgie, looking at them suspiciously.

Georgie took the initiative and moved forward. 'Hello. Our car's broken down along the lane back there.' She pointed. 'We're trying to find help. My husband's leg was injured in France and it's not fully better, so he's not able to walk far. Is there anyone who could help us find a mechanic? Perhaps drive us to see one? We'd pay them for their trouble.'

The older woman answered in a soft voice burred with the local accent. 'There ent no mechanics round here, dearie, and it's going to rain soon, if my rheumatics are anything to go by. But your husband do look to be in pain, poor soul. I noticed when we first saw you how badly he was limping.'

Patrick scowled so fiercely that Georgie dug her elbow in his side, before answering. 'Oh, dear. Then perhaps there's somewhere like a pub where we could stay for the night and look for help in the morning?'

The older one said, 'There ent anywhere near here as does rooms, but if you don't mind sleepin' on our hay bales, we could put you up for the night in our barn. There's going to be a hard frost, but it's snug and weatherproof, and I've got some old blankets I could spread over the hay. They're clean enough. And my husband can go and fetch your car straight away, so that it's safe and out of the weather too. Expensive things, cars. You don't want someone to run off with it.'

'Thank you. But how will he get the car there? The engine won't start.'

'We'll get our horse to pull it. She's a Shire and very strong, and *she* won't break down on you. Good old worker, she is, long as you feed her reg'lar.' She laughed heartily at her own humour.

Georgie forced a smile. 'That's very kind of you. I'm Georgie Farrell and this is my husband, Patrick.'

'Pleased to meet you, ladies,' he said. 'May we know your names?'

'I'm Mrs Needham and so is she.' More laughter. 'I'm her daughter-in-law. Our turn-off is just past the signpost, but we'll have to walk a few hundred yards. Will you be all right to do that, Mr Farrell, and shall I take that bag for you?'

Patrick stiffened visibly. 'I can manage, thank you.'

They walked back along the road together, their breath clouding the air and the first stars twinkling in the sky.

'This way now.' The women turned left onto a muddy farm track.

There was nothing Georgie could do to get Patrick to accept anyone's help, so she concentrated on avoiding muddy patches. She was relieved when they saw a cottage, which had been hidden from the road behind some trees. There were no lights showing there.

'That's my house,' said the younger woman. 'It belongs to our family farm, like we all do. I'll come with you to find Pa and then he can take you to fetch the car, Mr Farrell, while I set things up for you and your wife to sleep in the barn. My Jim's out visiting his cousin and he never comes home till late once the two of them get talking.'

'I'll make you a cup of tea and find you something to eat once we've sorted out your beds and got the car,' the older Mrs Needham said. 'There ent no one goes hungry under my roof.'

Georgie didn't dare offer to go with Mr Needham for the car, because it would have upset Patrick still further not to be considered capable. She watched him go across to the barn to help Mr Needham with the horse. His limp was definitely worse. When she turned round, the older woman was looking at her sympathetically.

'Men don't like to be helped, even when they're not well, do they?'

'No.' She found herself confiding, 'Patrick needs a special shoe on that foot to even up his walking, but he hasn't had time to get that sorted out, because he's only just been demobbed. He hasn't even been able to get a temporary piece put into the shoe yet. They don't waste time when they decide to dismiss you from the Army.'

'Well now, if that isn't a strange coincidence. My father lives with us and he used to mend the family's shoes. He ent a cobbler, but he's clever with his hands. We'll ask him if he can help, but he won't be able to do anything till the morning. He's eighty now and he gets terrible tired by this time of day, because he insists on helping out here and there.'

'You're being very kind to two strangers.'

'We should all help those who've been hurt fighting for our country like your husband has. My brother's son was killed at Ypres, poor lad. Never mind that old limp; you've got your husband back an' that's what counts.'

She patted Georgie's shoulder, dabbed at her own eyes,

then became brisk again. 'I'll get us all something to eat and you go out to the barn and help Minnie to make up the beds.'

It was a big barn with three horses housed to one side, partitioned off from the rest, which was partly filled with hay and a jumble of farm implements. The two men were there and Mr Needham was just finishing putting a harness on the largest animal, a Shire horse. Patrick was standing to one side looking helpless.

Instinctively, Georgie went across to join them and make the acquaintance of the mare. 'She's a fine lady, isn't she? What's her name, Mr Needham?'

'Queenie. I can see you've been around horses, Mrs Farrell,' the farmer said. 'Might be better if you come with me to get the car. Your husband is no doubt better than me at looking after motor cars, but he don't know much about horses, do he? You'll know what I'm talking about if I need help with her.'

Patrick opened his mouth to protest and Minnie Needham said quickly, 'I need to move some bales of hay, so you can help me with them, if you don't mind, Mr Farrell. It's not as if anyone needs you to drive your car, if it's broken.'

Georgie could see the moment when Patrick accepted the arrangements, because his shoulders sagged for a moment, then straightened again.

'My wife could drive the car, if she had to. That's what she's been doing during the war while I was over in France, driving injured soldiers round London.' He smiled ruefully at her.

'Just think of that, then,' Minnie said. 'Is it hard to drive a car, Mrs Farrell?'

'No. Well, I didn't find it hard. It just needs a bit of common sense and not to rush at things till you're used to handling the car on the road. I love driving.'

'There. I'm going to have a try one day, whatever anyone says.' She said this with a pointed look at her father-in-law, then turned back to Patrick. 'You get on your way, Pa. Me and Mr Farrell can rearrange the hay bales.'

Georgie walked back along the lane beside the farmer and the big, gentle mare ambled calmly along behind them. There was enough moonlight to see their way, though her companion was carrying a lantern. Mr Needham had tied a canvas bag to the mare's back, with what he called 'this 'n' that' in it.

When they came to the car, she thought the poor thing looked forlorn, standing on its own.

He studied it, head on one side. 'Small one, ent it? Shouldn't be much trouble for my Queenie to pull it, as long as we can attach ropes to it. Does it have a name?'

'It's called a Swift light car. And you can attach the ropes to the chassis underneath at the front. I'll show you.'

They crouched to look under the car and he nodded as she pointed out where she thought the ropes might go. 'Hmm. That should do it. I'll tell you what, though: your car might move more swiftly, but give me a horse any day. They can get back home under their own steam, horses can. Nor they don't go rusty on you or need filling up with that nasty smelly stuff!'

She didn't contradict him, watching as he pulled ropes and straps out of his bag and set about finding a way to fix them to the car's chassis, so that the vehicle could be pulled along the road.

'We'll go slowly, but I think this'll hold,' he said when he stepped back.

'I need to take the brake off the car first,' she said.

'You do that, Mrs Farrell, and then you get in and steer her, so we can head back without running into the ditch. I'm ready for my tea now, by heck I am. My wife's been to the monthly meeting of the church ladies' committee and tea's always late when them women get nattering.'

He fell silent till the horse had got the car moving, then carried on talking more loudly as they went back along the lane. 'It's good that the war is over, ent it? They're talking of setting up a war memorial for our three villages now, because we've lost a few lads from round here. It'd be nice to have something to remember them by. We didn't even get the bodies back for most of them, so there are no graves to put flowers on. There were too many being killed, I suppose.'

'My brother was killed in France.'

'Ah. I'm sorry about that. But at least we beat them rascals, didn't we, so it wasn't all in vain?'

'We did indeed.' People said that sort of thing, trying to comfort you, but it still hurt every time she thought of her twin. Always would, she supposed.

The car bumped along slowly. Mr Needham stopped the mare once to adjust her makeshift harness, then set her off again. It seemed to take a long time to get back to the farm and Georgie was feeling exhausted and chilled through by then.

Patrick came out to help push the car under a lean-to, then the farmer patted it as if it was one of his animals. 'There you are, little Swift. It's going to rain before morning, but you're out of the weather now, so don't try to go rusty on us.'

When Patrick thanked him, he clapped the younger ma. on the shoulder in a fatherly gesture. 'It'd be a poor lookout if we couldn't help the stranger at the gate. We'll fetch Eddie from down the road to look at your car tomorrow. He's as near as we've got to a mechanic round here. He'd be no use to you tonight, I'm afraid. It's his birthday and he allus has a drink or two extra when he can find something to celebrate, old Eddie does.'

Mrs Needham came to the door of the farm to shout across the yard, 'Dinner in fifteen minutes. I left a bowl of water in the barn for you to wash your hands in, Mrs Farrell. Be careful with that oil lamp. We don't want the place setting on fire.'

'We'll be very careful, Mrs Needham,' Patrick called, then led the way back inside the barn. 'No trouble with the horse pulling the car, Georgie?'

'None at all. Aren't they a nice family?'

'Very nice.'

She stood for a moment in the doorway, looking round. The lamp was hanging on a hook near the door, making a circle of bright light, but the far corners of the barn were still in shadow. In the other half of the building, Mr Needham was rubbing Queenie's muddy legs down and talking to the mare in a low, fond voice.

When Georgie turned back to Patrick, he was looking at her anxiously so she tried to keep her voice cheerful. 'I think we'll do fine here. I'm so tired I could sleep standing up.'

'No need to do that, though I've dozed on my feet before now. You get your wash first, Georgie. There's a privy through that side door. Take the lamp with you. I've already used it.'

She attended to her needs, then brought back the lamp and quickly washed her hands and face in the bowl of now tepid water.

Patrick used the bowl of water after her. 'I think we'll ask the Needhams and their neighbours not to mention that we've been here if anyone asks after us. I'm sure we can trust them. And actually, this incident might have a good side to it. No one will know where to find you, since you've no connection whatsoever with this farm. There isn't a telephone anywhere nearby, so we couldn't get in touch with anyone if we wanted to.'

'Well, I shall regard it as a chance to get a good night's sleep. And I bet your leg will be better for a rest, too. You're favouring it more than you were before.'

'It is hurting a bit. I've not walked that far for a while, though we didn't get much choice about it today, did we? It turns out Mrs Needham's father does the family's cobbling and he's going to look at my shoe and perhaps make me a leather wedge to put inside it in the morning.'

'There you are. It's an ill wind, isn't it?'

He hesitated, then asked, 'You're sure you're not worried about spending the night here with me, are you, Georgie?'

'Of course not. It's you who's doing all the worrying.'

'You're a wonderful woman to be in trouble with.'

She chuckled. 'Thanks for the compliment. Well, I think it's a compliment.'

'It is. And a very sincere one, too. The only other woman I've met with your fortitude was my mother, who would have soldiered on today without complaining, just as you have.'

'That really is a compliment, then. Your voice grows

softer whenever you speak of her. You must have loved her very much.'

'I did.'

'But at least you have a brother still.'

'Half-brother. And unfortunately, we don't get on.'

'That's sad. My twin and I were the best of pals. Most of the time, anyway, and we never fell out for long.'

'You'll have some golden memories of him, then.'

'Yes. Wonderful memories.' Something in her eased just a little. Patrick seemed to have a knack of saying exactly the thing she needed to hear whenever she got upset.

He finished drying his hands on the rough piece of towel hanging on a hook, then gestured to the door. 'Shall we join our kind hosts? Mrs Needham was saying how hungry her husband would be so we don't want to keep the poor man waiting.'

After he'd turned the lamp down low, they walked together across the moonlit yard towards the welcoming display of lights in the farmhouse.

'It's like a small kingdom here,' she said.

'Yes. They're lucky people. I don't know where I'll settle down now that Ma's not there in Rochdale. And to tell you the truth, I don't really consider anywhere home after so many years away. I was in the Army right from the start.'

'You'll find yourself a kingdom of your own one day, Patrick. You're too intelligent not to make a go of your new life.' She knocked on the kitchen door and followed the shouted instructions to 'Come on in, do, an' close that door quick'.

'Ah, Mrs Needham. Something smells wonderful . . .'

* * *

That same night three men met in London, each making his way to the rendezvous on foot. They exchanged what information they had, sharing worries about a traitor at the bureau or one of its related centres of activity.

'I can't think how we missed it,' Cotterell said.

'Easy to miss small details when you're working on major life-or-death projects. Anyway, I think the fellow was being held in reserve. But I think we're on the right track about him now.'

'Yes. But I'm afraid you're going to have to assume that no news is good news where your daughter is concerned.'

'We'll see about that. I have a couple of ideas to pursue.'

'Be very careful, Gerald. Our chappie isn't a fool and he won't hesitate to kill people to save his own skin.'

'I'm not a fool either. And I hope *I* get a chance to kill him first. I shan't hesitate. Hard times need hard measures.'

As he walked home through the darkness he thought grimly that if anyone hurt Georgie, he'd kill them if it was the last thing he did.

# *Chapter Eleven*

Aaron Tesworth, better known to his friends as Tez, had business in London, so he drove from Honeyfield to Malmesbury and left his motor car there, taking an early train to the capital. He visited his lawyer, then took a taxi across town, expecting to have lunch with Mr Cotterell at his club.

He had a new photo of his adopted son to share with the man whose own son had been killed in the war. But Philip had fathered a son and Tez felt honoured to be bringing up his best friend's child. He'd fallen in love with the boy's mother almost on sight, but it was only after Philip's death that she'd turned to him.

He walked into the club, nodding to the concierge at the door, whom he'd known for years. 'Mr Cotterell in yet?'

'No, sir. Haven't seen him for a day or two.'

'Oh? He invited me to have lunch with him today.'

'If you'd like to sit and read the newspaper in the foyer, sir, I'm sure he'll soon turn up.'

But half an hour passed and there was no sign of Mr Cotterell. This was so unlike his friend that Tez asked to see the head porter. If anyone would know what was going on, Jonnby would.

The dignified old man came out of his little office at the side of the foyer and beckoned to Tez. 'I gather you're looking for Mr Cotterell? Could we speak about it in private, sir?'

He took Tez into the office and explained that he'd had a phone call only an hour ago to say that Mr Cotterell had gone missing. 'I've been asked to report to the military police if anyone comes here asking for him. I wonder if you'd mind speaking to the captain in charge now?'

'Happy to. I hope Cotterell's all right.'

'I hope so too. I'll telephone the number I was given.'

After a brief explanation, Jonnby handed the earpiece of the phone to Tez.

A man's voice boomed out. 'Tesworth? Ralph Jordan here. We've met a couple of times.'

Tez leant forward to speak into the mouthpiece. 'Yes. I remember.' He hadn't taken to Jordan, who was rather given to barking orders at people, whether he had authority over them or not.

'About Cotterell, I wonder if you'd mind coming to the bureau and speaking to me? I'm at a bit of a loss about where to look for him.'

'Happy to help in any way I can, though I doubt I know anything pertinent.'

'Nonetheless, one would be grateful for your help.'

It sounded more a command than a request, however politely phrased, so Tez took a taxi to the building that looked more like an elegant private residence than a government bureau. He gave his name to the man stationed just inside the entrance and was quickly escorted up to a comfortable office by a young lieutenant who didn't attempt to make conversation.

A man rose to greet them. 'Ah, Tesworth. Thank you for coming. Please sit down.'

Tez recognised Captain Jordan, took the chair indicated and waited.

'Were you aware that Mr Cotterell was missing?'

'No, of course not, or I'd not have come up to London. We had an appointment to have lunch together today, only he didn't turn up at his club, which is unlike him.'

'He's been missing for a couple of days now and no one knows where he is.'

'That's strange.'

'Yes, very much out of character.' Jordan hesitated then added, 'Are you sure you haven't heard anything from or of him?'

Tez was dumbfounded at the persistence of the questioning. 'I'm certain. I only wish I could help you.'

'As Cotterell has been involved in some highly confidential matters, the bigwigs are rather concerned.'

'Well, yes. One would be concerned. Did you speak to his daughter? What does Georgie think?'

'I did speak to her. She said she knew nothing.'

'You'd think he'd at least have told her that he was going to be away. Perhaps I could have a word with her?'

'That's not possible. The day after he disappeared someone

tried to kidnap her. I'd hired some former soldiers to keep watch over her, but now they've vanished, and her with them, so we're not sure where she is or whether she's safe.'

Tez could only gape at him. It sounded like one of those moving pictures about gangsters and he almost expected to see captions appear in mid-air, as they did on the cinema screen. 'Did you trust the men you hired?'

'Of course I did. They had impeccable Army records and had been wounded in the service of their country.'

'Then perhaps they took her into hiding.'

'We hope so, but why didn't she tell us she was going away? Are you sure you haven't any idea where she might be? She hasn't contacted your wife, for instance? We know the two of them are particularly good friends.'

'No. Bella would have told me if Georgie had been in touch with her or was in trouble.'

'Since we're not sure whether Cotterell has been taken prisoner or not, what would *your* guess be about where either he or his daughter could have taken refuge?'

Tez frowned down at his hands, puzzled that the captain would ask him so many questions when he had nothing to do with Cotterell's work. The more he considered it, the more it seemed strange that he was being grilled like this.

'Well, Tesworth?'

He took a quick decision not to make any guesses. 'Sorry. Haven't the faintest idea where they might have gone, I'm afraid.'

'What did you say your current connection with Cotterell was?'

'It's purely social. He's the father of my best friend, who was killed in '16. Mr Cotterell and I keep in touch and we have lunch together sometimes when I come up to town, that's all.'

'What does he talk to you about?'

Why the hell was Jordan questioning him like this? 'Cotterell talks about the war in general, who's been killed recently, that sort of thing. He never talks about his work, if that's what you're getting at.'

'I see. Well, I won't deny this is disappointing. I won't take up any more of your time, but I must emphasise that if you hear anything or find out even the smallest piece of information, about either Cotterell or his daughter, you are to let *me* know, but no one else, for security reasons.'

'Yes. Right.'

Tez left the building but to his surprise, quickly realised he was being followed. He strolled on towards his mother's comfortable London home, giving no sign that he'd noticed. The man tailing him was good, with nothing about his appearance to draw attention, but Tez had learnt in France to notice every single detail of what was going on nearby. It had saved his life more than once.

He paused a couple of times, pretending to gaze in shop windows, but really watching the reflections from the street in the glass. The same man stopped each time he lingered like this but set off again as soon as Tez did, so he knew he hadn't been mistaken.

Once he was inside his mother's comfortable house, he let the butler take his overcoat and trilby, and stood frowning. Something about the interview had been . . . not quite right. Definitely.

But who would set a tail on him? Jordan came from

a good family, should be absolutely trustworthy, and Tez couldn't even work out why he felt so suspicious of the chap. But he'd learnt to trust his instincts.

He realised the butler was waiting for instructions. 'Sorry. Thinking about something. Mother at home, Potterly?'

'Yes, sir. She has a lady with her who's been there for well over ten minutes.'

Which was butler-talk for it being time this visitor left.

'I'll pop in to see her.'

Tez was shown into his mother's sitting room and greeted her and the friend with what he hoped was a pleasant smile.

The minute the elderly lady took her leave of 'dearest Marguerite' he stopped forcing the smile and said abruptly, 'Can you ask Potterly to tell callers you're not at home, Mother? I've something I need to talk to you about. It's important. At least, I think it is.'

She gave him one of her searching looks and nodded, ringing for the butler and asking him to bring refreshments and turn away any further visitors.

While they were waiting, Tez explained quickly about Mr Cotterell and the day's events, including his worries that something about Jordan wasn't quite right.

'I knew Gerald was missing,' she said quietly. 'I think we'd better send for Constance Berrens. She'll know what he's doing if anyone does. They've worked very closely together at times, though that's not general knowledge, and I've been privileged to help them when I could.'

'*You* have? You never said anything, Mother.'

'One doesn't when something is confidential.'

'Then maybe Lady Berrens will know if there's anything I can do to help. I don't like to leave matters like this.'

'You're sure Georgie hasn't contacted Bella?'

'Certain of it. Bella would have told me. She knows how fond I am of Georgie.'

While they waited for Constance to arrive, they chatted about little Philip and Honeyfield House, in whose management his mother was involved on behalf of the Greyladies Trust.

'Why exactly are you suspicious of Jordan?' she asked suddenly.

'I can't put a finger on what exactly was wrong. Yes, I can – now I come to think of it, he kept looking towards a connecting door at the side of his office. I bet someone else was there, listening in.'

'Well, if you're worried about him, then something is definitely not right. You've never been a fool.'

'Thank you for the compliment.'

'I suppose if Gerald Cotterell suspected there was a traitor in his bureau, he'd have expected John Garbury to look into it. The two have known one another for a long time. Is it a coincidence that Garbury's been knocked out of the picture at this moment, do you think?'

'What's happened to him?'

'Motor car accident. Serious injuries, but he'll live.'

She frowned. 'I'd not have thought Jordan a traitor. I've met him several times and he's very stiff and proper. Maybe—'

'Maybe what?'

'There's Butterly. I really can't take to the man.'

'I can't say I know him.'

'A tinpot dictator where paperwork and regulations are concerned, even at the bureau. No, it can't be him!'

'Now you have got me worried, Mother. I don't like to think of Georgie being in danger, for her own sake. If she gets in touch and asks to stay with us, Bella won't hesitate to help her, then *she* might be in danger as well, which would be worse.' Just let anyone lay one damned fingertip on his wife and he'd make very sure they regretted it. He might be missing some fingers but he wasn't missing his wits or his physical strength.

He looked up. 'Is that the doorbell? I hope it's Lady Berrens. She used to terrify me when I was a child, but she's been brilliant during the war. The woman deserves a medal.'

'The things Constance most deserves a medal for will have to be kept secret.'

Which left him gaping.

Constance Berrens was shown in by Potterly. She was all smiles until they explained what had happened, then she frowned and became very quiet.

'Surely *you* have some idea of where Cotterell and his daughter could be?' Tez asked. 'I know what good friends you and he are.'

She flushed slightly, biting the corner of her lip as if dubious about whether to say anything.

'Couldn't you even hazard a guess?' he pressed. 'Surely you trust us?'

'I think it'd be best to keep our thoughts on that matter to ourselves, Tez dear, but I'm sure we could both come up with fairly accurate guesses.'

He frowned. 'Well no, I can't guess where either of them is. After all, they vanished at different times. Except for Westcott, and that's too obvious, surely?'

'I must say it puzzles me that Georgie should have disappeared as well,' his mother put in. 'I'd swear Gerald always kept what he was doing completely to himself, even with her, so she can't be involved in it.'

'But she could be used as a hostage to force him to do something.'

Another silence, then Lady Berens said thoughtfully, 'I know he worried about her more than I expected and preferred to have her where he could keep an eye on her. He didn't even want her joining the VADs, which is why I offered her a job with my lady drivers' group in London. She was good at it too, a born driver.'

Tez nodded. 'My Bella is a good driver, too, and some of those ambulances she handled are unwieldy vehicles, I can tell you.'

'Both of them have more than done their bit for the war effort. Georgie isn't the sort to stay quietly at home. Like a bird released from a cage, she was, when she first got away from that so-called mother of hers.'

Tez grinned pointedly at the two ladies. 'None of the women I'm close to are meek little creatures.'

They smiled back but the smiles soon faded and Lady Berrens stood up. 'I'm sorry I haven't been able to help you, Tez. I must go now. I have a meeting to attend. If either of you hear anything about Georgie, you'll let me know? Or if she needs help, she can always come to me. My house is . . . fairly secure.'

It was only as he was waiting for his mother's car to pick him up at the front of the house, to take him to the railway station that Tez suddenly realised that Lady Berrens hadn't asked them to let her know about Mr Cotterell.

He'd bet she had a very good idea of where Georgie's father was. Or she might even be sheltering him herself. And whatever she was involved in, his mother must be part of too.

He was relieved that he hadn't said anything to Jordan about Greyladies or Honeyfield as possible refuges for Georgie.

As his mother's car drew up in front of the house and he got in, he watched the man dogging his footsteps run out into the street further along to try to flag down an approaching motor taxi. But it was already carrying a passenger, so he had no luck.

The chauffeur said, 'He'll not catch up with us, sir,' and drove off quickly.

Tez stared at the back of the man's head. Another surprise, that his mother's chauffeur should be aware of, or even involved in what was going on.

'Thank you.' Tez's thoughts were in turmoil. These people trying to cause trouble were clever enough for Mr Cotterell to judge it better to go into hiding, so he'd better be extremely careful how he went about things, too. He had a family to protect now.

As the train rattled its way through the stark winter countryside towards Malmesbury, Tez couldn't get Cotterell out of his thoughts. What was the man planning? His friend's father was one of the cleverest people Tez had ever met.

He wished he could help. He'd felt rather useless since he was invalided out. He'd done small jobs for his mother to help the war effort, and had taken over the financial reins of his little family. He'd also just been asked to chair the group getting together to raise money for a war memorial in the village, something many places in Britain were doing, because the sacrifices of those who'd fallen must not be forgotten.

But it wasn't enough, somehow. He'd gone into the Army intending to make it his career and had never held or trained for a civilian job. He was lucky that he'd inherited enough money to live on, but he did wish he could find something truly worthwhile to do with the rest of his life.

Thank goodness for Bella. She was the joy of his little world, and the next baby she bore would be his. The mere thought of her cheered him up. Thank goodness she was a practical woman who didn't dwell on the past. She'd had a whirlwind romance with poor Philip but it had been brief and Tez knew she was growing fond of him. Well, she was *his* wife now, in every way, and they were happy together. It was as simple as that.

Thinking of Bella brought him another worry. Surely he wouldn't be followed out into the country? The people at the bureau must know where he lived. Perhaps he should have stayed on in London? But then if he had done, there would have been no one in Honeyfield to protect Bella and little Philip.

Where the hell was Georgie? Not to mention these men guarding her? How could they just vanish?

He prayed they were to be trusted.

At Honeyfield, Bella came home to be greeted by her daily help with, 'That dratted telephone rang, Mrs Tesworth. About half an hour after you left, it was. Fair makes you jump, it does, when the bell goes off.'

Bella sighed. Nothing she said or did could persuade Ivy to pick up the telephone and take a message. The poor woman was convinced that she would do something wrong and 'break' it!

Bella wondered who had phoned. Probably Tez, who might have decided to stay overnight in London with his mother. He kept a change of clothes there because something occasionally cropped up where she needed his help, or wanted him to act as her escort.

Then she heard little Philip cry out for attention from the nursery and she hurried upstairs to play with him for a while. She had a girl from the village living in to look after her son or help with the household chores generally, as well as Ivy coming in daily, but she liked to play with little Philip herself. She hadn't grown up surrounded by servants and still couldn't get used to standing aside from jobs in her own home, and especially not from raising her son.

If it was Tez who'd called, he'd phone again, surely? But the hours passed and nothing happened, so maybe it hadn't been him. Who else could it have been, though?

When she saw headlights turn into the street just after six o'clock, she went to look out of the sitting room window and check it was her husband. Yes. Dearest Tez. She smiled to see him back.

How lucky she was to have had him to turn to after Philip died. He was such a dear.

Tez got out of the car, still undecided about what to tell Bella. Should he burden her with his worries about her friend Georgie and Mr Cotterell, or should he keep the fact that they were missing to himself?

When he'd had something to eat and they were sitting together in front of a cosy log fire, she said quietly, 'You may as well tell me, Tez.'

'Am I that easy to read?'

'I know you rather well now. You can put on that glassy-eyed bonhomie for others when you feel the need, but it doesn't fool me. What's wrong, dear?'

So he told her about the Cotterells.

She was quiet for a moment or two, then said slowly, 'Since it wasn't you, I wonder if it was Georgie who phoned earlier? You know how silly Ivy is about answering the phone. She just let it ring, as usual.'

'Could it have been Georgie, do you think? She might have been asking to take refuge here.'

'Would you mind if she did?'

'No. Of course not. Mr Cotterell has given most of his life to serving our country; I could do no less than support him or his daughter if they needed help against our mutual enemies. But I'd want you to be careful.'

'Of course. Only, if it was her, why hasn't she phoned again?'

'Maybe she's found somewhere else to hide.'

But the worry that Georgie might be seeking help and not finding it stayed with him and he slept badly that night till he came up with a plan to take a few precautions of his own.

In the morning he shared his idea with Bella. 'I thought I'd alert the members of the War Memorial Committee to keep an eye out for strangers acting suspiciously in Honeyfield. What do you think?'

'It wouldn't hurt. They're a nice group of people and I'd trust every single one of them. You'd better tell them to keep it to themselves, though. If Mrs Saunders at the baker's gets to hear of it, she'll tell everyone who comes into the shop, and there are a few people in the village I'd not trust.'

So he went out for a stroll and had a quiet word with the village policeman, the curate and his wife, and several others. It all seemed so peaceful, too quiet a place for trouble, surely? Though nowhere was exempt, and the war might have ended officially, but some would continue to carry their hatred of their opponents in their hearts, he was sure.

After that, he went along to Honeyfield House, where five women were currently taking refuge from troublesome husbands or families. He let the matron and Sal, the general maid, know to keep their eyes open. Sal would alert her husband Cole, a sturdy fellow partly employed to defend the women if necessary.

On the way back he stopped for a chat with Malcolm Leatherby, from whom he bought his motor spirit. Malcolm did minor car repairs, but he was looking old and tired these days, though he snapped at anyone who dared to suggest he take things easy.

'I'll let you know if any strangers come in for motor spirit,' Malcolm offered at once. 'Though I don't usually get many outsiders, just folk from round about, usually.'

'Keep it to yourself.'

Malcolm tapped the side of his nose. 'I can do that.'

As Tez walked back along the short street where he lived, he stopped to look at the gardens of the old house next door to his. It was called Orchard View but last summer everything had been so overgrown it had had no view at all.

Now things were winter bare, you could see that the garden was badly neglected and the house downright shabby. He wished someone would buy it, come to live there and set things to rights. It had become an eyesore.

His own garden was neat and tidy, with a few evergreens to brighten the winter. He wished he could give Bella more than a smallish house in Pear Tree Lane, but he wasn't a rich man and anyway, she didn't hanker after a large house and a life of luxury, bless her.

He shivered as he glanced up at the sky. It was looking like rain and the wind had become bitingly cold. This was a day to spend indoors, unless you were obliged to go out.

It was also a day to worry and be unable to settle to anything, as he soon found out. Poor Georgie! He hoped she was somewhere safe and warm.

# *Chapter Twelve*

The following day seemed long and tedious to the three people left behind at Westcott. They'd decided to stay on another day but were keeping a very careful watch for any signs of strangers in the area. During the afternoon, they asked Cecil to stroll into the village and see whether any strangers had been sighted by his friends. He came back and reported that all was quiet.

Marge provided them with a meal but Rosie found herself without appetite.

Dennis looked at her across the table. 'Eat a bit more, lass. You need to keep your strength up.'

She forced in two or three mouthfuls then shook her head and pushed her plate away. 'Shouldn't they be back by now?'

'You've been wondering that for a while and I'm no wiser now than I was last time you asked me,' Dennis told her.

'Oh. Sorry.'

She tried to smile at him but it was a poor attempt. He put an arm round her. 'I expect they'll be all right. Patrick's a sensible chap. He'll look after her.'

But it grew late and Patrick and Georgie still hadn't come home. The three of them were now seriously worried about their friends' safety.

'If they're not here by dawn, we'll set off for this Honeyfield place and hope to find them there,' Dennis said as they went up to bed. 'Wake me when it's my turn to keep watch, Martin.'

Some time later Rosie came awake with a start, staring round in the darkness. What was that? She was sure some sound had woken her, because she was a light sleeper.

She lay still, hardly daring to breathe in case she missed hearing it again. But she didn't miss it and realised with a sudden leap of terror in her chest that what she'd heard sounded like footsteps on the gravel of the drive that led round the side of the house. They were muffled and intermittent as if the person was trying not to make a sound.

Yes, there they were again! Footsteps definitely. And again. Whoever was there was walking quietly, but not quietly enough. Well, you couldn't avoid the gravelled areas completely, whatever you did, not if you wanted to get to the big house.

Thank goodness for gravel!

She was out of bed in a flash, glad now that she'd given in to the temptation to sleep fully dressed, in case she had to flee. She hadn't wanted to run round the countryside in her old flannel nightie!

As she was pulling on her coat, there was the faintest of taps on her bedroom door and it began to open. She grabbed the poker from the side of the bed and waited.

'Rosie? Are you awake?'

She whispered, 'Dennis! Oh, thank goodness it's you. Yes, I'm awake and dressed.'

'Good girl. Grab what you can and come with me at once. There's someone waiting at the front of the house and someone else is creeping round to the back. Martin's gone to wake Cecil and Marge and send them down to the cellar. You and I will meet him at the car.'

She snatched up her bag. 'I'm ready.'

'Good lass!' He led the way down the backstairs, through the silent kitchen and into the scullery. 'I don't think they'll have anyone watching the laundry door yet, but if there is, I'll thump them and you run for the car.'

She took a firmer hold of her poker, ready to do her share of the thumping if she saw the chance. Ma had always told her not to rely on other people protecting you.

Dennis led the way to the door that led out to the washing lines. For a moment he paused and they both listened. But they couldn't hear any sound from outside.

'Let's go.' He turned the key in the lock and opened the door, stepping to one side as he did so to let her pass.

That probably saved him because a cudgel thumped into the door frame making him stumble sideways.

It rose into the air once more, but before the man could bring it down again, Rosie jabbed out with her poker, catching the stranger in his middle and making him go 'Oof'. She followed that up by bringing the poker down on his shoulder as hard as she could.

He yelled and fell to the ground, letting the cudgel drop and rolling about in agony, cursing.

Dennis took her hand and dragged her past the man, who was still moaning and making no attempt to get up and follow them. He hoped she'd broken one of their attacker's bones! There couldn't be anyone else nearby or they'd have come running.

Without saying a word, Dennis tugged her across to the kitchen garden, where the bare earth would muffle their footsteps. Within less than a minute they'd reached the back lane.

He stopped and put one finger to his lips. She could see quite well in the faint moonlight now that her eyes were used to the darkness, so she stopped too, not trying to speak, just listening hard and trying not to pant loudly.

There was no sound of pursuit. 'Follow me along the edge of the ditch,' he muttered in her ear.

She nodded and did that, not caring about the mud, only wanting to escape from an enemy who was pursuing her new mistress so relentlessly she was sure these people wouldn't hesitate to harm anyone else who got in their way.

When they got to the car, they found Martin waiting for them with the crank in place.

As Dennis flung himself into the driving seat, Rosie got into the back seat and Martin swung the handle.

Rosie prayed as hard as she could that the motor would start first time.

It didn't and the sound of it must have carried to the house, because she heard shouts from that direction. As Martin cranked the car engine again, she had a sudden thought and opened the rear door of the car. When the ca[r] did start to move, Martin would need to get in quickly.

This time the engine coughed, hesitated, then started chugging steadily, so she pushed the car door wide open, saying, 'Get in quick!'

The vehicle was already moving as Martin jumped on the running board, scrambled from there into the back and leant out to snatch at the swinging car door and close it.

He looked to be leaning dangerously far, so Rosie grabbed the back of his jacket, holding on for dear life. She groaned in relief as he got the door shut and sagged back on the seat, panting and grinning at her.

'Thanks! You might just have saved my life, lass.'

'You're a quick thinker, Rosie,' Dennis said from the driving seat. 'First you bashed the man attacking me and probably broke his shoulder, then you thought to open the car door. Well done!'

'You have to think on your feet if you grow up where I did. At least, you do if you want to stay safe, especially when you're a woman.'

She blew out a deep breath, then another one. 'Eeh, my heart's still pounding, though.'

'So is mine.'

'Who are they?'

'Wish I knew.' Dennis's voice was grim.

'I'd not even recognise them if I passed them in the street.'

'No, nor would I.'

Silence as they all considered that. No one could even guess at the identity of their pursuers.

'Do you know where to go?' Rosie asked after a while.

'More or less. But what I don't know is how to warn Patrick about them coming to Westcott.'

'Patrick won't go rushing back there,' Martin said confidently. 'He'll do a recce first. They'd not have made him up to sergeant if he hadn't been good in tight corners.'

'I hope you're right. You two all right in the back there?'

'Snug as fleas in a blanket.'

'Good. I'm not going to stop to try to light the car lamps. We'll be better driving in the dark. Lights can show from a long way away at night. I don't want them to know which direction we're taking. We'll work out the details of finding this Honeyfield place later. For the moment I just want to get away from them, and I'd rather not meet anyone else who could remember us, either.'

'I doubt there'll be anyone out and about at this hour.'

'Pray that you're right.'

After a while Dennis turned off the road and bumped along onto a piece of rough land behind some trees. 'We need to find out if we're being followed.' He switched off the engine and got out of the car, standing on the running board in the darkness, listening as hard as he could and scanning the horizon all the time, eyes moving to and fro.

Suddenly he let out a low exclamation and got back to the car, pointing to one side. 'Is that light in the distance a pair of headlamps, do you think? Have a look, Martin, lad.'

'Could be.'

A light breeze touched their faces with its chilly fingers as they all watched the beam of light. To their relief, it seemed to be moving away from them. After a few moments it disappeared completely and then there was nothing except the faint moonlight and the shadowy landscape.

Dennis went back to keeping watch for a while but could see and hear nothing else, so got back into the car, shivering. 'It might be a good idea for us to stay here and not drive on till it's starting to get light and other people are out and about. That way no one will think it unusual to see our car passing by.'

Without waiting for their agreement, he got into the driving seat. 'Leave the car doors open and keep on the alert.'

'How long do you think they'll keep searching for us?' Rosie asked.

'Who knows? But since they've got their headlights on, we'll see them coming for as long as it's dark. And they won't easily find us here even if they drive past on the road, because the ground slopes downhill behind the trees.'

A short time later Martin said, 'How about I go and have a recce, make sure we can't be seen at all from the road?'

'Good idea.' Dennis sighed and huddled down in the driving seat. 'You all right, lass?'

'Yes. A bit cold, even with this blanket. You must be frozen. Do you want me to check if there's another one in the box on the rear luggage rack?'

'No. I don't want to do anything that makes a metallic noise, like opening the box would. That sort of sound would carry a long way in the quiet of the night and anyone would be able to tell it wasn't natural.'

'Oh. Yes. I see.'

He chuckled softly, 'This is comfort compared to what we've been through. Don't worry about us. It's you I'm concerned about.'

'I haven't had an easy life, Dennis. I've been cold and hungry many a time.'

'Me too.'

It seemed ages before Martin came back, then suddenly he was standing there beside the car.

'There's no sign of this car from up on the road, so I reckon we can stay here till it's fully light.'

'Good. Get back into the car, but I'll keep my window open so that I can hear if anyone approaches.'

Rosie shivered. 'It was kind of you to let me have the blanket, but I'm still cold and you two will be frozen since we none of us have any really warm clothing. How about we all sit in the back and huddle under the blanket close together? We'll be much warmer that way.'

'If you don't mind us cuddling up to you,' Dennis said.

'Mind? I'm freezing cold here. Just keep your hands to yourselves, that's all.'

After they'd settled down she said suddenly, 'We used to sit like this on winter evenings when we were little, cuddling close to keep warm, taking it in turns to be in the middle. Ma and Pa couldn't always afford to buy coal, even in winter.'

'Aye, we did that sometimes, too,' Dennis said.

They fell silent, glad of the warmth of the other bodies and the blanket.

'Shhh!' Rosie said suddenly. 'I heard something.'

They all listened, just about holding their breath and heard the sound of a car engine.

'I'm getting up on the car bonnet and having a look round,' Martin said.

When he'd got out, Rosie whispered to Dennis. 'They're not giving up easily, are they?'

'Do you think it's them?'

'Who else would it be out in the middle of nowhere at this time on a cold winter's night? I hope Miss Cotterell and Patrick are safe.'

'Aye. He's a good chap, should have been an officer. If anyone can save her, I reckon it'll be him.'

Martin got back into the car. 'I could see car lights for a long time going to and fro, so it's probably them. Well, even if they find us, they might have a few shocks. Chaps like me won't forget what we learnt about protecting ourselves – and our mates.'

'Someone will notice them if they keep blundering around the countryside.'

'Miss Cotterell didn't think they knew about her connection to Honeyfield, even if they know about her friend Bella. It's a refuge for women, so we'll be all right there, won't we?' Rosie asked.

'I hope so. I wish we had a map.'

'We'll find our way there. I can sense which way is east and west. But I prefer to arrive after it gets light, so that we look like normal travellers,' Dennis said. 'We'll see whether Miss Cotterell's directions were good enough for us to find this Pear Tree Lane without asking anyone.'

They snuggled down and soon Rosie was asleep. Not long afterwards, Martin began snoring.

But Dennis stayed awake and alert, regarding himself as on watch, listening intently to the night noises. He could do without sleep but he didn't want to lose his life after getting safely through the war – well, more or less safely. He fingered the scar on his forehead and sighed over the missing fingers. A lot of chaps had lost fingers.

Damned nuisance that was. And ugly. But Rosie didn't seem to mind it.

Eh, she was a grand lass. As good as a man she was, if you were in trouble.

# *Chapter Thirteen*

Georgie woke with a start as Patrick began to toss and turn. It took her a minute or two to work out where she was, but the lamp was still burning at its lowest setting and its light was enough to remind her they were in a hay barn and why.

It was still early, but a further light shone from the stables at the other side of the wooden wall dividing the interior of the building into two parts. Someone was already at work and she heard Mr Needham speaking gently to an animal. Even as she looked, a dog came to poke its head through the open doorway and stare across at them with a soft woof.

By the time her eyes had grown used to the dimness, Patrick was also waking up.

At first he stared round as if seeing something in the far distance and muttered, 'Keep your ammunition dry, lads.'

After lying perfectly still for a few seconds, still staring, he let out a whoosh of breath and came fully awake. 'Sorry, Georgie. I sometimes dream I'm back there.'

'Such memories are giving a lot of men nightmares, and no wonder. It must have been hell.'

He nodded. 'Aye. It was. I hope the others spent the night safe and warm at Westcott.'

They heard footsteps and Mr Needham peered round the doorway of the stables. 'Ah. Thought I heard voices. Sorry if I woke you but we start work early here. My wife says you're to go to the kitchen when you're ready to eat and her dad has already got his tools out and is sorting through his scraps of leather to see if he can do anything about that shoe of yours, Mr Farrell. Fair set up to be able to help an ex-soldier, he is.'

He went back to work and Georgie slipped out of bed. 'I'll just use the privy.'

When she got back, Patrick followed her example and the farmer showed them where to get some clean water. She had a quick wash of her hands and face, gasping at how cold the water was.

As she reached for the square of ragged towel hanging on a hook and started drying her hands, she spoke her thoughts aloud, 'I wonder where my father slept last night?'

Patrick answered obliquely. 'He sounds to be a clever man.'

'Yes, very clever.'

'Then your dad will have found somewhere safe.'

'Unless he was taken by surprise.'

'Worrying won't help. I'm sure you can trust him to look after himself.'

That was a comforting thought and Patrick was

probably right. She'd already decided that her companion was another clever man. It was one of the many qualities that attracted her to him.

It was still dark outside but lights shone from the farmhouse as they had the night before. It looked so cheerful and normal. It wasn't raining this morning but there were clouds in the sky. There was some faint brightening of the sky on what Georgie supposed must be the eastern horizon. She was completely lost as to where they were, but no doubt their kind hosts would be able to tell them what the nearest town was.

The kitchen was warm and Mrs Needham was cooking slices of bacon in a huge frying pan. An elderly man bobbed his head at them in greeting from the far end of the big table and their hostess turned to smile at them.

'Ah. There you are. We let you sleep in a bit.'

Georgie managed not to chuckle. The clock on the mantelpiece said six. What time did this family get up normally if that was considered 'sleeping in'? 'Thank you. Very kind of you. The food smells wonderful.'

Mrs Needham waved her hand towards the table. 'Sit you down. I'll have your breakfast ready in a minute or two. This is my dad, Ben Barton, only everyone calls him Grandpa. When you've finished eating, he'll take a look at your shoe, Mr Farrell.'

'I'll do my best to help, but I'm not a trained cobbler,' the old man warned them.

'Any improvement would be much appreciated,' Patrick said.

'I seen a man once as had a built-up shoe and he let me look inside, just out of curiosity. Neatly done, it were. Mine won't be as good as that but I'm sure I can do *something* to help you till you can get a proper shoe made.'

Another man came in just then and Mrs Needham said, 'Sit down, lad. It's nearly ready, then you can get back to your work.' She turned to their guests. 'This is our labourer, Alan.'

As she put a plate in front of him, he picked up his knife and fork with only a quick mumbled 'Hello' to the visitors. Clearly food was much more important to him.

Mrs Needham went back to her frying pan and soon afterwards served them large platters of ham, fried eggs and sausages with hunks of crusty bread. There were clearly no food shortages here.

She plonked a huge teapot on the table, then filled a big mug with tea and set two slices of bread and jam on a plate beside it at the head of the table. 'First meal of the day for my husband,' she said cheerfully. 'He has a proper meal at nine. Good eater, he is. My turn now.'

Patrick breathed in the smell of the fried ham with a happy sigh. He hadn't seen so much food for a long time. 'We'll pay you for this, Mrs Needham.'

'That you won't, lad. You've paid already with your service to our country.'

'Oh. Well, thank you.'

Silence and the occasional clink of cutlery bore witness to the excellence of the meal.

The old man cleared his plate then left with another nod. Once they'd finished eating, Mrs Needham took Georgie and Patrick along to a little workshop near the back door, whispering, 'He's a bit deaf, so speak up.'

Grandpa swung round as they went into the cluttered

little workshop. 'I bin watchin' you walk, young man. Let me have a look at the shoe from your bad leg. I need to see how it's worn.'

He studied it by the light of a good oil lamp, shaking his head. 'You're soon going to need new shoes, and make sure you choose better ones than these.'

'Army issue. I had no choice.'

'Shame on them as made the dangy things, then.'

He had some tools ready and picked up a piece of soft leather. 'Best I can do is make a pad to fit under your foot. Can't make it too high or your shoe won't hold your foot well enough to walk. But I think that'll make it a bit easier for you.'

'Any help would be appreciated.' Patrick moved his stockinged foot to and fro, sighing involuntarily.

'Gets bad sometimes, does it?'

'If I do too much. The doctor said it'd improve gradually if I was careful with it.'

'Thass all right for rich folk as don't need to earn their bread. Not for us ordinary folk, eh? *We* can't sit with our feet up waiting for things to improve.'

Patrick shrugged and watched what the old man was doing, in case it was something he could learn to do for himself.

Rain beat against the window panes in a sudden squall and they all looked up.

'Going to pour down for most of the day,' Mr Barton said cheerfully. 'My knees allus tell me when it's going to rain heavily. Fair aching they are this morning. If I were you, I'd stay another night. It'll be dark afore you're finished here because Eddie sent the lad over to say he can't come to help with the car till this afternoon.'

'Oh, dear. But we can't impose on you folk.'

'Bless you, Joss won't mind you being here, and as for my Dulcie, she enjoys a bit of company. Best daughter a man could have, she is.'

'I'll go and have a word with her,' Georgie said. 'See if it's all right, and whether I can help in any way.'

Mrs Needham was bustling to and fro. She clearly had her small world well organised and when Georgie told her what Grandpa had said, she volunteered an invitation at once. 'You'd better stay another night, then. It'll be no trouble.'

She hesitated, then asked wistfully, 'Can either of you play the piano? I do love a bit of music, but I've never had the time to learn to play myself. I like singing, though. My Peter says I don't know when I'm singing as I work, and that's the truth. Good thing I can hold a tune, eh, or I'd drive everyone mad?'

'I play a little,' Georgie admitted. What girl from her sort of family wasn't sent to piano lessons, whether they had talent or not? 'Perhaps I could have a look at your music, see if you've any pieces I know. I'm not good enough to play in public, but I could manage the accompaniment to a little singalong, maybe.'

Mrs Needham beamed at her. 'That'd be grand. I've lots of sheet music because even if I can't play the piano properly, I can read the words and pick out the notes with one hand.'

Minnie Needham came in just then and was informed by her mother-in-law that they were going to have a sing-song that night.

'Jim will like that. Has Grandpa finished the shoe?'

'Still working on it,' Mrs Needham said cheerfully. 'But since you offered to help, Miss Cotterell—'

'Georgie, please.'

'Georgie, then. Are you any good at sewing? I've a basket of mending.'

'I'm afraid I'd make a mess of it because I'm hopeless with a needle. But if there's anything else you need doing, don't hesitate to ask.'

'Minnie can get on with the mending, then, and since it's baking day you can lend me a hand in the kitchen.'

'I've not done a lot of baking but if you tell me what to do, I'll give it my best go.'

Both women looked at her in surprise.

Georgie felt guilty as she admitted, 'We always buy our bread from the baker's.'

'Well, my old Gran allus said every woman should learn to bake her family's daily bread, however rich she was, so I'll give you a lesson as well as getting me a helper.'

When Georgie went to take the men a mid-morning cup of tea, she had a quick word with Patrick, because she was fretting more than a little at the prospect of another day's delay and the safety of their friends if they waited too long at Westcott.

He gave her one of his kind smiles, as if he'd read her mind. 'No use worrying because there's nothing we can do about it till I get the car fixed. We'll leave tomorrow, so make the most of your restful day. These are good people. We've fallen lucky, haven't we?'

After which, time passed quickly and busily, and even the bread Georgie had helped knead turned out reasonably well.

It was mid-afternoon before the neighbour came with his tools to look at the car. His breathing was a bit wheezy, which made Patrick wonder if he'd been gassed in the war or had he always had difficulty breathing, as a few folk did.

Eddie hummed and hawed when the stranger wanted to take over the repair work, but as Patrick's superior skill quickly became apparent, the two of them ended up sorting out the blocked carburettor, swapping knowledge, and making adjustments so that the engine ran better.

When they'd finished, Eddie stood back, rubbing his dirty hands on a rag. 'Nice little car, this. Never seen one before, 'cept in a picture.'

'I'd offer to take you for a ride, but I daren't because we have to use our motor spirit sparingly.'

'Where are you going next?'

'Not sure. We have to make a phone call first and find out where our friends are.'

Eddie looked at him with a grin. 'Keeping that information to yourself, are you?'

'Yes. You might let something slip without realising it, and we don't want to give some nasty fellows a clue as to where we've gone.' He held up one hand to stop Eddie interrupting. 'It's not that I don't trust you: I do. But this is actually a matter of national importance.'

'*National!*'

He saw the doubt on the other man's face, so looked him steadily in the eyes as he added, 'I'm not telling you lies, or even exaggerating. I'm just . . . being very careful with everything we do.'

Eddie studied him. 'I bet you were a good sergeant.'

'I did my best. Tried to look after my lads. Were you in the Army?'

'Aye. For a while. But I was gassed early on, so I come

home to help on the farm. I can breathe better here than in a town. And I won't betray you, I promise.'

'I knew that or I'd not have told you.'

They exchanged nods that said they understood one another, then Eddie patted the car again and packed his tools away. 'You should be all right now. That engine sounds to be running smoothly. Good luck with whatever it is.'

'Thanks.'

The evening's sing-song was a great success and Georgie's occasional missed note on the piano was more than made up for by the soaring beauty of Dulcie's voice.

'You have a glorious voice,' she said in awe, 'and it's clearly been well trained. You must have had a good music teacher.'

'She was wonderful. Dead now. She was old when I went to her.'

To Dulcie's delight, Patrick too had a good voice and was able to harmonise effortlessly with her.

'You must have had a good music teacher as well,' she commented.

'No. Only what they taught us at primary school. I just like singing.'

'But you sing the harmonies perfectly.'

'I just, sort of, you know, feel my way.'

Dulcie nodded and tapped her head. 'Born with it. Lucky you.'

Mr Needham caught sight of the clock just then and exclaimed in surprise, 'Eh, it can't be that time already! Better get to bed now, folk. Them animals will still need feeding in the morning. I thank you for giving my Dulcie so much pleasure.'

His son and wife nodded and went back to their own cottage.

Georgie helped clear away the cups. 'You're good enough to be on the stage, Mrs Needham.'

She blushed.

'My Dulcie used to sing in concerts here and there,' Mr Needham said proudly, 'but the war stopped that. She were needed here on the farm, with our best lad gone to fight in France.'

'The war stopped a lot of things,' Patrick agreed. 'I'm sure you'll sing for people again, Mrs Needham. Your voice is truly beautiful. It was a pleasure to sing with you.'

Mr Needham nodded, then said firmly, 'Bed now, everyone.'

'We'll leave as soon as it's light tomorrow, if that's all right with you,' Patrick said.

'I'll make sure you're both awake in plenty of time.'

As they were lying in their improvised bed in the barn for the second night running, Georgie said softly, 'Salt of the earth, aren't they, the Needhams?'

'Yes. They were what I was fighting for, honest folk trying to make a decent living for themselves and their families. That's what our freedom's for, to me, not for the kings and queens and politicians who're squabbling with one another.'

## *Chapter Fourteen*

Dennis roused the other two as the grey light of predawn became bright enough to show the details of the landscape around them.

Although he moved cautiously, Rosie woke up at once. 'Oh! We're still in the car. I didn't think I'd sleep well, but I was that tired I went straight off. Ooh, I'm stiff all over. Could I get out and stretch, do you think, Dennis? And, um, I'll nip behind those bushes while I'm at it, too.' She couldn't help blushing as she said that.

He had to shake Martin, who was a solid sleeper, to wake him up, but by the time it grew light, they were all ready, so hungry they were eager to leave.

'How do we know which way to go?' Rosie asked.

'We have to head roughly north-east, so the sun will help us get started in the right direction. Luckily for us, the sky is only partly cloudy this morning.'

He managed to find a road that let them head in the right direction and presently they came to a signpost indicating the way to Malmesbury.

Dennis came to a decision. 'I don't think we should stop anywhere to ask the way. I don't want to be remembered if anyone asks about strangers passing through. I've a good sense of direction and we know Honeyfield is to the east of Malmesbury so we'll try to find our way on our own.'

'Let's stop at a bakery first,' Rosie begged. 'I'm so hungry I can't think straight.'

'If we go past one that looks busy, you can nip in and buy whatever you like. Do you have any money?'

'A little. Enough to buy some food.'

'We'll all pay our share when we stop.'

'I'm a good eater,' Martin said, 'and I've enough to pay my way, so don't stint.'

She got out and came back with a bag of broken pieces of bread from the night before, some iced buns and two new loaves. 'I thought I'd better get enough for more than one meal. We'll have to find a stream to quench our thirst, though.'

Martin sighed. 'I could murder a cup of tea.'

'We all could.'

They drove on to a suitable stopping place near a stream, ate the iced buns and some of the bread, scooped up some of the clear water to drink, then set off again.

'I feel much better now,' Rosie said cheerfully. 'And there were two other women in the shop pestering to be served quickly, so I don't think the baker noticed much about me.' She giggled. 'I spoke with a Scottish accent, too. I have a friend from Glasgow so I know how to do it.'

The two men were grinning as they drove along.

'You're a tonic, you are, Rosie,' Martin said. 'Go on, do us a Scottish accent.'

So she 'spoke Scottish' for a few remarks, then Dennis did some Welsh like his mother's voice.

They made a couple of turns that led only to small villages, and had to turn round and go back to the main road each time, but when Dennis spotted a signpost pointing the way to Honeyfield, he braked and pointed, letting out a yell of triumph. 'Told you I'd get us there, didn't I? Now all we have to do is find this Pear Tree Lane. Through the village, Miss Cotterell said, past the shops and turn right.'

Rosie beamed at him as they jolted slowly along by a long, narrow village green. 'You are clever, Dennis! And it's been such a comfortable ride. I've never even sat in a big fancy car like this before, only been in a couple of rattling old cars and a van.'

Pear Tree Lane was indeed on the other side of the village. It proved to be a cul-de-sac, with only a few houses on either side.

'The house is called Pear Tree Cottage and she said it was the last one on the left,' Dennis reminded them. 'Aha! There's the name on the gate.' He let the car roll to a halt and switched off the motor. 'We did it. We're here.'

There was silence and no sign of anyone in the street. The only car apart from theirs stood in the drive of Pear Tree Cottage. 'Looks like Patrick and Miss Cotterell haven't got here yet, unless they've hidden their car behind the house. No, they couldn't get round it, could they? The path's too narrow.'

'I hope they're all right,' Rosie said.

'Only one way to find out. Come on. Let's see if her friends know anything.'

He got out of the car and led the way to the front door.

From the sitting room window Tez saw a large black car stop outside their house. 'I wonder who that is?'

Bella came to join him. 'I don't recognise the people who've got out of it, but they're all coming up the path. Do *you* know them?'

'Never seen them before. I'd better answer the door. You stay in here.'

He opened the door just as Dennis was reaching for the knocker. 'Hello. How can I help you?'

'Miss Cotterell and Patrick Farrell told us to meet them here today. We'd expected them to be here already. I believe Miss Cotterell is a friend of the lady of the house.'

'That's my wife, Mrs Tesworth.'

'Would her name be Bella?'

Tez nodded, and took the man's knowledge of his wife's first name as probable proof that they really did know Georgie. He wondered who this Farrell person was. All the strangers looked to be decent folk. The men were ex-servicemen from the looks of it, one of them with a hand injury similar to his own, the other with a badly scarred face.

Based on that, he took a sudden decision and held the door open. 'Come in and tell us what's been going on.'

'Thank you, Mr Tesworth.' Dennis introduced his companions, then stood back and gestured to Rosie to go first.

The fellow had good manners too, Tez noted. Another point in his favour.

In the sitting room the three visitors stood in an awkward group just inside the doorway as Tez introduced them to his wife.

'Come and sit down next to me on the sofa, Rosie,' Bella said. 'And perhaps you two gentlemen would take those chairs?'

Tez went to stand by the crackling wood fire, one hand on the mantelpiece. 'Now, tell us about yourselves and what's going on with Georgie.'

The other two looked at Dennis and he took over the explanations.

When he'd finished his tale, Bella said immediately, 'We don't get a lot of phone calls, so I think our mysterious phone call must have been from Georgie. The caller didn't try to ring us again, though.'

She looked at Tez anxiously. 'Where can Georgie be? If she's not here and she daren't go back to Westcott House, where else could she have taken refuge?'

'With Lady Berrens in London, perhaps?' Tez suggested.

'We all left London together,' Dennis said. 'Georgie was with us then. I don't think she and Patrick will have gone back there.'

'And she can't be staying with my mother, either, because I was up in town yesterday and Mother would have said something. What about Honeyfield House? Could Georgie have gone there?'

His wife shook her head. 'If she had, they'd have sent me word.' Like her husband, Bella had been studying their visitors carefully. 'In the meantime, you three are going to need somewhere to stay. We'll find you beds here.'

Tez frowned. 'I'm not so sure about that, not because I object to your presence, I promise you, but because you'd be found very easily if you stayed with us. Georgie and Bella's friendship is well known among her London acquaintances. But of course you must stay here for the rest of the day until we think of somewhere else where you can sleep in safety.'

'I'll tell the maids that you've popped in to see us, say you're friends of my mother-in-law,' Bella said.

Tez looked thoughtful. 'Perhaps they could be put up at Honeyfield House, Bella? Shall I phone and ask my mother? She can authorise it, being one of the trustees.'

'At a pinch we could do that. But I think it'd make the women nervous if they had strange men staying there, so I'd rather not, if we can manage. Some of them have suffered so dreadfully at their husbands' hands that they don't trust any men now.'

Dennis looked at their comfortable surroundings and sighed. 'Well, if we could just wait here for a while, perhaps Georgie and Patrick will turn up, then we can work out with them where to go. We could sit in the kitchen to be out of your way and we'd try not to be a nuisance.'

Bella shook her head before he'd even finished speaking. 'Better not do that. It'll look as if you're not friends and then people will wonder what you're doing here. The slightest thing can set off gossip in a small village, believe me.'

Tez was looking thoughtful. 'I've got an idea about where you might be able to go, but I'll need to phone someone first to ask about it.' He smiled. 'What did we do before we had telephones? I think some day everyone will have one, rich and poor alike.'

'I can't imagine that,' Rosie said. 'My mum has enough trouble putting bread on the table, the idea of having a telephone isn't even in her dreams. No, you're wrong. They're only for rich people and always will be.'

Tez smiled at her. 'Meet me here in thirty years and we'll see who's right.'

Rosie smiled back. 'All right. It's agreed.'

Bella stood up. 'I'll go and put the kettle on.'

'Can I do anything to help?' Rosie offered.

There was the sound of a baby crying. 'Oh dear, Philip's awake early. Yes, please do come and help, Rosie. It's the nursery maid's day off and once that young man wakes up, he wants to be with people.'

The two men were left in the sitting room while Tez went to use the telephone.

'Where can Patrick and Georgie be? It worries me that they're not here,' Dennis muttered.

Martin just shook his head and spread his hands in a gesture of helplessness.

When Dennis next looked, his friend was asleep.

Nathan picked up the telephone in his office when it rang. 'Nathan Perry here.'

'It's Tez. Do you have a moment to chat and if so, can you please make sure no one overhears us?'

'Yes to both. I'll go and shut my office door.'

He came back to the phone and picked up the earpiece again. 'All set.'

Tez explained about the three people who'd turned up. 'They seem honest to me, but from what they told me, I'm worried about Georgie.'

'Not to mention her father.'

'Hmm. I think Cotterell can take care of himself. I can make a good guess as to where he's gone.'

Nathan chuckled. 'Yes, of course. Either Greyladies or Lady Berrens' house. But won't his enemies guess that too?'

'His connection with the Latimers is very tenuous and Constance Berrens is as clever as he is about keeping things secret. Even if he is with her, it won't be immediately obvious, I'm sure, and she's had the same servants for decades so can rely on them absolutely to keep quiet about a visitor. The pressing problem is, assuming Georgie and her friend arrive here today, we don't have enough room to put all five of them up and yet they need somewhere safe to stay. I wondered . . . Are you still keeping an eye on the old house next door to us?'

'Orchard View? Yes. The man who inherited it before the war has been wanting to sell it for a while, but no one is interested in buying. It's in a terrible condition, needs decorating and bringing into the twentieth century.'

'Don't I remember that it's still got some of the original furniture?'

'Yes. But what's left is old and half of it's broken. The new owner took away anything decent.'

'Beds?'

'Yes. But the mattresses will need a good airing, Tez. They've been lying around for several years.'

'How about we let those three stay there? They could do some cleaning and even perhaps a bit of whitewashing, and we'll tell people in the village that you've hired them to brighten the place up so that it'll sell. We'll also hint that they're ex-soldiers and short of money.'

Silence, then, 'Actually, that's a good idea. I've been meaning to get round to brightening the place but I've been rather busy lately, I'm glad to say. I'll come over with the keys. You'll need some bedding and towels. What do these people look like? Could we say they're brothers and sister?'

'I doubt it. They're all three very different in appearance.'

'Then the woman will have to pretend to be married to one of them, and the two men can be mates who got through the war together. We don't want to start any rumours of immorality.'

'Good idea, Nathan. You have a fertile imagination.'

He chuckled. 'I have to have when I show people houses that are for sale and want to persuade them that they could live there with a few minor adjustments. Most people can't see how to rearrange a residence.'

'You're still enjoying selling houses better than accounting?'

'Much more. And it's going to be a lot more profitable now the war has ended. My family firm is getting back on its feet after the mess my father made of things, so I'm leaving the accounting side of things to my chief clerk and those he hires. Mr Parkin loves fiddling with figures.'

'And how's Kathleen?'

'She's well and so are the children. Look, I've got a house to look at shortly, Tez, and it's halfway to Honeyfield from Malmesbury. How about I carry on afterwards and bring you the keys to next door? I'll feel better if I see the people who are going to stay there myself, then I can tell the owner I've found some ex-soldiers who'll do some of the work in return for their keep and a small payment.'

'I can pay for their food, if necessary.'

'The new owner can afford to pay them for their work, then they can buy their own food. He's not short of a bob or two but he lives too far away to make arrangements himself, even if he was interested, which he isn't. He'll do what I suggest, believe me. Especially if he thinks he'll be able to sell it at last. So many civilian things are going to get going properly now.'

'Good. That's settled, then.'

Tez went back to join the others and explained what he'd arranged. All three visitors brightened visibly. Then he and Bella left the three of them on their own to decide who was going to pretend to be married to Rosie.

As Bella was getting ready to go shopping, Tez said, 'Why not drop the word that it's some of my former men from the Army who are going on this job for me? No one will be surprised at their presence then.'

Tez kept an eye on the baby while Bella went off to buy some extra food to cater for their visitors. Other men rarely seemed to play with their children when they were this small, but he loved being with Philip, loved to feel the child's soft little arms go round his neck.

He was enjoying himself so much that it seemed no time at all till Bella returned with the food.

Once the three of them were alone, Rosie stared down at her clasped hands, forcing herself to keep them still in her lap, trying not to betray how embarrassed she felt.

She couldn't help jerking in surprise when Dennis asked quietly, 'Who do *you* want to pretend to be married to, Rosie?'

'I don't want to *pretend* to be married to anyone,' she muttered.

'We have to or we'll not seem respectable.'

'It won't be respectable, anyway, if it's only pretend.'

'No one else in the village will know that and you can trust us not to take advantage of the situation, can't she?'

Martin shrugged and looked embarrassed. 'It's only fair to warn you, though, Rosie, that I snore, so if we have to share a bed, I won't have to touch you to keep you awake.'

She chuckled, relaxing a little. 'I heard you in the car. You could win a prize for snoring.'

'I'm a quiet sleeper mostly,' Dennis said, 'and I'm a light sleeper too. I'll wake if anyone comes prowling round the house, believe me.' He waited, then prompted, 'All right to pretend to be Mrs Petley?'

'Yes, all right.' She hoped she hadn't betrayed the fact that she thought Dennis was a very nice man and half-wished this was real and she was indeed his wife. At other times, she'd have tried to encourage him to come courting, but things were in such a mess in all their lives at the moment, she didn't know whether she was coming or going. She certainly hadn't expected to be gallivanting all over the countryside with two strange men. Her mam would throw a fit when she found out.

'We'll make sure we have separate beds,' Dennis said.

It was as if he'd read her mind. 'Yes.' She sought desperately for something to change the subject. 'Um, I've never been out of London before. I don't know how they do things in the country.'

'They'll expect strangers to ask questions, anyway, so we needn't be afraid to ask for information or help.' He walked across to stare out of the window. 'I'm not used to sitting around idle but we'd better not show ourselves in the village ıll we've been given permission to move in next door.'

The minutes seemed to tick past slowly and after a while, he went to sit down, trying not to fidget openly.

This made Rosie smile, because he failed completely. First his foot twitched in time to some imaginary drumbeat, then he tapped his fingers one by one on the chair arm till he realised what he was doing and quickly flattened his hand.

Eventually they heard the sound of a motor car and Dennis was up in a flash and back at the window. 'It's a chap who's a bit older than us, but not old. Got a fine big nose on him, he has.'

Footsteps moved along the hall and Tez's voice rang out. 'Come in, Nathan. I'm glad to see you.'

'It must be the man about the house next door,' Martin said unnecessarily.

'He's got a nice smile,' Rosie said. 'I always judge people by their smiles. And the nose might be big—'

'It *is* big.'

'Yes, but it suits him. He looks like a friendly eagle. I've seen pictures of eagles in library books, always liked the noble look of them.'

She couldn't help glancing sideways as she said that. Dennis had a nice smile, too – a very nice smile – and the scar didn't worry her, or the lack of two fingers.

Gerald Cotterell was coldly furious when the man he'd gone to meet after dark for news of his daughter confessed that she hadn't been seen for two days.

'How can you possibly have lost her, Jordan? I thought we'd agreed that you'd keep her in the London house with a guard posted there.'

'I tried. But it takes time to summon suitable people to do that, and I haven't got your authority to move men from elsewhere at the drop of a hat. I thought three ex-servicemen would be able to hold the fort for a day or so, with Mathers being there as well.'

The older man's voice was burred with scorn. 'One man who met her in the street and two complete strangers!'

'I did check out Farrell's details with his regiment, sir, because I know one of the officers. He was highly thought of and if it hadn't been for the severity of his leg injury, he'd probably have ended up as a regular junior officer in peacetime.'

'Well, he wasn't good enough to keep her safely under guard in her own house, was he? And what *she* was thinking of, to go down to Westcott after all that trouble blew up, I cannot understand. As if they wouldn't know where to look for her when they realised she'd gone. Mathers will answer to me for that.'

'He's still there, keeping an eye on the house, sir.'

'He'd better be. I shall be speaking to him myself about this.'

There was silence for a few moments, then Cotterell shook his head, muttered something to himself and snapped, 'Now that you know how to contact me, send me a message to let me know the minute there's news about my daughter. If they tried to use her to blackmail me, I couldn't protect her, because my country would have to come first.'

He glared at Jordan. 'Damned well go out and *look* for her yourself, if necessary, then keep her safe if you have to tie her down. But don't reveal what you're doing to anyone, not even people at the bureau.'

'Yes, sir.'

But he was talking to himself. After Cotterell had delivered his ultimatum, he'd slipped away without a word.

Jordan stared in vain into the darkness for signs of where Cotterell had gone, then pulled his scarf more tightly round his neck so that his face was concealed and strode back home through the dark streets. It was easier fighting openly in the trenches than chasing shadows and mirages as they were doing at the moment. Why did these *Siebenzeit* sympathisers always seem to know what they were doing?

If he didn't find Georgie, he would never redeem himself in her father's eyes, and such was Cotterell's power, that his hoped-for peacetime career might be blighted before it started.

But if she was as clever as her father said, she might not even be at Westcott, and if so, it'd be hard to find out where she'd gone.

He should have stayed at the house himself to keep an eye on her. But how could he have done that without certain people at the bureau finding out, especially when he'd had an unexpected summons to a meeting, with instructions that he was expected to attend *in person* – underlined.

He stopped suddenly as the thought of who had sent that particular message sank in.

Oh, hell. Was it possible? It could be. Only, how on earth could he prove anything? He didn't have the authority to obtain some of the necessary information.

He heard the whisper of footsteps behind him in time to flatten himself against the wall and face his opponent.

But the man had a knife already raised and jabbed at him with it so suddenly, he sliced one arm.

Before he could do anything, someone yelled from across the street and his assailant ran off, leaving Jordan to grab his arm and pray that the knife hadn't sliced into an artery. He assured his shocked rescuer that he'd be all right. Yes, really. He had to argue about going to hospital and in the end allowed the person to call a taxi to take him there.

Once they were under way, he gave the driver directions to another place whose address he'd been given for emergencies if injured. There a doctor was summoned to deal with the knife slash and while Jordan waited, he made his report to the man in charge, who was sitting behind a screen.

What next? Jordan wondered wearily, as the doctor lectured him about resting that arm.

What the hell next? Talk about secrets within secrets.

# *Chapter Fifteen*

Patrick drove along the lane leading from the farm and stopped at the main road. 'You're sure we'll be able to take refuge with your friend Bella?'

'Yes. Either with her or at Honeyfield House, which is nearby.'

'Then I'll head towards Malmesbury. I found out which direction that's in from Eddie yesterday. I don't think he realised we wanted to go there, at least I hope he didn't. He wouldn't give us away voluntarily, I'm sure, but some people know how to question a man in such a way that he doesn't realise what he's revealed.'

She smiled and drew an answering smile from him by saying, 'Which is what you did with him, right? Anyway, once we get to Malmesbury, I can direct you to Honeyfield.'

It was a chilly morning, but even if it had been sunny, they'd have kept the hood of the car up. Both were wearing their scarves in a way that partially obscured their faces as well as helping keep them warm.

At Malmesbury she started giving directions, but as they were leaving the outskirts of the town, a child ran out right in front of the car. Patrick braked immediately but couldn't stop in time and the front bumper caught the little girl and sent her flying.

Georgie was out of the car as soon as it stopped. She bent over the child, who was unconscious, and to her relief found that she was breathing steadily and there was no sign of bleeding. 'She's alive.'

'Thank goodness!' Patrick looked round. 'There's a cottage over there. I'll see if I can get help. They may know who she is.'

He was back in a couple of minutes, followed by a woman in a wrap-around pinafore, who was still wiping her hands on a cloth fastened to her waistband.

She let out an incoherent cry and ran towards the child, calling, 'Dodie! Dodie, love!'

'Don't move her!' Georgie ordered sharply. 'We need to check that she hasn't broken a limb.'

The woman gulped but contented herself with brushing the child's hair gently back from her face. 'She must have sneaked out to watch for cars going past, which she knows she isn't allowed to do. Eh, she's been in a naughty mood ever since she got up today. Whatever will she do next?'

'I'm so sorry. She ran straight out in front of our car and there was nothing we could do to avoid her,' Georgie said. 'Is that her name, Dodie?'

'Yes. Short for Dorothy.'

The child stirred just then and moaned.

The woman clapped one hand to her mouth and stared at them with tears in her eyes. 'Is she going to be all right?'

Georgie put out her arm to stop the mother moving the child. 'I think so. Let's check a couple of things. Dodie, can you move your arms?' She'd been taught to do that on a first-aid course she'd had to take before she started driving the convalescent officers around London.

'Mammy!' wailed the child suddenly and waved both arms around without any sign that they hurt.

'Her arms are definitely all right,' Georgie whispered, then raised her voice. 'Dodie, can you move your legs?'

The child ignored her, staring at her mother and holding out her arms to be picked up.

Georgie whispered, 'Get her to move her legs.' The woman moved forward to hold the child's hands.

'Dodie, love, can you move your legs?'

In answer the child used her legs to push herself closer and cuddle against her kneeling mother.

'She's not broken a limb, then, thank goodness,' Georgie said.

'Shall I carry her into the house for you?' Patrick asked. 'You can talk to her as we walk.'

'I'll move the car to the side of the road and switch off the engine.' Georgie noticed that the mother looked at her in surprise as she said this.

She was glad the child wasn't badly hurt. She'd be glad to be away from severely injured men for the rest of her life now that the carnage had stopped. She desperately wanted to build a new life now, one in which her father didn't keep trying to wrap her in cotton wool.

Unfortunately, it seemed he'd had good reason. Surely that would stop now the war was over?

On that thought she looked round, relieved that no other car was in sight. She watched as Patrick carried the child into the house. He was limping only slightly today, so the new pad in his shoe must be helping.

She got into the driving seat and moved the car on to the verge, glad the engine was still running, so she didn't have to waste her energy crank-starting it. Better get it out of sight as soon as possible.

Only after another glance along the road did she go inside to join them.

'You're hurt too!' the woman exclaimed as she led the way into the house. 'Have you sprained your ankle?'

'No. It's just a war wound. It's much better now, actually.'

By the time Georgie joined them, an older child had brought the father in from the barn and the small kitchen seemed full of people. To everyone's relief, the father took charge and sternly ordered his younger daughter to sit still and keep quiet.

When he found out what had happened, he looked furious. 'Didn't we tell you not to play on the road, Dodie Evans?' he roared.

The little girl began to cry even more loudly than before.

The mother looked pleadingly at him, but he shook his head and she held her tongue.

'Didn't we tell you?' he demanded again. 'Answer me, Dodie!'

'Yes, Da.'

'If you do that again, I'll tie you up in the barn every

day and you won't get to play outside at all. Promise me faithfully, cross your heart and hope to die, that there will be no more going out on the road.'

She nodded several times in quick succession, making the crossing-heart gesture. 'I promise, Da. It hurt.'

Georgie saw him close his eyes in relief and knew it was only love making him shout at the naughty child.

'Are you hurting anywhere in particular, Dodie?' she asked.

The child rubbed her forehead and when Georgie bent closer she could see that the bruise that had been starting to form now covered that side of her forehead. 'Anywhere else hurting?'

'I'll check her out,' the mother said. She picked the child up and whisked her into the room next door, coming back a few minutes later with the child clinging to her skirt. 'Only a couple of bruises on her shoulder. Your car isn't damaged, is it, sir?'

The husband put his arm round her. 'If it is, we'll pay for the repairs.'

Georgie looked at Patrick and shook her head slightly.

He picked up what she wanted instantly. 'No, thank goodness.'

The woman's whoosh of relieved breath could be heard clearly.

'Would you kind folk like a cup of tea?' the father asked. 'I certainly would. Put that young madam to bed, Mary, love, and she's to stay there until I let her come downstairs again. I'll put the kettle on while you take her up.'

It was an hour before they were able to leave the little farm.

As they got into the car, Georgie asked in a low voice,

'I'm sure my father won't mind about the damage. It's only a scrape and a slight dent, after all.'

'That child must have a hard head.'

'Yes. I'll pay myself if Father complains, because in spite of their generosity with the cream cake today, I could see that those people didn't have a lot of money to spare.'

'They're not alone in that,' he said curtly. 'It sounds as if that little girl is very naughty.'

'Yes, but this'll probably have taught her one important lesson, at least. A lot of people don't realise how fast cars are travelling, or that cars can't get out of your way like horses do. You read about serious motoring accidents in the newspapers all the time, people getting killed or maimed.'

He leant across from the driving seat and kissed her cheek suddenly. 'Well, I'm most relieved *you* weren't hurt. You did well today, lass.'

As they drove off, she asked flippantly, 'Whatever will happen to us next, do you suppose?'

He answered more seriously. 'Nothing dramatic, I hope. We'll find a place of safety and leave a message with someone about where you are. Then we'll lie low till your father sends for you. End of the adventure.'

'Mmm.' She could still feel the warmth of Patrick's lips on her cheek and wished she'd had the courage to kiss him back. It suddenly occurred to her that he was probably being careful about what he said or did because he knew he'd not be considered a suitable man to court her.

And yet she'd never felt as comfortable with anyone else except her twin. If she was interested in Patrick, she'd have to pluck up her courage and make it clear that she wanted him.

Could she do that? She hadn't had a lot of experience in flirting, let alone conveying her feelings to a man about that sort of thing. Well, let's face it, she hadn't had much experience with men, because her so-called mother had kept her tightly penned up.

She looked sideways and caught Patrick looking at her. She smiled involuntarily and blew him a little air kiss.

He looked surprised then pleased.

Yes, she decided. She could and would find ways to make her feelings clear. She wanted very much to get to know him better. A lot better.

She liked to think she was a thoroughly modern woman when it came to driving motor cars. She now intended to be just as modern when it came to finding a husband. No one was ever again going to push her into an unsuitable relationship. Not even her father.

Just before they got to Honeyfield, Patrick began worrying about the car running out of fuel, so when he saw a big wooden shed at the side of the road, he slowed down. 'That looks like it might sell fuel – yes, it does! Look at the sign.'

Painted on the dark wood in white were large uneven letters saying *Motor Car and Cycle Repairs*. Below it was another smaller sign saying *Carburine Motor Spirit Sold Here*. He heaved a sigh of relief and drew up in front of the big double doors.

'That sign's a bit crooked. They must have painted it themselves. Let's stop and see if we can buy a couple of cans of fuel.'

As he got out he said 'Aha!' and pointed to the right, just inside the open door. There was the familiar pile of wooden crates each containing a couple of tall, narrow two-gallon cans.

A lad came out to see what they wanted and looked distinctly relieved when they told him they wanted to buy some motor spirit.

'Are you alone here?' Patrick asked, not seeing anyone else around.

'Yes, sir. I was worried you wanted something repairing, but my master, Mr Leatherby, isn't well today, so he can't repair any cars. One man got angry with me about that, but I haven't learnt enough to do repairs on my own yet.'

'Well, I'm not angry with anyone. I'd like to buy three cans of motor spirit, please. I'll use one straight away to fill my car up.'

The lad nodded and lugged out a crate containing two full cans, then brought another full can and a funnel. They traded in their empty cans and paid him.

The lad was in a chatty mood and it didn't take much to keep him talking. 'Mr Leatherby's been ill all week, getting old, he is. When he sells this place, I might lose my job, but he's going to try to get the new owner to take me on.'

'He hasn't sold it yet, then?'

'No. He thought he could sell it himself, because of being on the main road here, but he hasn't managed to, so far. Well, he's a bit sharp with folk sometimes. He's going to get Mr Perry from Malmesbury to sell it for him. Everyone knows Mr Perry's the best in the county for selling houses and businesses.'

'I wish your master well. Um, you don't know how much he wants for the place, do you?'

'No, sir, sorry. He wouldn't tell me, said I'd only blab

it to my friends.' He let out a huff of laughter. 'He was probably right. I might have let it slip by mistake. My mam says my tongue's hung in the middle and wags at both ends. Are you staying in the village, sir? I can ask him to send a message to you about the price.'

'We may be staying. Not sure yet. If we do, I'll come back and knock at the house door and ask him.' He handed over the money.

'I'll crank-start your car for you, sir, if you like. I'm good at that now.'

'Yes, please.'

So Patrick handed over a threepenny bit for him to swing the starting handle and left a smiling young fellow pocketing his tip as they drove away.

'Thinking of buying that little business?' Georgie asked with a smile.

'I might be. One like that is my only chance. It's not much of a place now but that might make it cheap enough for me to be able to afford it. Eh, I'd work my fingers to the bone to have my own workshop and build the trade up into a decent living. That one is well situated if you had bigger signs.'

'And properly painted ones!'

'Yes, definitely. I'm good at repairing cars – well, all motor vehicles, actually, and motorcycles too. The Army taught us well.'

'And that's what you'd most like to do with your life.'

It was more of a statement than a question but he answered it anyway. 'Yes.' Then he sighed, glanced quickly sideways at her and back at the road.

'I like being around cars too,' she said. 'I think my father plans to stop me driving myself and hire a chauffeur once things have settled down, but I'm not going to let him dictate how I live. At the very least I'll buy a car of my own and possibly move into a house of my own too.'

'Not many women are that interested in cars.'

'Well, I am. I'd like to learn to repair them. It'd be fun.'

'And get your hands dirty?'

She chuckled and waved one to and fro. 'I can always wash them more often. Now, carry on along the side of the village green till you reach that big tree, then turn right after it.'

He followed Georgie's instructions for getting to her friend's house and said, 'Thank goodness!' when he saw Mr Cotterell's big black car standing in the street outside the end house.

'They got here safely. Oh, Patrick, what a relief! They must have been so worried about us.'

The front door burst open and Bella rushed out towards them, throwing her arms round Georgie the minute her friend got out of the car and giving her a big hug. 'We've been so *worried* since your friends arrived and told us what's been happening! Where on earth did you get to?'

Tez came to join them. 'Calm down, love. They're obviously all right.'

Georgie stepped back and took Patrick's arm. 'This is Patrick Farrell, who helped me get away. We've had such a time of it.' Then she saw Rosie, Dennis and Martin standing further back and called, 'I'm so glad you all got here safely. We'll have to swap tales.'

Tez put an arm round his wife and pulled her gently

back towards the house. 'Come in, love. Let's not give the neighbours a free show, eh? Come in, everyone, do.'

Talking and laughing, they crammed into the sitting room and Bella refused point-blank to do anything about refreshments till she'd heard about their adventures.

The telling took a while, with interruptions and exclamations stopping the narrative.

It was lovely to be part of such a nice group of people, Georgie thought wistfully. She hadn't had much experience of this in her lonely life, wanted more of it, much more.

While this was going on, Nathan arrived and knocked on the front door but no one heard him, even when he repeated the action more loudly.

There was quite a hubbub inside, but it sounded happy, so in the end he simply opened the door and walked in. Standing in the sitting room doorway, he waited for a lull in the conversation to say, 'I did knock.'

Tez turned round and chuckled. 'As you can see, my dear friend, we're having quite an exciting time catching up on news.' He summarised what his visitors had been doing, indicated a chair for Nathan and said, 'I suppose I'd better put the kettle on myself since my lazy wife refuses to lift a finger.'

Bella pulled a face at him. 'I don't want to miss anything. There'd be more room if we all sat round the kitchen table. Come on, everyone. Let's go through to the back. We don't need to stand on ceremony, surely?'

Nathan held out his hand to the nearest stranger and introduced himself, then nodded to the others, repeating their names and hoping he wasn't giving away how carefully he was studying them.

As Tez had said on the phone, the three men looked like returned soldiers and the young woman with them had a cheerful, honest face. Nathan was a big believer in faces being the mirrors of the soul. He took after the Latimer side of his family in that, with a touch of fey understanding about people. He was usually able to see through any attempts at deception and feel whether they were decent folk or not.

Once in the kitchen, the conversation turned to refreshments and Tez left Bella to sort that out with Rosie and Georgie's help. He managed to get Nathan into a corner and say quietly, 'They seem all right to me.'

'Yes. I like the looks of them, too. After we've finished our cups of tea, we can show them round the house next door, if you like. Apart from any other considerations, it'd be good to get it cleared out. If we do that and ask a slightly cheaper price, we'll sell it more easily.'

Bella had come close enough to overhear this. 'Let's all go round it. I'll need to see what furniture is missing if everyone is to have a proper bed for the night.' She turned to her friend. 'You'll stay here with us, won't you, Georgie?'

'Thank you, yes.'

Patrick frowned. 'Then one of us ought to stay here as well. We still need to keep a careful watch on your friend, I'm afraid, Mrs Tesworth. I've no doubt these people will come here, and quite soon too. They seem very determined to capture her and get a hold over her father that way, I suppose.'

'Desperate men can be particularly dangerous,' Tez agreed.

Bella's face fell.

'In that case, I think it'd be better if I stayed at the house next door,' Georgie said at once. 'I don't want to put you and little Philip at risk, Bella.'

Her friend betrayed herself by laying a hand protectively on her stomach in the age-old gesture of a woman expecting a child, but no one was rude enough to comment openly on that, though a couple of the men smiled briefly.

Georgie broke the silence. 'That's settled, then, and it solves another problem: Rosie and I can share a bedroom, and our three heroes will keep watch over us.'

Her voice was teasing but the glance she shared with Patrick betrayed her own secret feelings to her friend Bella, who immediately turned to study him more closely.

Dennis didn't say much but he was sorry he wouldn't be spending time alone with Rosie. She didn't seem to care in the slightest that his hand looked so ugly. She was such a lovely lass. Could his life really have turned the corner and brought him a chance for the family life he craved? He really hoped so.

Just let these villains try to get in the way of that!

# *Chapter Sixteen*

Nathan led the way next door and took out a large, old-fashioned key. 'I'm afraid the whole place is in a terrible condition and needs a thorough going through, inside and out.' He opened the door and stepped into the hall. 'Oh dear! It's worse than I remembered. If the house wasn't so pretty, it might be better to knock it down and build a new one, but the outside fits in well with the others in the street and a modern building might not.'

He stopped to look at one side of the entrance hall, then the other, frowning. From it, open doors showed dusty rooms with rubbish on the floors, occasional pieces of shabby furniture and peeling wallpaper. 'I haven't been here since the new owner took away some furniture. He has left it in a mess, hasn't he? Can you gentlemen clear up the floors, throw away the rubbish and perhaps whitewash the kitchen and laundry areas, do you think? That alone would be a great improvement.'

'Yes, of course, but could we walk round it all first?' Patrick asked. 'Before we agree to stay, we need to be sure that we can keep Georgie safe here.'

'Yes, of course. Good thinking. I think it's slightly larger than the house next door. There are three rooms as well as the kitchen and a housekeeper's room on the ground floor, plus the usual scullery and laundry. Oh, and there's a lavatory beyond them with inside access.'

'Thank goodness for that!' Georgie said fervently.

'The main thing we need to do is inspect the ground floor and study its ways of accessing the outside,' Patrick reminded him.

'Yes, sorry.' Nathan set off and they followed.

When they got back to the hall, Patrick said, 'I think we can manage to look after Georgie here. All windows are weak points when defending a position, though, especially sash windows like these.'

'Let's go upstairs and make sure there are enough beds for everyone,' Tez suggested.

'And that the mattresses aren't damp,' Georgie added.

They inspected the four bedrooms, which all had sagging beds. There was no bathroom, of course, and though there were three other bedrooms in the attic, they were tiny, presumably for maidservants.

Georgie felt all the beds and grimaced. 'These are only cheap flock mattresses but the ticking looks clean. They definitely feel damp, though, so we'll have to dry them out. Is there some coal or firewood available? There are plenty of fireplaces, after all.'

'*If* the chimneys aren't blocked,' Rosie put in.

'Pray that they aren't,' Dennis said. 'We've no equipment or time to get chimneys swept.'

'We can do our best to clear some of it for you, Mr Perry,' Georgie said. 'Come on! Let's make a start and light some fires to air the mattresses. I'm sure I saw a pile of wood outside at the back.'

With the help of Tez, who fetched some old newspapers and kindling from his own home, they got fires started in several rooms. Soon the mattresses were propped up in front of their warmth and the rooms started to get a damp feel to the air.

Brushes were found and more borrowed. The men swept the floors, while the women tied clean rags from torn sheets in the linen cupboard round soft-bristled brooms and went round the house clearing the crevices and cornices of spiders' webs.

'I can put up with dust but not with spiders. I hate the horrible things.' Georgie shuddered as one ran out from a crevice and Rosie disposed of 'the fearsome beast' for her, laughing.

Nathan stayed longer than he'd expected, because Patrick and Georgie both wanted to know about selling houses and how much this one was worth.

After a while, Tez suddenly stopped collecting rubbish and his voice echoed across the hall. 'Oh dear! I forgot. We ought to telephone my mother and tell her you're here, Georgie. She'll know how to get in touch with your father, if anyone does, or her friend Constance Berrens will.'

'I suppose we'd better.'

Patrick came out into the hall to join in. 'You don't sound enthusiastic.'

'To tell you the truth, I don't want to go back to my old life with my father. When I wasn't out on driving duties,

I had to find things to fill my time because he didn't like people coming to the house unless he was going to be there too. And the car wasn't always available for me to go out. He didn't like me going out on foot on my own, you see. So it was hard to make friends or have a social life.'

'Did he give you a reason for all these precautions?' Patrick asked.

'No. Just that the modern world wasn't a safe place for a young woman.'

'I'll make a quick call to my mother,' Tez said. 'I won't mention any names, so even if the operator is eavesdropping, I won't be giving your presence away, just hinting.'

He went across to his own house and returned a short time later. 'Done. Thank goodness my mother is quick on the uptake. I didn't have to say much at all for her to realise why I was calling.'

'But she didn't say anything to hint at where my father is?'

'No. 'Fraid not. Well, she might not know.'

'Sometimes I wish I had a less inscrutable father,' Georgie said bitterly. 'It's hard to work out what he's thinking or planning at the best of times – and this isn't the best of times.'

She shrugged and went back to work. When she looked at Patrick, he winked at her, and she felt herself relaxing a little.

By early evening the house was more or less habitable and beds had been made up from a motley collection of yellowing old sheets, thin old blankets and eiderdowns. Nathan left once he'd made sure they needed nothing else, anxious to get home to his wife before dark, in case she worried about him.

A simple meal of stew, bread and a bought cake from the baker's had been prepared for them by Bella and her daily maid, who was always glad of some extra hours' work.

Tez was happy to see friends old and new gathered round his table. The only thing to mar the pleasant mood was the decision that one person would keep watch outside the house at all times. Seeing Martin walk past the window outside, looking very alert, Tez frowned and decided to take his revolver to bed with him.

After he'd been invalided out of the Army, he hadn't felt safe without a way of defending himself, even back in England, and had bought a handgun from an acquaintance, not asking where it came from. A lot of men he knew had done the same thing, either retrieving an enemy gun or 'finding' a gun from their own side among the chaos. Tonight he was particularly glad to be armed.

He had a quiet word with Patrick after the meal ended, on the excuse of giving him a set of keys to all the doors of the other house. 'I have a handgun. I'll load it and keep it easily available. If you need help, yell, and I'll come running.'

'We brought two from Georgie's father's store,' Patrick said grimly. 'And I won't hesitate to use mine, if necessary. Who knows what lengths these villains will go to? Perhaps you could borrow a gun for Martin. He was a sniper so he'll be the most accurate of us, I should think.'

'All right. One or two chaps round here have guns, legally or illegally (I don't ask which), and will no doubt oblige. Oh, and we do have a village policeman. You know, I should have thought of him sooner. Perhaps we should let Browning know there may be trouble brewing. He's a sensible older chap.'

He pulled out his pocket watch and flipped open the lid. 'It's not late. I could stroll over to his house and let him know what's going on.'

'Shall I come with you?'

'Yes. Good idea. Let's do it straight away.'

Georgie went out into the hall to find out why they were putting on their hats and overcoats. 'Where are you going?'

Tez hesitated.

'If I'm the reason for your outing, I ought to be kept informed.'

'She's right.' Patrick explained what they were doing.

By that time Bella had joined them as well. 'Why don't we ladies come too, then we'll only seem like two couples out for an evening stroll.'

'People don't usually go out for strolls in the dark in such cold winter weather. I'd not be surprised if there's a frost during the night.'

Bella smiled. 'Then I'll have to hold tightly to your arm to prevent myself from falling in case the ground is slippery.'

Tez rolled his eyes, but gave in to her, as he usually did.

Which left Georgie the pleasure of taking Patrick's arm and chatting quietly as they walked along.

She had thick fleece-lined mittens, but noticed that his gloves were well worn, knitted ones and that one finger had come partly unravelled. She wished she had the right to take care of him properly.

Constable Browning opened the door to them, looking anxious, and Tez acted as spokesman, as they'd agreed.

Given that he was a respected member of this small community, he would have more credibility than strangers.

'There may be trouble brewing, Constable, and we thought we should tell you about it.'

'Quite right. Better come in, though I'm afraid the fire has gone out in the police station part of the house.'

'Doesn't matter. This will only take a few minutes.'

The constable listened intently to Tez, then stared at Patrick and Georgie as if he could see into their souls, following that up with a little nod, which presumably meant that he liked what he saw. 'Well, if you need any help, don't hesitate to telephone me, night or day, Mr Tesworth. I can be round to your place in five minutes at most, yes, and collect a couple of helpers on the way. It's a blessing that both our places are connected by telephone, eh? Some of these modern inventions are marvellous, are they not?'

'They are indeed. We'll definitely phone you if we need your help.'

When they got back, Tez suggested he and Patrick go round the inside and outside of the old house to make doubly sure everything on the ground floor was secure. Georgie said she'd help them, but Bella was looking tired and Tez insisted she sit in front of the fire with her feet up.

Tez watched Georgie stop at the gate in the fence between the two properties to study the old house.

'You know, this could be so pretty if it were painted and rethatched, not to mention being brought up to date inside.' After another long stare, she added softly, talking more to herself than her companions, 'Imagine living in a village where you know all your neighbours and can walk to the shops without calling for a car.'

Patrick didn't comment on this revealing remark, but he was staring at her like a hungry man looking into a baker's shop window. Poor chap, Tez thought. He's very taken with her but I doubt Cotterell would consider him a suitable son-in-law.

She seemed to have forgotten Tez's presence and was speaking only to Patrick. 'I don't hanker for a life of luxury, you know. I hate sitting round idle. What I want more than anything is a family to keep me busy: husband, children, home and helping in a family business would be perfect, too. If it's not too late for that.'

Tez took a couple of steps backwards, realising that were they to become aware of him, they might not continue what obviously could be an important conversation.

Wishing them luck from the bottom of his heart, he walked quietly back next door, giving thanks mentally that here in his own home, he had all that Georgie longed for – all that he had yearned for, too, while serving in the trenches.

Patrick stared at Georgie's face in the moonlight, thinking how striking she looked. Not strictly beautiful, but so very attractive. 'What you describe sounds like paradise to me. Perhaps we can make it come true one day. I know I'm not . . . well, the sort of man your father would choose for you, but if you like, if you're sure you want to, we could see how we get on together.'

She chuckled. 'We've already spent a lot of time together and not a cross word exchanged.'

'No. Not even one cross word. Before we do anything about our future, though, we do need to deal with the present dangers, which means checking the house carefully, then getting a good night's sleep.'

'Yes. I suppose you're right.'

He allowed himself to add, 'I too hunger for what you described and—' He broke off and looked behind them, feeling a bit embarrassed about Tez overhearing this private conversation.

But they were alone, so he gave way to temptation and drew her into his arms, delighted when she came willingly.

When the kiss ended, they stayed close together and she whispered, 'I've been wanting you to do that – kiss me wholeheartedly, I mean.'

'Not as much as I've been wanting to do it, I'm sure.' He took a deep breath and made himself step backwards. 'Let's go inside now. We mustn't let ourselves get distracted. Anyone could have crept up on us while we were kissing. Your friend's husband is a very tactful fellow to slip away and give us a quiet moment or two together. I like them both.'

'So do I. You fit in well.'

'Do I? Good.' Taking her hand he walked towards the house, opened the front door with the key Nathan had given them and locked it carefully behind them. Once inside, he didn't take her hand again, wanting no distractions to this inspection.

'We have candles but no holders, and anyway, they'd probably blow out as we walked round in such a draughty house, not to mention dripping hot wax on our hands.'

'Even a hand torch would be a help. Still, there aren't

any curtains in most rooms, so there's probably enough moonlight for us to see what we need to.'

They walked through the house and soon he found her hand again and their steps slowed to a companionable stroll as they only let go of one another to check that every window was locked in place.

When they got to the kitchen at the rear of the house, however, Patrick froze and let go of her hand, hissing, 'Shhh!' They both saw the silhouette of a man standing outside, watched his hand reach out towards the window.

'What the hell are we going to do?' he muttered. 'We're not armed. Why the hell didn't we wear our handguns? Who knows what sort of weapons he's carrying, or how many others there are with him? If it comes to a fight, I'll yell for the others and you're to run next door the front way. Here. Take the key. Scream for help the minute you get outside.'

The man began fiddling with the catch of the window. He was obviously trying to get in without breaking the pane, the noise of which would attract attention.

Just as Patrick had decided to go and fetch a chair to jab at the fellow and keep him from opening the window, they heard a voice from the garden next door calling their names.

The figure at the window froze, then stepped backwards, disappearing into the shadows.

Someone hammered on the front door, calling their names again, yelling, 'Supper's ready.'

'I think that's Dennis,' he said.

She listened. 'Yes. Undoubtedly. Let's open the door quickly.'

They ran into the hall and as she fumbled with the key, Patrick muttered, 'That was too close a call for my liking. I have to concentrate on guarding you properly, not courting you.'

'Forewarned is forearmed. I don't think the intruder knows we saw him.'

'We'll have to keep a very careful watch tonight. How the hell did they find where we were so quickly?'

'Tez was right. There has to be a traitor in my father's bureau. Perhaps this person has been eavesdropping on my father, or on other people's conversations over the past few weeks to get information about me. Who knows? He won't have found it from the servants in the London house, though. I'd trust Mathers and Nora with my life.'

'Are you all right in there?' Dennis called.

'We're having trouble with this damned key again, Dennis.' Patrick lowered his voice and continued speaking to her. 'Let's hope your father knows about what's going on. He's been gone for several days now, hasn't he? I'd have expected him to reappear by now.'

'Me too. It isn't like my father to vanish for so long, leaving people wondering. When he acts, he usually does so quickly.'

Patrick got the key to turn at last and flung open the door, saying curtly, 'There was a prowler out at the back just now, Dennis. We need to let Tez know.'

He locked the door again behind them, cursing under his breath as the key continued to be stiff and hard to turn, then they walked back to Pear Tree Cottage, with Georgie sandwiched between the two men.

They didn't see anyone, but the prowler could have

been watching them leave – probably was, he decided.

'You look different, Patrick,' Georgie said as they went inside the brightly lit house and closed the front door.

'Do I? How?'

'Alert and grim.'

'That's how I feel. We must all stay alert every single second from now on. We can't afford to relax in any way. That mess of a garden is perfect for spying on someone from.'

# *Chapter Seventeen*

The warmth and bonhomie had vanished, Georgie thought, as she clasped her hands round her cup of cocoa, grateful for the warm comfort it gave. It was the same group of people sitting round the table as before, minus Martin who was keeping watch in the next-door garden, but this time the kitchen was filled with tension and conversation was only stuttering along.

Every now and then one of them would turn suddenly to stare towards the outside as if able to see through the walls and curtains. It made her feel furious that these traitors were spoiling the happiness of the early days of peace for them.

Like most people, she had been filled with hope when she went out to join the revellers in London – was it only a few days ago? Now, she was fleeing for her life and it felt as if the celebrations had taken place in another world.

Most of the time she sat quietly, listening to the men, thinking about what they were saying. She didn't feel the need to add to their plans or to participate in their discussions. They'd had far more experience than she had of dealing with dangerous situations, after all.

One thing they were discussing caught her attention suddenly, however: how best to protect themselves. That, she did need to join in. 'Personally I'm going to carry my gun and a small sharp knife, just in case.'

'You won't need one,' Patrick said curtly. 'You and Rosie will be staying here with Bella.'

'And what if these people realise there's only one man and a few women and children in Pear Tree Cottage and turn their attention to it? It's me they're after, not Tez and his family, so I won't put them in danger by staying here. I absolutely *insist* on joining you men next door. We don't even know how many people have been sent to Honeyfield to find me.'

'I'm surprised at the way this pursuit is continuing,' Patrick admitted. 'I don't think Captain Jordan expected such a vigorous effort to capture you, either, or he'd have found somewhere safe for you in London.'

'Unless *he* is the traitor.'

He stared at her in shock. 'No, surely not? We'd have noticed something.'

She stared right back at him. 'Patrick, it has to be someone who's very good indeed at deceiving others to have escaped my father's attention. Anyway, I'm coming next door with you, whatever you say.'

Tez nodded across at her. 'I think you're right, Georgie. It will be far better for you and Rosie to stay with your three companions. They can defend you better than one man like me, who is trying to protect his family as well.'

'Of course you are!' she said warmly.

'I can defend myself,' Bella muttered.

'Against how many?' Tez sighed. 'I don't want to draw anyone's attention to this house. I'm going to spend the night downstairs near the telephone and believe me, at the slightest sign of trouble – and I'm a very light sleeper – I'll be calling Constable Browning.'

He turned to his wife. 'I think you'll be all right.'

'I intend to make sure of that. I still have my own gun and I'll load it before I go to bed.'

Everyone stared at her in surprise.

'What's more, I can scream loudly enough to bring our neighbours running to help me, if necessary. No one will get near our son while I'm with him, Tez darling, and the nursery maid can sleep with us. Pippa's a strong lass and we'll give her the rolling pin for protection. So you go ahead and keep watch downstairs without worrying about us.'

'That's my girl.'

The look those two shared made Georgie envious, so bright was the love that shone between them.

Dennis joined in the discussion. 'We four should definitely go back to the other house and keep a very careful watch, Patrick, but I don't think they'll notice if Rosie stays here.'

Georgie shot him a quick glance. Not another pair!

'I'm coming with you.' Rosie folded her arms and gave them all just as determined a look as Georgie's had been.

'But—' Dennis began.

Rosie held up one hand and continued speaking, 'I didn't grow up soft, believe me. I've had to look after myself in rough streets from a very young age, yes *and* protect my younger brothers and sisters. So I want a knife and a poker. I'll not be afraid to use them if I'm attacked.'

Patrick raised his hands in a gesture of defeat. 'All right. Point taken. Those men might not return tonight, but we'll be ready for them if they do.'

Dennis frowned in thought. 'You know, I don't think they've realised we're on to them, which might give us a bit of an advantage. We'll give them a hard time if they come after us, a very hard time indeed. I didn't lay my life on the line over in France to put up with this at home in Blighty.'

There were nods and murmurs of agreement from all the other men.

When the others had gone next door to Orchard View for the night, Tez locked up his home carefully, checking every door and window, then had a quick word with his wife.

'I'm going to try to discover where these people are hiding. They can't be staying in the village itself. I don't think any of *our* people would shelter traitors.'

'They might if they didn't know why the intruders were here and were being well paid. You go and see what you can find out. I don't think they'll strike so early in the evening, but I'll keep my gun handy.'

'You're a plucky woman.'

'I hope so. Are you going on your own?'

'No. With Cole, I hope.' He picked up the telephone and rang Honeyfield House, asking to speak to Sal's husband, who was both handyman and guard there.

'Are you any good at tracking people, Cole?'

'Not bad, Mr Tesworth. Why?'

He quickly explained the situation, ending, 'How about you come for a look round with me? I can let you into our garden through the back wall without anyone who's watching the house next door noticing. Then we'll go and have a look round the village.'

'Happy to help, sir.'

'Good. I thought we could dress so that we seem to be poachers going out for the night. I've got some dark clothes. What do you think?'

There was a chuckle on the other end of the line. 'I'll be there in ten minutes, sir. And I'll bring some clothes for you because yours won't be nearly ragged enough. Mine will smell a bit ripe, but you won't mind that in a good cause.'

He would mind, Tez thought ruefully as he hung the phone up. He hated to be dirty in any way. But this was definitely in a good cause, so he'd put up with it.

# *Chapter Eighteen*

In London, Captain Jordan decided to pretend that the injury to his arm was much worse than it really was in order to do some scouting round. He telephoned the bureau and left a message for Major Butterly, who was in charge of day-to-day administration among other duties, saying he wouldn't be able to come in for a few days due to an injury.

To his surprise, he got a phone call back almost immediately, and from the major in person, insisting he couldn't be spared and telling him to damned well pull himself together.

That was . . . strange.

He didn't intend to comply, however, so went back to see the military doctor who'd dealt with his wound, a man he knew from school and university, and trusted absolutely.

His friend listened carefully. 'I know where you're

working, Ralph, and how important it is. What do you want me to say in the note?'

'That on no account must I use that arm and risk infection or I might lose it. It should advise me to go and convalesce in the country.'

'This job you're doing must be very important?'

'Oh, yes. Crucial. Why do you think someone attacked me in the first place? The outright war is over, but we're now facing some serious jockeying for power. Between you and me, they think it's that group who call themselves *Siebenzeit*.'

His friend let out a soft whistle of surprise. 'You'd think even they would acknowledge defeat, as Germany itself has done.' He sat down, took out his fountain pen and wrote a medical certificate on headed official notepaper.

Jordan sent his note to the bureau by messenger and didn't wait for an answer, but went round to Mr Cotterell's house to speak to Mathers.

'You work closely with your master, so you must have some idea of where I can look for Miss Cotterell.'

Mathers stiffened and gave him a suspicious look. 'No one has informed *me* of her whereabouts, sir – why would they? – so I'm afraid I can't help you.'

'Look, this is extremely important, a matter of life or death, and her father isn't around to look after her. You must be able to make a reasonably accurate guess, given how long you've worked for Cotterell.'

'No, sir. I couldn't do that.'

'Have you been into the bureau since Mr Cotterell vanished?'

'Why would I, sir? My employment was directly with him and my visits there were only to assist him or drive him somewhere if the official chauffeur wasn't available or else he wanted to use another car.'

Silence fell, but Jordan wasn't satisfied. 'Whatever you say, I'm still certain you have an idea of some possible places to look for her.'

Mathers shook his head, his face quite expressionless. 'I'm sorry, sir. I couldn't take it upon myself to guess, let alone share those thoughts with anyone.'

'Hell fire, man! How many times do I have to tell you that Miss Cotterell is in very real and present danger.' He saw the door handle turn slightly. Someone must be standing outside in the hall. Were they going to come in? But the handle turned noiselessly back into place again and he didn't think Mathers could have noticed anything, because his back was to that door.

He raised his voice a little as he added, 'Do you *want* someone to kill Georgie Cotterell?'

'I'm sure she'll have found somewhere safe to hide, sir. She's not a stupid young lady. Now, I must get on with my work. Allow me to show you out.'

'I can show myself out, thank you very much.'

Mathers sighed and as they both left the room, he frowned at Jordan and ran lightly down towards the basement kitchen, leaving the visitor to use the front door. He paused at the bottom to make sure the door was opened, nodding in satisfaction at the sound of it opening and closing.

Jordan didn't leave the house, however. After closing the door again, he slipped into the room across the hall and left its door partly open. Through the narrow gap he watched Mathers come up to the ground floor from the basement, lock the bolts on the front door, then carry on up the stairs to the first floor.

When he heard the sound of a door shutting upstairs, Jordan crept across the hall and down to the basement. He found Nora standing near the kitchen window, arms clasped around herself, looking upset, so cleared his throat to alert her to his presence.

She spun round. 'Ooh, sir, you did give me a shock! I thought you'd left.'

'Not yet. Look, I think you overheard what I was saying to Mathers a few moments ago so I wanted to speak to you as well. Do *you* have any idea where Miss Cotterell might be?'

She hesitated.

'Please! It's vital that we find her. She's in terrible danger. These people won't hesitate to kill her. Just like that.' He snapped his fingers to emphasise his point.

Nora pressed one hand across her mouth, then pulled it away again and said in a rush, 'I reckon she'll be at Honeyfield, sir. Either at the big house or at Pear Tree Cottage in the village. But please don't let anyone know I told you.'

'I won't. Thank you. You may just have saved her life.'

'Does Mathers know you're still here, sir?'

'No. He thinks I left.'

'Then I'd better let you out the back way, sir.'

When she returned to the kitchen from the mews behind the house, Nora found Mathers waiting for her, arms folded, expression furious.

'I saw who you let out and I know what Jordan wanted to find out. What did you tell him?'

She swallowed hard. 'Nothing.'

'Don't lie to me, Nora.'

'I couldn't *not* tell him, Mr Mathers. He said Miss Georgie's life was in danger and he *is* working at the bureau, after all.'

'So is a traitor. Why do you think Mr Cotterell himself went into hiding? What if the traitor is Jordan?'

Her mouth fell open and she stared at him in horror.

'Miss Georgie may be in even greater trouble now, so you'd better tell me *exactly* what you revealed!'

She told him, then burst into loud, noisy tears after she'd finished her tale.

She couldn't believe it when Mathers walked out of the kitchen without another word.

'What have I done?' she whispered and began crying again. 'Oh, Miss Georgie, what have I done?'

For once, Mathers made no attempt to comfort Nora. He was too angry with her. He went to his master's study, unhooked the telephone earpiece and waited for the operator to respond. He asked her for the special number he was only allowed to use in emergencies.

When he heard someone clearing their throat at the other end, he gave a little cough, the pre-arranged password, and said, 'Something's come up. I need to speak to you know who and it's urgent.'

He waited impatiently while his employer was fetched to the phone.

A voice he recognised at once spoke suddenly. 'It had better be important.'

'It is, sir.' Mathers went through what had happened and waited as silence greeted the information.

'You were right to contact me. We'll have to speed things up. I'm just getting proof of the main person involved, because he's too well connected in the upper levels of society to be accused otherwise. If I do this carefully, we can act at once. What worries me most is whether your recent visitor is also involved. I haven't been able to confirm J's role either way yet, not to my own satisfaction, anyway, though I *think* he's all right, just rather tactless. Sadly, the country's needs must come first if . . .'

His voice trailed away but they both knew what he meant.

'Yes, sir.' If the worst came to the worst, his master would sacrifice Georgie's life to his country's needs.

'Get the car ready for action and pick me up here, at the side entrance, tomorrow afternoon. Bring all the guns from my special cabinet with you.'

'What shall I do about Nora?'

'She can stay there tonight with you. You'll be quite safe because I'll arrange for a guard to be posted both front and back. Tomorrow you can leave her here when you pick me up.'

Mathers was startled. 'What about after we leave? This place will be totally unprotected, sir?'

'Not quite. That will be taken care of. We may even trap one or two minor fish in our net there.'

Mathers knew he'd get nothing further out of his master unless and until he needed to know so asked simply, 'Is that all, sir?'

'Hmm. Oh yes. I was just starting to think over the details for speeding up the next stage. Be careful tonight, but *you* ought to be all right.'

The phone line went dead. Mathers sighed. Mr Cotterell

could be very frustrating to work for, given the way he rarely confided in anyone. On the other hand, it felt good to serve your king and country, even if what you did would never be publicly acknowledged. He was very proud of playing his part.

At least this matter was in the best possible hands. Mathers was very fond of Miss Georgie. If anyone could keep her safe, it was her father.

And if anyone did hurt her, he would be as keen as her father to make them sorry. By hell he would! He had grown very fond of that young woman in the two years she'd been living with them.

He went to find Nora, who looked at him apprehensively.

'Mr Cotterell has need of me tomorrow.'

Her voice wobbled. 'Will I be left here on my own?'

'No. We've found you a place of safety.'

'Thank goodness!'

'People will be on guard outside this house tonight, too, but just in case anyone gets past them, I suggest you and I sleep in the same bedroom. The guest room with twin beds next to the master's would be the most suitable, I think.'

She flushed.

'You will have a separate bed, woman, and I for one will not be getting undressed.'

She relaxed a little. 'Then I won't, either. Sorry. I'm being silly. It's all getting me down, especially the worry about Miss Georgie.'

He hated to see her looking so subdued and fearful, and was glad she'd be out of this whole messy business from now on. She was a very capable housekeeper, could turn her hand to almost any job indoors, but she was too fond of Miss Georgie to think clearly about this problem. Look at what had happened today!

'I don't think Captain Jordan is a bad 'un, Mr Mathers, I really don't,' she volunteered suddenly.

'I don't think so, either, but one can't always tell. Even the master isn't sure about him.'

From Mr Cotterell's house Jordan went straight to a place where he could occasionally take refuge or change clothes if necessary. The room was in a sleazy area and had been rented for him by the bureau. He intended to pack an overnight bag and leave London within the hour.

As usual he paused at the corner to look along the street before he went any further, and what he saw made him step hastily back against the wall, sucking in his breath in shock.

*He hadn't left his bedroom curtains like that last time he was here!* He always placed one curtain in a certain position when he left – always! It moved to a very different position if anyone touched it or even just brushed against it accidentally. He'd been told the trick by an old colleague years ago.

Its position today showed clearly that someone had been in his room, might even still be there. Only one person at the office could have got hold of the information about this bedsitter, which settled his worries about whether to act independently today or not.

He went into the newsagent's on the corner, relieved to find no other customers there. 'Can I use your special rear entrance, Burtill?' He slapped a half-crown down on the counter, the price agreed.

'Yes, sir. You know the way.' The coin vanished quickly into the shopkeeper's hand even as he lifted the end of the counter. He set it back into place immediately the captain had passed through.

When two men burst into the shop a couple of minutes later, Burtill gaped at them, not needing to pretend to be startled, they looked so fierce. They weren't from round here, that was sure.

'Where did he go?' one of them asked sharply.

'I beg your pardon, sir?'

'The man who just came in – where did he go?'

'He went out of the side door, sir.' He pointed to a door to one side of the counter. The shop was on a corner and he liked to catch potential customers going both ways. The third door, accessed from behind the counter, led into the rear and out into the back alley, but they wouldn't know about that.

The men strode through the shop without a word of apology, slamming the side door open and leaving it banging to and fro.

Burtill didn't even try to close it but retreated hastily to his living room, where he locked the solid wooden door between it and the shop. He half-expected them to try to kick it in when they didn't see any sign of his recent visitor, but they'd have difficulty doing that quickly. It was a very solid door, chosen on purpose.

Picking up the earpiece of the phone, an extravagance that had paid off a couple of times already, he telephoned the man to whom he paid regular protection money, getting through straight away.

'Burtill here. There's trouble from two men I don't

recognise. Can you come round straight away, Andrew? And better bring a gun. I think they were carrying weapons from the way their jacket pockets bulged.'

'On my way.'

When the two men returned to the shop a few minutes later after a fruitless search of nearby streets for Captain Jordan, they found a burly man standing behind the counter.

'Where is he?' the taller man snapped.

'Who, sir?'

'The shopkeeper.'

'I'm the shopkeeper, sir. Oh, you mean my friend. He was just minding the shop while I nipped out for a snack. What would you like: cigarettes, pipe tobacco, matches?'

As they hesitated, exchanging quick glances, one of them moved a hand towards his pocket, trying not to show what he was doing. The man behind the counter had his own gun out before the other could complete the move, pointing it at them.

'Keep your hands away from your pockets. Bit rough, this area, so I've learnt how to protect myself. We don't welcome outsiders causing trouble here, so I think you'd better leave my shop. And don't come back to this district, either, if you know what's good for you. I never forget a face and I have some good friends round here.'

They looked astounded at this curt ultimatum.

He watched them hesitate, look at the gun he was pointing steadily at them, then leave without a further word.

When they'd gone down the street, he called in a low voice, without turning, 'I think I'd better stay here with you for a while, Burtill. You were right. Nasty-looking types, those, and definitely not from round here. They'd better not try to poach on my employer's territory. Powerful man in this district, Mr G, and doesn't like others intruding.'

'I was never so glad to see anyone as when you arrived. Thanks, Andrew.'

'That's what you pay protection money for. Don't say you didn't get your money's worth today.'

'I got excellent value today, Andrew. I'm grateful.'

'I'll stay on here for a while, just to make sure. You wait in the back. I can serve any customers who come in.'

The shopkeeper let out a huge sigh of relief and stayed where he was. The takings in this shop were good, but at times the area round it could get a bit . . . difficult . . . well, let's face it, downright rough.

He hoped Mr Jordan had got clean away. Always polite, that gentleman was, and bought cigarettes here regularly.

The neighbour who owned the house along the street said he was a good tenant. Only used the room now and then, kept it clean and paid his rent on time. What more could you ask?

Burtill wished he had a tenant like that in his own upstairs room.

# *Chapter Nineteen*

Tez let Cole into the garden through the secret back door of the summer house for a moment but didn't lock the gate. 'I thought we'd go through the orchard. That way, perhaps?' He pointed in the opposite direction to the way Cole had come. It would be easy to slip unseen along the rear wall of the neighbouring orchard, even now when the branches were bare of leaves, because it was about six foot high.

'Fine by me. But I think it'd be better if you changed into these first, Mr Tesworth. Your clothes are too clean for a poacher, and they're gentleman's things, anyone can see that at a glance.'

Tez shuddered at the smell of the bundle that was thrust into his hands and made one last protest. 'But if we stay in the shadows no one will see me that clearly.'

'They might see enough to make them suspicious if it

was them villains looking at who's out and about. Please, sir. Just to be safe.'

'Oh, very well.' Tez took off his outer garments and put on the borrowed ones – baggy clothes with large inside pockets to contain small game like rabbits. The smell of sweat and dried blood made him gag.

Hoping he now looked like a poacher, he followed Cole out into the orchard again and in the opposite direction to Honeyfield House, locking the gate to his own garden carefully behind them.

When they got to the lane, they clambered over the low gate and started on a circuit of the outer parts of the village. At first they saw nothing but dark cottages presumably full of sleeping people.

Then Tez's hunch about needing someone more used to the country at night to help him track down the intruders paid off, because it was Cole who spotted a very faint light flickering in an abandoned labourer's cottage on the far side of a field. Tez had barely glanced at the cottage, knowing it to be a near ruin.

Cole stopped dead and tugged at his sleeve, whispering, 'Why is there a light when there ent nobody livin' there? Well, they can't be livin' there, can they, because half of it's fell down? And look, there's a car parked behind it, a big one. You can just see its bonnet. What's a big posh car doing outside a tumbledown cottage, eh? You tell me that, Mr T!'

'We'd better check it out.'

As the two men moved closer, following a narrow lane with a ditch to one side, the sound of low voices could be heard in the still night air, though not clearly enough to make out the words.

Then another car drove towards the village from the north and to their surprise, turned into their lane.

Cole vanished into the ditch and Tez only just managed to leap after him before the car drove past and stopped behind the cottage.

'What d'you reckon is goin' on?' Cole whispered.

'A German group called *Siebenzeit* is trying to cause trouble, my mother thinks.'

'Germans? But we've won the dangy war.'

'These are British traitors, people with relatives or interests in Germany. I'm not positive if it's them doing this, mind. No one is. But it's likely. The newspapers are already suggesting there will be a lot of tricky dealing going on behind the scenes as the various nations prepare for the coming peace negotiations.'

'I still don't understand what that has to do with Miss Georgie.'

'Our best guess is that they're intending to capture her and use her to force her father to act as an informer both before and during the coming peace negotiations. He's bound to be at the centre of what's going on. He's a very important—'

'Shh!' Cole moved a few steps closer, listening intently. This time the voices carried more clearly because the newcomers were standing outside the ruined cottage. 'They sound to be speaking the King's English.'

'Yes.'

'Why would they want to help the enemy, then, if they're English?'

'There's been a lot of intermarrying between the Germans and the British upper classes over the last couple of centuries and sometimes even rich people can't be trusted.'

Cole didn't say anything, just muttered a few choice swear words under his breath as they watched the two men. They were so muffled up against the cold that from this distance there was no telling whether they were young or old, tall or short.

The number plate of their car must have been deliberately covered in mud, Tez thought, because neither the letters nor the numbers had been visible when the vehicle passed close to them, even though the moonlight was bright enough to have made them out. If they'd been able to see what its one or two initial letters were, they might have had some idea where the car came from. Though you couldn't always tell these days, because with so many people having cars, the local licensing authorities simply added a second letter when the number got beyond 9,999 and started counting again. How was anyone to keep track of it all?

Time seemed to pass slowly as they kept their eyes on the cottage. He pulled his pocket watch out and checked it every now and then. It was nearly half an hour before one of the men came out again and got into the back of the car.

It drove away almost immediately but though they waited, no one else left the cottage and after a while the light inside winked out.

'Don't look like they're intending to do anything else tonight, do it, Mr T?'

'No. I'm not sure whether it's worth staying here longer or not. What do you think?'

'I'll stay on a little while if you like, sir, and keep an eye on things, just to be sure.'

'Don't go causing trouble, Cole. We don't want them to know we've found their hideout.'

'I'll be careful. You'll want to get back to your wife, and anyway, you make a lot more noise than I do. I can get right up to that cottage if I have to without them hearing me. I'll nip back across the fields and warn you if these sods look like attacking the old house next to yours tonight, you can be sure of that.'

'They'll not get into my house, whether I'm there or not. I have good locks and my wife has a gun – knows how to use it too. Just the sound of it being fired would bring our visitors running from next door. And if Bella screamed for help, all the neighbours would come running as well.'

'Rare determined lady, your wife is, if you don't mind me saying so, sir. She'd give 'em what for. Only it ent her as they're after, is it, from what you say? It's them other folk what's stayin' next door.'

'I daren't leave the back gate from my garden through to the orchard unlocked. You'll have to find your own way back to Honeyfield House, if necessary.'

Cole chuckled. 'Bless you, sir, I know more than one way to get back there and no one any the wiser, I promise you. I'll have a potter round the village before I go home. I want to make sure *my* wife is safe, too, because she don't have a gun.'

'I'd back your Sal against anyone who tried to attack her, gun or not.'

Cole chuckled. 'Aye. She's a fine, strong woman, not one of them scrawny, wambly types. A *proper* woman, as gives a man something to hold in bed of a night.'

'Yes. I'm sure she does. Thanks for your help.'

'We all have to pull together, don't we? Oh, and leave them clothes near your front gate. Someone will pick them up for me. Never know when they might come in useful, even though I don't do no poaching these days, sir. My Sal won't stand for it.'

When Tez had left, Cole stayed where he was for half an hour or so, went to check that there was no sound from inside the end of the cottage that still had a roof over it, then left to prowl round the village. He knew it well enough to keep out of sight most of the time, in case someone else was about. But he didn't meet anyone.

He made a few stops en route to see certain people, tossing gravel at windows or knocking on doors in a certain way to wake them up, then having a quick word with the occupants.

Mr Tesworth wasn't the only one to have friends ready to help him, Cole thought as he left the last house, pleased by the responses he'd got. Satisfied he'd done his best for the moment, he ambled back home to Honeyfield House.

Of course, Sal woke up the instant he opened the back door. Well, she would, wouldn't she, because she wasn't in their bedroom but dozing in the rocking chair near the still-warm kitchen range.

'Don't light a lamp, lovie,' he warned.

'Trouble?'

'It's brewing, yes. Mr T an' me poked round a bit, found where them villains were hiding, which was in Sam Bunkle's old cottage. When Mr T went home again, I let a few of my old friends know what was going on. Eh, he made a right old noise as we walked, he did. Poaching teaches you more about moving around quietly than them townies will ever learn.'

'I thought we'd agreed: no more poaching.'

'Bless you, I've no *need* to catch my food when I get fed so well here. But you don't forget how to move quietly.' He pulled her to him for a hug.

She pushed away for long enough to say, 'You will help keep Mrs Bella safe, won't you? I'm rare fond of her, I am. Taught me to read, she did, when she first come here. I'd always wanted to learn.'

'We're all fond of her, and of her husband too. Nice chap, Mr T is. *He* don't look down his nose at anyone like some I've met. No, you've no need to worry, love. There's quite a few people who'll be keeping an eye on her, yes, and on them London friends of theirs too.'

After a moment's thought, he added fiercely, 'Mr T says these people attacking 'em are traitors, an' such as them ent going to mess up *my* village. Now, are you coming to bed, woman, or are you going to sit here all night a-watchin' the fire?'

# *Chapter Twenty*

No one at Orchard View slept soundly that night. The men took it in turns to keep watch, but they saw no signs of intruders nearby.

They breakfasted on bread and butter, with ham and a boiled egg each – the latter thanks to Bella's hens.

Patrick hardly noticed what he was eating. He didn't feel hungry because he'd had a fitful night's sleep worrying about the ongoing problem of Georgie's safety. He waited till everyone had taken the edge off their appetites then said, 'Look, we have to decide whether to stay here in Honeyfield or move on and try to find somewhere safer, somewhere they'd never think to look for us.'

Georgie didn't hesitate. 'I feel safest of all in Honeyfield. There's something about the place that makes me happy. So I vote we stay here. We've got friends nearby who'll come to our aid if there's trouble and Bella says the neighbours would pile in as well if we yelled for help.'

He looked doubtful, so she hurried on, 'And there are the people at Honeyfield House. Wait till you meet them, Patrick. They're such kind, caring people. We'd have help from Cole, I'm sure. He's a big, strong fellow. And Mr Doohey and his dog would help out as well, if we needed him.'

Dennis nodded but was clearly more interested in buttering another slice of bread and laying his last piece of ham reverently on it than in discussing what seemed obvious to him. He beamed down at his plate. 'Eh, it's been a long time since I've eaten such good food. I vote to stay here as well because we've already got allies here. It's a nice village. I'd like to live here or somewhere like it if I could find a job. I've had enough of crowds and cities.'

She was grateful for his support and his comment made her even more certain that she'd like to live here permanently.

Martin simply nodded and grunted what sounded like agreement. She could see that he too was enjoying the ham.

Rosie added her piece. 'I like it here as well. But we'll need to buy some more food today, whatever we decide to do. A lot more food, if we're to keep you chaps satisfied, because the shops won't be open tomorrow, remember.'

'Is it Saturday already?' Georgie asked in surprise. 'What a week it's been!'

Dennis reached out for the final piece of bread on the central plate. 'Shame to leave one piece to go stale. Haven't had bread as good as this for years, except for one time in France when the captain found a Frenchie baker to do a batch of bread for our unit. Funny shape he made it, long and thin and crusty. Eh, it tasted grand.'

He smiled at the memory as he buttered the bread.

Patrick looked at his companions. 'I think we should stay here too, but I wanted you to have a say. So it's decided. We'll stay here till we get word from the captain or your father, Georgie. Should we drive into Malmesbury for the food to hide how many we are or buy it here, do you think?'

'Buy it here,' Rosie said immediately. 'If these folk in the village are anything like the ones in my mam's street, they'll have a fair idea already of who's staying in this house and why. And they'll be more on our side if we buy food from the local shops and farmers than if we buy it from outsiders. Stands to reason.'

'There are some nice people in the village shops,' Georgie said. 'I'm looking forward to meeting them again.'

Patrick gave her a worried glance. 'I don't think *you* should leave the house at all. Rosie can do the shopping and one of us men will go with her.'

'What? Even in the middle of the day? They're not likely to attack any of us while we're walking down the main street of the village in broad daylight, surely?'

'They might risk a quick snatch if they spot an opportunity. It's what I would be on the lookout for in their place, anyway. So I'm trying not to give them a chance.'

'Well, I don't agree. They can't keep watch on this house every minute of the day and night without someone noticing them. And there are always people around in the village centre.'

'Georgie, if what we suspect is true, these people will keep on trying until they succeed. You must *never* go anywhere on your own till it's all sorted out – and that includes outside in this street, even. We're not in the village centre here.'

She gave him a pleading look but he shook his head.

'They'll probably still be planning to take you from the house during the night, so that's the time we have to be most careful of all.'

Her frustration escaped her. 'In other words, I'd better not go outside and I'd better not sleep too soundly, either. Patrick, I'll go mad penned up here.'

His sigh was audible. 'Well, perhaps you could walk along to the village shops with a couple of us in attendance. That ought to be safe enough. It's only about three hundred yards.'

He looked round and grimaced. 'We've made this house as secure as we can but it'd still be easy to break into it.'

'They'd not get in without making a noise,' Dennis pointed out.

'We hope not. But if they have someone good at picking locks, they may find a way to sneak in quietly. There aren't enough of us to leave more than one on watch at a time during the night. I've heard tales from men I fought with about how easy it can be to break into buildings.'

He turned back to Georgie. 'We just want to keep you safe. Hanging around can be wearing, I know. Let's hope your father will get in touch soon.'

'I know you're right to be careful, but I hate being idle. Perhaps I could put on some of those old clothes and help with the whitewashing?'

'You don't want to get yourself all mucky. Ask your friend Bella if she can lend you a magazine to read.'

'I couldn't sit still and read while you all work. I'll help Rosie with the cleaning.'

He opened his mouth to protest, then closed it again when she gave him a fierce look. He knew he'd pushed her as far as he could. She was an active sort of lass, which was another thing he found attractive about her – but unfortunately this made it harder to keep her penned up indoors with nothing to occupy her.

When Tez came in from next door soon after breakfast and told them what he and Cole had seen during the night, Patrick knew his worries were well founded, though it didn't comfort him to be right.

'I hate to sit here and wait for *them* to act,' he said.

'I've been wondering if we should take you somewhere else. We could do that tonight, if you like,' Tez offered.

'They'd only follow us and try again.'

'I think I've worked out a way to spirit you all away without them being any the wiser, and then I know exactly the place to hide you.'

'Oh? Where?'

'Honeyfield House.'

Patrick frowned. 'Everyone talks about it, but you can't see it from the village centre, so it must be quite isolated. And anyway, from what you saw last night, we'd be sitting ducks if we tried to drive there, with only one way through the village. We know now, thanks to you and Cole looking round last night, that they've got *two* cars. It's not impossible for them to have other cars at their disposal. They can't be short of funds if they're bringing in all these men.'

'I can't believe this is happening in England!' Rosie exclaimed. 'You'd think you'd be safe in your own country after just *winning* the war, wouldn't you?'

'I agree with Patrick,' Dennis said. 'If we leave here, they'll see us going, however careful we are.'

Tez gave them a smug smile. 'The beauty of my idea is that you only have to get across to our house without them seeing you in order to escape. It'd be quite easy for you all to sneak across the back gardens on foot after dark and there's a gate through our back wall from inside the summer house. It's so well hidden that even if they searched the garden they'd probably not find it.'

'What about our car?'

'You'd have to leave that here, I'm afraid.'

'And what's on the other side of this gate?'

'It opens into a walled orchard, a big one. The farmhouse isn't close by, so it's not overlooked by anyone. You just have to keep quiet and turn right, then walk along the perimeter walls to Honeyfield House and enter that the back way too. We'll get Cole to wait for you outside our garden once it's dark. He not only knows the way but he'd be a good chap to have on your side if it does come to a fight.'

'I thought the big house was for women only,' Patrick said. 'Are you *sure* they'll take in us men as well?'

'I'm going to phone my mother this morning and I'm sure she'll be able to arrange it. She's on the board of trustees for Honeyfield House, you see. It all fits in very neatly, considering.'

One after the other, they nodded, Patrick last of all. 'Could be a good idea to keep them guessing for a while longer.'

'I'll come back to see you later, once I've spoken to my mother, just to confirm that it's all right. She's always busy, so I may not catch her straight away, but if I say it's urgent, her housekeeper will get word to her.'

* * *

'We might as well carry on working to pass the time,' Patrick said.

'We'll need to do some shopping before dinner time,' Rosie warned them.

'Leave that till later.'

Georgie helped Rosie with giving the kitchen and pantry a thorough cleaning while the men continued to throw out rubbish and broken furniture, working their way slowly through the house, room by room.

The cleaning of the pantry and kitchen was slow and difficult because they had trouble heating enough water to scrub the floor and shelves in the couple of saucepans which were all they had to use. The kitchen range seemed to have a leak in its built-in water tank and when he gave permission for them to stay, Mr Perry had said it wasn't safe to use.

By late morning, both women were ready for a change of task.

'The pantry's clean now, so once it's dry we can put our food in it.' Rosie looked at Georgie anxiously. 'We really ought to go and do that shopping soon because we've nothing here for our dinner, let alone our tea this evening. And we'll have to cater for tomorrow, even if we plan to leave tonight, just in case something goes wrong, because the shops won't be open on a Sunday. I'm happy to go and do it only I don't have enough money to buy food for us all.'

Georgie felt for her embarrassment and spoke lightly. 'Don't be silly. Of course I'm paying for any shopping we do, since you're all here because of me. What's more, I'm still determined to come shopping with you. No! Don't argue. I don't care what Patrick said. I just don't believe I'll be in danger in the centre of the village at half-past eleven in the morning.'

'Are you sure?'

'I'm not sure about anything except that I'll go mad if I'm shut up in here all day with dust flying and that horrible smell of whitewash.' She looked round, stretching her aching muscles. 'We've made a big difference in the kitchen at least, haven't we?'

The younger woman gave an equally satisfied nod. 'More than I'd expected.'

Patrick, who was working in the next room, must have overheard their conversation because he walked into the kitchen to join them, rolling his shoulders to stretch the stiffness out. He looked from one woman to the other. 'Are you two going to the shops?'

'We'll have to or there won't be any dinner.' Georgie gave him a challenging look. 'Do you want me to get you anything in particular?'

'Couldn't you . . . leave the shopping to Rosie?'

'Patrick, do we have to keep going through this? I'm going shopping with Rosie.' She held her breath when he didn't answer immediately.

'Well, since I'm the one in charge of keeping you safe, I'd better come with you. I wouldn't mind getting a breath of fresh air. Just give me a few minutes to clean myself up and change my clothes.' He held out his arms and grimaced at the white spatters on his sleeves, hands and bare forearms. 'Good thing Tez had some old clothes for me to work in. They're messed up already.'

He turned back to look at her sternly. 'Promise me you won't go out till I'm ready.'

'I promise.'

She watched him leave, wishing now that Rosie wasn't coming with them. She hadn't had much time alone with Patrick since their stay at the farm. It was so frustrating! How were the two of them going to get to know one another better if they were always caught up in problems and crises, and never alone?

Come to that, how would they even know when the current danger had passed? All she could hope was that her father was as omniscient as people said and would sort out this set of problems quickly, then come and find them. Surely he would?

Rosie came back to join her, dressed to go out. 'Not ready yet?'

'What? Oh, I was thinking about something.'

'You've got a smear of dirt on your nose, so you'd better wash your face.'

'No!' She rushed across to the speckled old mirror on the wall. 'Oh, my goodness what must he think of me?'

Rosie chuckled. 'Patrick won't let a bit of dirt put him off. You still look pretty. I'm just going to nip next door and see if I can borrow some shopping baskets while you tidy yourself up. Dennis will stay with you and make sure no one gets into this house.'

They were taking it so seriously that someone had to be with her at all times. Georgie felt humbled by their care. She wiped away the smut, combed her hair standing in front of the hallstand mirror, put on a beret in lieu of a hat and dragged on her gloves. Dennis waited in the still-dusty front hall, then followed her back into the kitchen.

Rosie came back from next door with two huge

shopping baskets, letting in a gust of cold air. 'Here you are. Where's Patrick?'

'He hasn't come down yet.'

There were footsteps on the stairs shortly afterwards and he appeared in the doorway. 'Ready? I'll take one of those baskets.'

Rosie nodded, then nudged Georgie. 'Better put a scarf round your neck. It's turned cold and windy outside, and the sun's gone behind some clouds. There's rain brewing, if you ask me.'

'I didn't bring a scarf with me.'

'Take mine. I rarely feel the cold.' Patrick unwrapped it from his neck and handed it to her.

'Thank you.' It was warm against her skin, almost as if he'd touched her.

'Oops!' Rosie spun round again. 'Just a minute! I've left my list in the kitchen.'

Georgie had wanted to be left alone with Patrick, but now that they had a moment together, she couldn't think what to say to him.

'We'll get our time together after this is all over, my bonny lass.'

It was as if he could read her mind. She felt tension drain out of her. Something about him seemed to set her world to rights. 'I'm looking forward to that.'

'So am I.'

But then Rosie came clattering back again and the lovely feeling of togetherness faded. But she still had his scarf round her neck. She stroked it and rubbed her cheek against it, then flushed as she saw that Patrick had noticed and winked at her.

* * *

Tez's mother wasn't at home so he had to leave a message to call him back urgently. It was noon before the phone rang, however. He ran into the hall to pick it up. 'Is that you, Ma?'

'Yes. How are you, dear?'

'Fine. I'm trying to find a place for some friends to stay. They're a bit desperate.'

'I'm sure you'll find somewhere easily, you have a lot of friends nearby. Some of them are bound to have a spare bed.'

He was sure she'd guessed what he'd been going to ask and thank goodness for that! 'I'll phone again soon. Bye.'

After hanging the earpiece up, he watched it swing to and fro gently as he ran through what they'd said in his mind. Yes, she had taken his meaning, surely?

# *Chapter Twenty-One*

Clouds were scudding across the sky as they left the house. A gust of wind blew the ends of her scarf up into her face by way of a greeting and Georgie breathed in the cold, fresh air with deep pleasure.

She stood for a moment to watch the wind whisking the last of the dead leaves to and fro. It was like a child, piling them in corners and chasing them out again to play more games. She wished she wasn't too old now to go and wade through the dead leaves and make them crunch beneath her feet. They'd soon be gone and who knew where she would be this time next year? There were no leaves to crunch where she lived in London.

At the end of their little street Patrick said, 'Just a moment!' and held out one arm to bar the way, stopping to scan the village green and the few shops dotted among the houses along the upper edge. 'Hmm. There are fewer people out than I'd expected. I really don't think you should have left the house, Georgie.'

'We're still going to need some food,' Rosie protested.

'You and I can get that after we've taken her back.'

'I'm *not* going back! There's no sign of any strange car lurking near the village green. You hardly ever see cars round here at all, in fact, so we'd definitely notice one. I'm sure I'll be safe.'

He looked round again. 'Well . . . let's get it over with.' He set off walking at a brisk pace, his limp not as bad now and they had to hurry to keep up.

But after a hundred yards or so, a big dark car surged out of the narrow dirt side road further on to their left. It drove along the side of the village green coming towards them, accelerating.

Patrick knew they'd never get back to Pear Tree Close in time to avoid trouble, so he tossed his basket aside and yelled, 'In here!' Opening the nearest gate, he shoved the two women through into the garden of a shabby cottage, muttering, 'I hope to hell someone's in.'

At the sound of the gate crashing back against the wall, a dog began barking furiously from inside the building and the front door opened before they got to it.

Patrick called out, 'Thieves after us!'

A large man surged out, yelling, 'Let my dog get out, then you two ladies go inside. *Gate, Rex! Gate!*'

The two women flattened themselves against the house wall to each side of the door as one of the biggest dogs they'd ever seen pushed past them. The man shoved Rosie and Georgie inside then followed his dog.

It stood at the gate next to him and Patrick, barking furiously.

With its paws on the top rail, it came up to their shoulders.

The car had slowed down and was creeping the last few yards to the cottage, as if the driver was uncertain what to do next.

With the man beside Patrick and his dog, the three of them completely barred the way in.

'Word's out that someone wants to hurt your young lady,' the man said. 'Soon as I saw you through the window, I come running out.'

'Who told you?'

'Cole passed the word to me and some others on his way home last night. By now everyone in the village knows.'

The car stopped just across from their gate, its engine purring smoothly.

'Just let 'em try to get in here!' the man muttered. 'My Rex will bite them if they so much as poke their noses out of that car. You tell 'em, boy! You tell 'em.'

The dog renewed its furious barking, showing a fine set of big white teeth.

The people in the back seat of the car couldn't be seen clearly because the glass of the side windows was darkened. The driver had a chauffeur's cap pulled down and a scarf round his lower face. He seemed quite young and the lock of hair that had escaped from one side of his cap was dark.

For a moment or two the car lingered, then it drove off along the street, speeding up quickly.

'Cheeky devils. In broad daylight, too. I'll recognise that car if it comes back and see if I don't chuck a rock through one of its windows. Allus wanted to do that.' The man grinned at Patrick. 'Don't worry. Everyone will be watching for them sods twice as carefully now.'

He turned to yell towards the cottage. 'You can come out again, ladies.'

They did so, looking cautiously round.

'How about I take a walk with you to the shops. Me *and* Rex. Let me introduce you to him.' He laid a hand on each of them in turn, saying, 'Friend, friend.' The dog wagged its tail each time as if acknowledging that.

Afterwards Patrick stuck his hand out and gave his name. The man shook it and said, 'Gregory Clarke.' He nodded to the two women and picked up the discarded shopping baskets for them.

Two older women had come to their front doors in the row of cottages to watch what was going on.

Gregory scowled in their direction. 'Trust them old gossips to be watching the show from inside. They'd not think of coming out to help you, though, would they? No, not them two.'

A flurry of large raindrops sent the women scurrying back into their houses.

'Going to pour down soon,' Gregory said. 'Better get your shopping done quickly, ladies. Should have brought an umbrella. I ent got one to lend to you. I allus cover my head and shoulders with a sack if it looks like rain is setting in.'

He was obviously a man who liked the sound of his own voice, Georgie thought. But he'd saved them, so she was happy to let him chat away.

Before they went into the first shop, she said in a low voice to Patrick, 'I've got plenty of money from my father and you're doing this to help me, so I'm paying.'

He scowled but nodded.

Unfortunately, it was impossible to follow Gregory's advice and hurry because each shopkeeper was delighted to see Georgie again and had to enquire how she was and how long she was staying this time. They had noticed or been told about the car and every single one wanted to know if it belonged to 'them rascals'.

At the baker's they bought four big crusty loaves, an apple pie and cinnamon buns. He said he'd send the lad to carry it all back for them once he'd seen them turn for home.

At the grocer's they bought two pounds of butter, a jar of jam, a big wedge of cheese, tins of salmon and peaches, a jar of Marmite, sugar, tea, bacon and eggs, and at the shopkeeper's suggestion a jar of pickled onions to go with the cheese. It didn't have a fancy label on it.

'My wife makes these, best you can buy,' he told them proudly.

They watched him start to weigh out the butter and cheese, and use a big knife to slice the bacon thinly from the piece swathed in muslin and hung from a hook in the back wall.

Georgie turned to Rosie. 'What else do we need? I'm sure I've missed something.'

'Biscuits?'

'Oh, yes. What sort do you like?'

'My favourites are *Nice* biscuits. I love the coconut taste and I like to lick the sugar off the top.' She flushed slightly. 'Sorry. That's not good manners, I know.'

Georgie grinned at her. 'That's how I eat them too, when I'm on my own. My father would have a fit if he saw me. He's a stickler for table manners.' She turned back to the shopkeeper, 'Two pounds of *Nice* biscuits, please.'

Patrick moved forward to join them at the counter as they waited for the biscuits to be weighed and put carefully into two white paper bags, with the top corners twisted to hold the bags closed. 'How about some humbugs, ladies? My treat.'

'Good idea, but I'm still paying.'

He looked at Georgie.

'You can buy us some sweets another time,' she coaxed.

The shopkeeper finished weighing and put down the second bag of biscuits near their other purchases, then got down the big jar of humbugs from a shelf. He looked from one to the other. 'Do you want some humbugs or not? I don't care who pays as long as I sell them.'

The tension eased and they laughed. Patrick was touchy about money, Georgie thought. She didn't care about it, but then she'd inherited enough to live on comfortably if she didn't spend lavishly, which made a big difference to your life, she was sure. So many people had trouble putting enough food on the table for their families.

As they left the grocer's Georgie realised she would have to tread carefully with him if she hoped to . . . Her thoughts faltered, then she grew angry at her own feebleness and told herself not to be so stupid. Everyone wanted to be happy, have a family, have someone to love. She had to be brave to achieve that. If Patrick continued to show signs of being attracted to her . . . She could feel her cheeks heating up at the thought of where that might lead.

She was glad they arrived at the butcher's door at that moment, just as another heavy shower started, and hoped her blush hadn't been noticed in the bustle of getting inside the shop quickly. Its floor was covered in clean sawdust and its wooden chopping bench had been scrubbed white so many times over the years it had a dip in it.

After that there was the greengrocer's. Not as many things for sale here as in summer but they needed potatoes, parsnips, onions and carrots to go in the stew she and Rosie planned to make for tea.

When they came outside, it was still raining, so they walked home briskly, the men carrying the laden baskets, leaving the butcher's lad to bring their meat and sausages, and the baker's lad to bring the loaves and cakes on the front basket rack of their delivery bicycles.

There was no further sign of the black car, or any other car, come to that, but Gregory and his dog escorted them right to the kitchen door.

Georgie, who had seen Gregory eyeing one of her purchases with particular longing, had bought two tins of salmon. Now she pulled one out of her basket and thrust it towards him. 'This is to say thank you for your help today.'

He made no attempt to take it from her, holding out his hands, palms outwards, fingers spread wide. 'I don't need paying to help a neighbour, miss.'

'No, of course not. But I can buy a present for a friend, if I want. And you are my friend after today, I'm sure. Go on. Take it, Gregory,' she coaxed. 'It's only a tin of salmon.'

He hesitated, then took it from her. 'Well, that's a rare treat, so me and the missus will relish some for our tea and think of you kindly.'

'We're all in your debt today, Gregory.' She was glad to see him straighten his shoulders proudly.

'You can always count on my help if you need it, miss.'

'And I won't hesitate to ask.'

Inside the house Georgie leant on the back of a kitchen chair and let out a long shuddering sigh of relief, before taking off her beret and shaking the moisture from it. 'Who'd have thought they'd try to grab me in daylight? That car with the darkened windows was frightening.'

'It's my fault. I shouldn't have let you go out in the first place.'

'It's just as much my fault because I was determined to get some fresh air and you'd have had to tie me up to stop me. Today's taught me a lesson, though, believe me. I'll be far more careful in the future and listen to your advice, Patrick.'

'I doubt they'll try that trick again, but what *will* they try next? That's what keeps me awake at night worrying.'

'It's a good thing Tez and his friend Cole spread the word that we might be attacked, isn't it?'

'Yes. Gregory made all the difference today. Stout fellow, he is, and that's a fine dog. I knew a lot of men like him in the Army. I can't help wondering why he isn't in the forces.'

'He squinted at the stuff in the shop, as if he found it hard to read the labels. I should think he's not got good enough eyesight to aim a gun. He probably needs spectacles but he wouldn't consider them a necessity. Poorer men don't usually do a lot of reading or close work, anyway. It's the women who bother to get glasses to do jobs like mending.'

'You sound as if you know something about that.'

She nodded gently. 'I've seen the difference spectacles can make to women's lives and I've helped a few people to buy them. Doesn't cost much to make a difference. Anyway, enough speculation, let's get this lot unpacked.'

Patrick stayed with them in the kitchen while the two women put away the food in the newly scrubbed and whitewashed pantry, using the big marble shelf at waist height for the things that needed to be kept as cold as possible and keeping out in the kitchen only what they'd need for a simple dinner, bread and butter with some cheese and the pickled onions they'd just bought.

'I wouldn't like to be kissed by one of the men after this meal,' Rosie whispered to Georgie.

'Would you like it otherwise?' Georgie saw her blush and added, 'By Dennis, perhaps?'

The blush deepened. 'Don't be silly. I've only just met him.'

She didn't press the point. She'd only just met Patrick and that didn't stop her liking him in that special way and wanting him to kiss her.

Rosie stepped back and looked round the large pantry. 'Not much to show for our outing, is there? What must this place have looked like with all its shelves filled?'

'Like my father's pantry in London. Well, let's put some food together for our lu—I mean dinner.' Georgie was trying to remember to use the same words for the various meals that her companions would: 'dinner' at noon and 'tea' at the end of the afternoon.

She saw by Patrick's quick grin that he'd understood her near slip but she didn't want to embarrass people who were trying to keep her safe, so she just elevated her chin as if to challenge him.

He gave her another of his quick winks and she couldn't help smiling back before turning to deal with the food. Why did one man make you feel warm inside and others not affect you at all in that way?

Once they'd eaten, it was a question of waiting for Tez to report on his conversation with his mother. His idea of hiding at Honeyfield House seemed by far their best option. They didn't want to start any more major jobs on this house until they found out what they were going to be doing, so they tidied up the kitchen and went up to the bedrooms to bring down their few possessions, ready to leave.

After that was done, they gathered again in the kitchen to chat about this and that. Georgie felt at ease with them. Such decent people and they seemed more relaxed with her now. At first they'd stumbled over whether to call her Miss Cotterell or use her first name as Patrick did; now they were on first-name terms.

After a while he pulled out his battered pocket watch in response to Dennis asking what time it was. 'Ten past two.' It was awkward in a house with no clocks on the mantelpiece. He was the only man with a pocket watch, while Georgie had a neat little fob watch.

Dennis fidgeted around. 'We could get on with a few jobs.'

Patrick shook his head decisively. 'No. I know there's a lot we could do to clear up the house, but we won't be able to leave suddenly if we're covered in whitewash, or dust and cobwebs.'

'I suppose not. I don't like sitting idle, and this place still smells of whitewash. I hope Mr Tesworth comes round soon to let us know what's been arranged.'

'I'll just get the newspaper we picked up at the shops. We can share the pages out, if you like, and see what's happening in the world.' Georgie had been intending to read it later but it'd fill the time nicely if Tez was late. Without waiting for anyone to go with her, she slipped into the sitting room to find it.

When she glanced out of the window, she saw her friend Bella coming across the winter-bare garden between the houses, carrying a basket and holding up an umbrella because it was raining again. Without thinking, she hurried to unlock the front door and let the visitor in, worried something might be wrong.

'Cheer up, love!' her friend said at once. 'Everything's all right. If you get the others together, I'll only have to tell my story once.'

'Good afternoon, Mrs Tesworth!' Patrick called from the back of the hall. 'We finished whitewashing the kitchen, pantry and laundry this morning, so you won't want to sit in the back. Why don't we bring the kitchen chairs into the front room? I was just going to do that, anyway. A bit of dust is easier to bear than the smell of whitewash.'

He locked the front door again and disappeared into the back part of the house with a frown in Georgie's direction. What had she done wrong now? she wondered as she followed Bella into the sitting room.

Patrick brought in two kitchen chairs, set them down and gestured to Bella to take one, but grabbed Georgie's arm and stopped her taking the other chair. 'Just need a quick word with her,' he said cheerfully to their guest and tugged Georgie back into the hall.

'What the hell were you thinking of, opening the front door on your own?'

'I'd seen Bella coming so I knew it was safe.'

'You can never be totally sure it's safe. Two women and one of them expecting! Someone much stronger than you two might have been lurking round the corner of the house and could easily have knocked her out of the way and grabbed you. You agreed not to open any of the doors without one of us nearby.'

'You didn't worry when I left the kitchen. She'd have got wet if I'd left her standing outside. It was *raining*.'

'Damn the rain. It's your *life* I'm thinking of. And you should have locked the door again straight away.'

She felt hurt by his rough tone and it must have shown in her face because his expression softened.

'I'm sorry, but you must learn to take every detail of this situation seriously. It's life or death, Georgie – and I shouldn't say this to you, have no right, but I can't bear to think of anything happening to you.'

Her anger faded at once. 'I'm the one who should be apologising again. I'm just not used to thinking in that way.'

He pulled her to him for a quick kiss, then they heard the others coming back and separated hastily, she to join Bella, he to check that the others had brought enough chairs through.

# *Chapter Twenty-Two*

Once everyone was settled in the otherwise bare sitting room, Bella began her explanation.

'Tez sent me round so that it'd look like a woman calling on a neighbour. He's arranging for you all to stay at Honeyfield House. He's going to nip round there the back way when I get home to make sure they're expecting you.'

Patrick's expression was now so grimly attentive he was like a figure carved in granite. My goodness, Georgie thought, that man can certainly concentrate hard. He looked very much in charge at such times, someone you'd turn to instinctively and know you could trust. Which she did, with both head and heart. She continued to listen to Bella, but couldn't prevent her eyes from straying to Patrick occasionally.

'Tez wants you to slip out of this house one by one as soon as it gets dark. If you go the back way, you can bend low and go right to your back fence without being seen from the street. Then you can edge along the fence behind the bushes till you get into our garden. It's a good thing the side fence has mostly fallen down, isn't it?'

She looked round as if checking that they were listening. 'Don't come to our house. Make your way across the back of the garden till you get to the summer house. Tez will leave the door of it unlocked and he'll be waiting for you inside. Then he can let you out via its other door, which leads through the garden wall into the orchard.'

'Georgie mustn't go across a dark garden on her own,' Patrick said at once. 'That's asking for trouble.'

'Tez wondered if she could dress as a man, then even if they catch sight of her, they won't realise who it is.' Bella looked at her friend. 'I have some clothes in my basket that ought to fit you. They're mine. I used to wear trousers when I was working as a VAD ambulance driver.'

'I have my own trousers with me, thanks,' Georgie said. 'But I don't have a proper top and jacket.'

'Even wearing trousers, she's not going anywhere on her own.' Patrick stood for a moment, so visibly concentrating that no one spoke until he offered an alternative suggestion.

'I think we should go in two groups, so that only one of us will be on their own, and even then he'll be within earshot if he hears a call for help. Dennis, will you do that solo job?'

'Yes, of course.'

'Good. If you go out first with Rosie and Martin, you can wait with your back against the fence and keep watch while they go across to the summer house. Yell for help if there's trouble. We'll hear you and come running. Right?'

'Fine by me.'

'If everything goes smoothly, I'll bring Georgie out five minutes after you, then all three of us will cross the final stretch together and join the others in the summer house.'

People were quiet for a moment or two as they took this in, then one by one they murmured agreement.

'What about the car?' Martin asked.

'I've been wondering what to do. Is this Leatherby chap to be trusted, do you think, Bella? If so, I can take it to that little workshop of his near the edge of town when we've finished here. I'll claim it's not running smoothly and needs looking at.'

She nodded. 'Malcolm's a decent chap. He's lived all his life in Honeyfield and is well liked. I'm sure you can trust him.'

'Well then, perhaps I'll explain that what I really want is for him to keep the car safe for us till we need it again. He and I can disable the engine so no one can drive it away. When that's sorted out, I can hurry back here on foot. That's the good thing about a small village. Nothing's far away.'

'It'd be safer for you to call at Gregory's house as you go and take him and his dog with you for protection,' Georgie objected. 'You keep saying *we* shouldn't go anywhere on our own, and *you* shouldn't do that, either. We all rely on you to organise things.'

There was another of those murmurs of agreement.

'All right. I'll try not to let you down. Anything else we should think about?'

Rosie signalled that she wanted to speak. 'How about we leave a couple of the rooms here with candles alight in them when we set off tonight? If we use candle stubs, they'll burn down and go out, then it'll look from outside as if we've blown them out for the night. The front room downstairs and one of the bedrooms, maybe?'

'Good idea. We'll only put them in rooms that have proper curtains, though, so that no one can see there's no one here.'

As he looked away, Rosie cleared her throat to get his attention back. 'There's another thing: Mrs Tesworth could take some of the spare food back with her in the basket now and we could carry the rest if there's anything left from our tea. I can't *bear* to think of good food going to waste.'

'Another excellent idea, Rosie. You're good at details. Only I don't think we should carry any leftovers with us, in case we need our hands free. I'll tell Gregory to pick it up tomorrow.' Patrick turned to their visitor. 'Is that all right with you, Mrs Tesworth?'

'Yes.' Bella took a pile of clothes out of her basket. 'Here you are, Georgie. Leave anything you don't need here. If you'll put the food in the basket, Rosie, I'll get off home. I don't want to appear unfriendly, but Tez said I shouldn't stay too long.'

Patrick turned to Rosie. 'Could you sort out the food we won't need?'

'I've already worked out in my mind what to leave for our tea.' She packed as much of the rest as she could into the basket. 'It's a bit heavy and some of it's bulky, so I think we'll have to leave one loaf behind. Will you be all right carrying this, Mrs Tesworth?'

Bella hefted the basket in her hands. 'Yes. I'm not a weakling and it isn't far. I shall—'

There was a knock on the front door and everyone froze.

Patrick stood up. 'I'll answer that.'

'Just a minute. I can peep out.' Georgie didn't wait for

him to agree to that, but got up and pressed herself against the edge of the bay window, hidden, she hoped, by the edge of the heavy curtain.

'He looks vaguely familiar but I can't quite place him. He's got a cap on pulled low and it's hard to see his face clearly.'

'Let me.' Bella took her place at the window. 'Talk of the devil. It's Malcolm Leatherby.'

'What on earth can he want?' Patrick wondered aloud.

'Let me answer the door,' Bella said. 'Malcolm knows me.'

'I'll be close by,' Patrick said at once. 'Stay inside the entrance, Mrs Tesworth. Don't go out on the doorstep till someone's with you.'

They heard the front door open and the murmur of voices, then the door closed and Bella brought Malcolm into the sitting room, followed by Patrick, who remained standing by the door, as if on guard.

'I'd better stay to see if there's anything else to think about. Tez will want to know.' Bella turned to their visitor. 'You said you wanted to see the people staying here, Malcolm. Tell us why.'

He took a moment to study them all before he spoke again. 'Cole knocked me up in the middle of the night and asked me to watch out for strangers. He said to let you people know if I saw anyone hanging round the village as had no business here. He said there are some villains after Miss Cotterell an' they might hurt her. Can't have that. We all look after one another in Honeyfield, see.'

The visitor had everyone's full attention but he stopped his narrative to ask, 'Could I ask who's in charge here, Mrs Tesworth?'

'Mr Farrell.' Bella pointed to Patrick.

'Thanks for coming, Mr Leatherby,' he said at once. 'We're grateful. Tell us exactly what you saw, every detail.'

'Well, sir, people who're driving past the village on the main road sometimes stop at my workshop to buy cans of motor spirit. There's some as ask for petrol, but my sign says motor spirit an' that's what I call it. Brings in good steady money these days, that does.'

He paused and Patrick nodded encouragement to go on.

'You see all sorts driving about the country, so I'd ha' thought nothing of what happened today, only for Cole knocking me up last night. Eh, I wondered what were going on when tapping at the window woke me up.'

He paused again and Bella gave a little shake of her head as if to warn everyone to be patient with his long-winded explanations.

'There was a car stopped by my workshop mid-morning today. Three fellows, but only two got out. They bought four cans of motor spirit. Four! I don't often sell that many to one person, I can tell you. It was a big car and it must use more than most, but still, four cans is a lot to buy at once.'

'Go on,' Patrick urged, almost twitching with impatience.

'Strange, I thought. Perhaps they're going on a long journey.' He nodded once or twice to emphasise this. 'Only they hung about afore they paid, asking me about the village, who were the important people and such questions. I didn't like the looks of them even though I was glad of their money, so I played dumb and told 'em the curate was the most important person, him an' the baker.'

'What did they say to that?'

'One of them asked if there were any gentry living in big

houses. I remember his words clearly, because he talked all la-di-dah, for all he were roughly dressed.'

'Baker and butcher have the biggest houses in the village, sir, says I. They looked at me like I was daft, so I acted dafter still and started talking about the grocer as well and how good the ham is there. That's when the one who'd stayed in the back of the car called out to hurry up. An' he had a posh voice, too. So they strapped the last can of motor spirit on the luggage rack, paid me and left.'

'And you'd never seen these men round here before?'

'No, never. I'm good at faces, better at faces than names these days, and I'd have remembered 'em because one chap had an old scar on his cheek – big straight one, it was right down the middle of his cheek.' He demonstrated with the side of his hand on his own cheek.

'Ah.' Patrick looked at the others. 'I've seen scars like that on some German officers. Duelling scars, they are, my captain told me. Not from war, but from playing at duels.'

'I don't know how he got the scar but I'd recognise those fellows if I saw them again, oh yes. I've been treated like an idiot before just because I live in a village and it fair gets me mad, it does. I may be old and I ent as strong as I was, I will admit, but I've still got enough wits left to make a good living, yes, and to save enough to see me and my wife through our old age.'

He ran out of steam and looked back at Patrick expectantly, head on one side. 'Was I right to come and tell you, sir?'

'Yes. Very right, indeed, and we're grateful. Now, I wonder if you can do me a further favour? I'm going to bring my car round to your workshop just before teatime and pretend it's not working properly. You could say you're repairing it for me if anyone asks.'

'Won't matter if folk in the village know I'm just looking after it, ent no one will tell them strangers.'

'But the strangers might come back, see it and ask. They'd recognise it as mine.'

'All right.'

'So if I disable the motor after I bring it to you, can you keep the car safe for me till we need it again, Mr Leatherby?'

Again, their visitor looked at Bella, who nodded as if to say this was all right. 'Yes, a-course I can do that.'

'I'll make it worth your while,' Patrick added.

He brightened. 'Thank you, sir.'

'You can say you have to send for a new part, in case people wonder why the car's been left there.'

The old man grinned. 'Ah. I can do that.' He tapped the side of his forehead. 'I'm good with engines so I can even tell folk it's the distributor an' I'll take it out for you, too.'

'I'm sure you're a very capable mechanic. You sound knowledgeable.'

'Thank 'ee. I'll say one thing afore I go, since you're all outsiders: if there's someone planning mischief, it ent one of us. No one in Honeyfield is a *traitor*. There's some as go poaching, there's some as drink too much, an' there's some as is a bit sharp to drive a bargain, but there ent no damned traitors here.'

'I'm sure not. And who would know better than you?'

The old man nodded calmly, accepting this as his due. 'Ah. Lived here man and boy, I have, know all the families. I better go now, in case there are any other people wanting to buy motor spirit. My wife can't serve them these days.

Poor old lass has rheumatics bad an' can't hardly walk.'

Patrick moved out into the hall. 'I'll see you to the front door, Mr Leatherby.'

'I'll leave too, now,' Bella said, picking up the basket.

They saw her walk next door, but there was the murmur of men's voices from the hall still and Leatherby didn't leave for a few minutes. Patrick was looking pleased about something when he returned, but as he didn't volunteer any information, Georgie didn't ask him.

It was a question now of waiting for dusk. Rosie started cooking the stew and Dennis said he'd take a nap sitting with his back to the kitchen door while she worked, so as to be there if she needed help.

He sat down, eyes closed and seemed to go instantly to sleep.

Georgie looked at him in bemusement and whispered to Patrick, 'How can he just go to sleep like that? Or is he pretending?'

'A lot of men learnt to nap when they could during their time in the Army. You didn't get regular hours for sleep when you were fighting at the front.'

Martin had stayed awake, but Patrick suggested he grab a quick nap too. 'I can keep watch on the front of the house, and I'll see anyone who tries to sneak past. I doubt they'll try to do anything else in broad daylight, especially not with people next door as well as in here.'

'I'll go in the dining room for my nap if you don't mind, Mr Farrell. I can be awake in an instant and come running.'

'When did I become Mr Farrell?' Patrick asked in surprise.

'When you took charge of our group. Can't call you sergeant now, can we, so it's *Mr* Farrell, as far as I'm concerned.'

'Oh. Well—' But he was talking to himself. Martin had already gone into the dining room on the opposite side of the entrance hall.

This left Georgie and Patrick alone together in the front room and he gave her one of his slow, warm smiles.

'They all respect you,' Georgie said. 'And rightly so.'

'Tell me that when I've got you safely through all this trouble.'

'What next, do you think?'

'I couldn't even guess. We just have to be ready for trouble.'

She sighed. 'I sometimes wonder if this whole situation is real. Maybe I'm simply having one of those nightmares that goes on and on.'

'Surely what's happened over the past few days isn't all nightmarish?'

His eyes were on her face as he said that, his smile so tender that she smiled back involuntarily. 'No. Some of it is very good, Patrick. Or it will be when the nightmarish part ends, I hope.'

'It will if I have any say.'

'I agree. Don't forget that after you meet my father, though.'

'Is he so intimidating?'

'He can be, yes.'

'I had a bit of practice at dealing with intimidating officers in the Army.'

'Not as bad as my father, I'm sure.'

'We'll see how I go with him when the time comes.'

After that she leant back in the dusty old armchair to have a little rest.

She came awake with a jerk when someone said her

name and shook her shoulder gently. 'What? Oh, I'm sorry, Patrick. I didn't mean to nod off.'

'Good thing to do. Who knows how much sleep we'll get tonight.'

'Did you manage a nap?'

'Well, no. But then, I'm in charge.'

'Is something wrong? Is that why you woke me?'

'Not at all. Rosie says tea will be ready in an hour and I have to take the car to the workshop first, so I can't leave you sleeping in here on your own.'

'Can I come with you?'

'Better not.'

She sighed but this time she didn't press the point. She didn't want to put him in danger. 'Take care how you go. You will pick up Gregory on the way, won't you?'

'Yes, I will. Martin is on duty in the front hall again, and Dennis is in the kitchen. I woke him up as well, now that I'm going out. You should sit in there. We'll eat our tea straight after I get back, then leave as soon as it's fully dark.'

'All right.'

'Before you do anything, how about changing into the men's clothes your friend brought across? Then we'll all be ready to sneak out at a moment's notice. Until then, you will stay with the others, won't you?'

'I won't break my promise, Patrick. Hurry back, though. I'll not feel comfortable till I know you're safe.'

He nodded, blew her a kiss and walked to the front door.

As she went up the stairs, she heard the front door close and the clicking sound as Martin shot the door bolt into place behind Patrick.

As she changed her clothes and took her bundle of things

down, she wondered how long they were going to be living like this, watching out for an attack every minute?

No wonder the war had marked men, if they'd had years of this sort of tension.

Only the war was officially over now. Why couldn't these horrible people understand that?

When Patrick stopped the car outside Gregory's cottage and tooted the horn, the front door opened at once and he came out, accompanied by his dog.

'Feel like earning a bob or two doing a short stint of guard duty, Gregory?'

'Any time. What about Rex?'

Patrick frowned, not liking the thought of Rex spreading mud and scuffing the car's leather upholstery when the vehicle didn't belong to him. On the other hand, the dog was big enough to make a powerful guard in its own right. 'He can come in the back of the car, if he'll be all right on the floor there.'

'He's never rid in a car afore, but he'll settle quickly if I tell him to sit. Where are we going?'

'We're driving to Leatherby's workshop, leaving the car there and walking back. I don't think we'll be long but I don't want to take any risks by walking back on my own.'

'Quite right. I'll just tell the wife.'

He came back with the dog ambling along beside him.

'Don't you need a leash for him?'

'Bless you, no, sir. My Rex is the best behaved dog I ever did have.'

And the dog proved it by settling down in the car as told, once he'd given it a few exploratory sniffs.

Patrick watched enviously. He'd never had a dog and would like to have one if ever – no, *when* he settled down somewhere. Georgie had seemed quite at ease with Rex earlier on. Maybe she'd like to have one, too?

The big doors of the workshop were open ready for them, and Malcolm gestured to Patrick to drive in.

The place was bigger than Patrick had remembered. This time he studied it very carefully. 'Plenty of room to work in.'

'Ah. An' I own it, don't I? Took me years to pay off the loan, but I did it. So now I can rent it out to someone when I retire and have an income from it as well as the old age pension. Seven shillings and sixpence a week for a married couple, they give you, as long as you don't earn more than thirty pounds – now was it that or was it thirty-one pounds? Anyway, it don't matter. I'll be over seventy soon and I fit all the rules. Wonderful idea to give honest, hard-working folk a pension, makes all the difference to growing old, don't it? Eh, my dad would have thought himself a king if he'd had it. Still working, he was, the day before he died.'

Patrick was getting used to how much Malcolm talked. He wasn't used to sharing his own hopes, but there was a sense of camaraderie between them that he'd experienced before with mechanics, so he said it aloud. 'After our talk I had a good think, and now I've seen this place I'm sure it'd suit me. I'm looking for a workshop of my own now I'm out of the Army. I've some money put by, could pay the rent and buy the equipment, if you're selling it.'

'Ah. Might you now? That'd be worth discussing. I do want to sell my things, though I'll be sad to lose them.'

'This isn't the time to discuss it, but once we've sorted out these villains and got Miss Cotterell safe, perhaps you and I could get together?'

'You're a proper mechanic, ent you? I'd not want this place used for anything else. Proud of it, I am.'

'Yes. I was trained in the Army.' He mentioned a few types of vehicle he'd worked on, said nothing about wanting to sell cars as well, then helped Malcolm to disable the motor.

After that, he and Gregory set off back for Pear Tree Lane.

He kept his eyes open for trouble, of course he did, but at the same time he felt a sense of hope running through his veins, hope such as he hadn't felt in years. If he had his own workshop, he'd not feel so much at a disadvantage with Georgie. And she loved it here in Honeyfield.

Would what he could offer be enough to appease her father, though?

Did she *really* care about him?

He had never wanted anything as much as he wanted to spend the rest of his life with her.

# *Chapter Twenty-Three*

Captain Jordan spent the rest of the day in the quiet little hotel where his mother always stayed when she came to London. He slipped out to do some shopping for clean underwear, a shirt and toiletries, buying them from a backstreet gentleman's outfitters where he wasn't known. He hadn't felt it safe to retrieve his possessions from the private room he rented in the working-class suburb, even after the men who chased him had gone.

He made no attempt to go back to his own flat, either, because he was quite sure there would be someone waiting there to arrest him – or worse. It was a serviced flat, so would be clean and ready when he did return, with his washing done, his clean shirts hanging in their place. On that thought he looked in the mirror and grimaced at the quality of the clothes he was now wearing. Needs must. At least they were clean.

This whole situation was a strange turn of affairs, very strange indeed. He'd better be right in his suspicions and was hoping desperately he could manage to get away from London and find Cotterell. He had to pin all his hopes on that. Fancy Major Butterly, the most pernickety bore of a man you could ever meet, being a traitor!

Jordan ordered the evening meal the hotel provided for its residents, but asked for it to be served in his room.

'Have to charge you a florin extra, sir, I'm afraid.' The young man on the desk was thin and looked unwell, wheezing slightly as he moved around.

'That's fine.' It'd be well worth two shillings to keep out of sight. 'Um, you don't have any magazines or books I could read, do you? I'm just recovering from an illness and need to live quietly, but I forgot to bring a book and that room is a bit too quiet for my taste. My mother stays here and she says the staff are very helpful so I hope you don't mind me asking.'

'It's Captain Jordan, isn't it? I remember you visiting your mother here once.'

'You have a good memory. Gassed, were you?'

A tight little nod was his only answer, then the man said, 'You could buy a second-hand book from the shop two doors away.'

'I wonder if you could do that for me?'

There was a pause, then the clerk nodded.

'Thank you. Don't say who it's for, there's a good chap. And please don't mention to anyone that I'm staying here.' He mentioned the types of novel he usually read, with the proviso that anything was better than nothing.

The clerk hesitated, frowning. 'Are you on leave

from the Army, sir? I was wondering why you weren't in uniform this time.'

'I've been assigned to somewhere else for the time being, a security matter. Hence the secrecy. Helping me means you can still serve your country.'

The young man straightened up. 'Then I'm your man, sir.'

Later on, Jordan made sure to tip him well for his help.

The young man accepted the coin. 'Sorry to take your money, but I have a wife and child at home. Every single farthing helps these days.'

'I understand. And a book will help keep me sane, so I'm happy to reward you. What time will the desk be manned in the morning? I need to leave early.'

'I'll be here by six o'clock, sir. And if you'd prefer to leave by the rear entrance, I can show you the way without anyone being the wiser.'

'Good chap. That's an excellent idea.'

When he'd left again, Jordan looked at the book, a dog-eared copy of *The Thirty-Nine Steps* by John Buchan. He put it beside the bed, was about to don his new pyjamas, then packed them away again. He'd sleep in his clothes tonight 'in case'. With his revolver to hand.

There was electric lighting in the room but the bulb was rather dim, so reading wasn't easy and his eyes soon grew tired. Anyway, he couldn't concentrate on the story, though it was well written, so he put it aside and switched off the light.

It was hard to get to sleep, even harder to stay asleep. He kept jerking awake every time he heard someone moving about nearby.

The night seemed longer and darker than usual.

* * *

At last it was time to get up and dress. It was still dark outside and few people were stirring, which suited his needs perfectly.

Once he'd paid, Jordan asked about leaving the back way. The obliging young man suggested he put on an overall then carried his shabby bag and showed him the way out. Jordan took note of that efficiency for future reference. The fellow might be a potential clerk in the bureau, if things were ever put to rights there.

It was still too early for other guests to be around and the maid they passed in the corridor was yawning and didn't even give him a second glance, probably assuming he'd been there to repair something.

'Thank you. I don't even know your name.'

'Albert Dodham, sir. If you need me again, I'm always here. Good luck.'

Jordan took off the overall and slipped his helper a further half-crown for his trouble, which brought a brief smile to the thin face.

Then he set off through the still dark streets, heading for a friend's house. The friend was over in France but would forgive him for borrowing without permission the car kept there once he explained why, he was sure.

The house was dark, no sign of life in it or the neighbouring properties, thank goodness.

He picked the lock of the back door and left a cryptic note that only his friend would understand nailed to the wall in what had once been the coach house and now lodged a Model T Ford. It started first time, thank goodness, probably because his friend paid a man to come round and run it round the streets for half an hour or so every month.

He hoped he'd bring the car back intact. If not, he'd have to get funding from the bureau to replace it, always supposing the bureau was out of Butterly's hands then. If not, Jordan might not be around to care about any car.

He only stopped once, to buy some motor spirit and visit a village bakery for a couple of rolls, which the shopkeeper there obligingly buttered for him.

And all the time he kept wondering where Cotterell was and what that enigmatic man was planning. This whole thing would have been much easier if he occasionally took others into his confidence about his plans.

The main thing Jordan feared at the moment was falling into the clutches of Major Butterly and the thugs he seemed to have hired. He wasn't sure he was heading to the right place for finding Cotterell, but had overheard enough over the years to have one or two ideas about where to start his search.

He was rather good at eavesdropping, if he said so himself. Nearly everyone who worked at the bureau had unusual skills of some sort.

That same morning Mathers and Nora rose early, since Lady Berrens had changed her plans and had decided they should go to her house in the morning darkness, instead of hanging around all day. Or, as he guessed, Mr Cotterell had revised his plans at the last minute, as he often did.

They made do with a quick cup of tea and a jam sandwich for breakfast, eating in silence.

Before they went out to the car, he peered out of a rear bedroom window into the darkness. He could see no sign of movement in the back alley but that didn't guarantee they'd be safe going out, so he'd taken the precaution of employing a lad who occasionally helped out around the house and was willing to do anything to earn money.

This time Jim had been instructed to keep watch on the car and to stay awake all night, so that he'd hear any movement outside in the laneway. If anyone tried to break into the former coach house, he was to fire a gun in the air, a prospect that made him dizzy with delight.

Jim jumped up to help as Mathers and Nora went out with their luggage.

'Everything all right, lad? You didn't hear anything?'

'Not sure, sir. I'd have heard if there'd been anyone creeping about on Mr Cotterell's property, or trying to break in here. I did wonder if I heard footsteps outside further along the laneway a time or two, though. Slow, as if someone was stretching his legs but trying to keep quiet.'

'You're sure about that?'

'I got good hearing, Mr Mathers. My mam reckons I could hear a mouse breathe under the floorboards.'

'Then we'll assume that someone is out there waiting to follow us. If so, you know what to do after we leave.'

'Yessir.' His teeth showed white in the moonlight as he grinned. 'I shall enjoy that.'

'Make sure you stay safe and never mind the enjoyment. These men are dangerous.'

'They won't catch me, Mr Mathers. If I could stay out of my stepfather's reach when I was younger, I can stay out of anyone's now I'm older.'

'You're a good lad. When you're old enough to leave school, I'll make sure you get a job. Don't lose that key, now.'

'Nossir. An' thank you, sir.'

Well, he would help Jim – if he was still around, Mathers corrected mentally.

He helped Nora into the back of the car and suggested she crouch down out of sight.

Working for Mr Cotterell and serving your country were not without danger, he thought as Jim crank-started the motor.

The lad darted back to the garage and watched the car reverse out into the laneway, keeping an eye out for attackers. He stayed hidden behind the dustbins while Mr Mathers got out and shut the garage doors, locked them and got back into the car.

No one watching would realise there was a lad left behind, but Jim was ready to give anyone who tried to follow Mr Mathers a right old shock.

He patted the key in his pocket. It would let him into the house again if he needed a refuge from some lads he was on bad terms with. That had happened a couple of times recently because he wouldn't pay them twopence a week safety money.

The car stayed in the lane a little longer, its engine running, giving Jim time to get ready for his part in this. He grinned as he removed the lids of the dustbins standing at the rear entrance and crouched down again behind them. He was going to enjoy this.

When Mr Mathers drove off, Jim heard another car start up and watched as it rolled slowly out from the bit of spare ground further along the lane. It hadn't lit its headlights even though it was still dark. There was no reason for a strange car to be here at this early hour, anyway, because only residents were supposed to use the laneway. What's more, that particular house had been empty since the beginning of the war, Mr Mathers had said when telling him what to watch out for.

'Oh, no you don't! I'm not having Mr Mathers hurt,' Jim muttered and as the car moved forward, he sent two lidless dustbins rolling out into its path, spilling rubbish and broken bricks everywhere. He followed that by hurling two heavy spanners Mr Mathers had given him when they made this plan towards the car's windscreen.

After that he ran for his life, delighted to have smashed the windscreen, showering the occupants with broken glass. He'd always been a good bowler when they played cricket in the street!

He risked a peep behind him. The men in the car were too busy dealing with shards of glass and a punctured tyre to follow him but they'd not have caught him even if they'd tried.

He fingered the two half-crowns in his pocket. His mother would have enough money to feed them all for several days, thanks to Mr Mathers.

Good start to the day, this had been.

Pity the war had ended. If he'd gone as a soldier, Jim could have sent his wages home to his mam. But he was small and scrawny for his age and no one would ever have believed him if he'd pretended to be older and tried to enlist.

Perhaps one day he might join the Army anyway. You got fed well if you were a soldier and they taught you trades. It was the only way he'd ever have a chance of getting a decent job. Unless Mr Mathers had meant what he said. But he hadn't said what sort of job.

* * *

There was hardly any traffic on the dark streets at this early hour, just a few gaslights burning dimly here and there. The lamplighters hadn't even started extinguishing them yet.

Mathers stopped the car once to make sure no one was following them, then smiled as he set off again. 'That lad is a treasure, Nora, an absolute treasure, sharp as a tack. I'll get Mr Cotterell to take an interest in him when everything settles down again. He always tells us to keep an eye out for likely people for the bureau.'

'*If* everything settles down,' Nora said. 'I never expected this sort of thing to happen *after* peace had been declared.'

She was always grumpy in the early mornings, though cheerful enough once she got going. He liked to tease her about that.

They went round to the back of Lady Berrens' elegant terraced house, as ordered.

Mr Cotterell came out of the house carrying a carpet bag.

'Hop out, lass. Don't forget your bag.'

Mr Cotterell gestured to the back gate. 'Get inside quickly, Nora. You're expected and you'll be safe here.'

He watched her inside, then tossed the carpet bag into the rear seat and took the seat next to the driver. 'No trouble?'

'They were waiting and tried to follow us. I had young Jim ready to help deflect their attention, sir.' He explained what he'd arranged.

Mr Cotterell chuckled. 'Your protégé sounds to be a good lad. You must introduce him to me once this is over.'

'I thought you were bringing someone else with you today?'

'I wasn't sure of him, not sure enough to risk my life, anyway. I've given him another job. You and I will manage.

We've been in some sticky situations together over the years and got out of them again. Head for Swindon.'

A little later, Mathers asked, 'Do you know where Miss Georgie is, sir?'

'I gather from one of my staff at Westcott that Georgie found out who her real mother was. I'd been looking for our letters for years, because my wife stole them and hid them. I asked my staff to keep an eye open for them, just as I'd asked you. They found a couple that must have fallen out of a bookcase.'

He sighed and stared into the distance for a few seconds, then resumed his explanation. 'I wouldn't put it past Georgie to try to make contact with the Baxters. I doubt any of her enemies would look for her in Swindon, and she might have realised that, so we'll go to them first. If she's not there, she'll be with her friend Bella in Honeyfield, but that's a more obvious place and I shall be disappointed in her if that's where she went.'

'Is this Bella's connection to our Miss Cotterell known, then?'

'Yes. And Bella has visited us a couple of times. If the main traitor is who I think it is, he would have made it his business to find out about all my daughter's friends when he decided to use her to get to me.'

'I see.'

'It won't take us long to call on the Baxters first. It's more or less on our way. If she's not there, Georgie can only be in Honeyfield, in which case I'll need to get her away from there as quickly as possible.'

He was silent for a few moments, then said in a low, calm voice, 'If anything happens to me and you survive, your first priority will be to get Georgie to safety. Take her to Lady Berrens.'

Mathers didn't say anything, but he was astounded that his master thought this situation so perilous.

As if he'd read his mind, Mr Cotterell said, 'If they can't control what I do, these men may get desperate. I have no doubt that if all else fails, they'll shoot to kill if they can get me in their sights. I hope to settle Georgie's safety before they can do anything to either of us. Or to you. I apologise for putting your life in danger today, Mathers.'

'I'm here willingly, sir, as I'm sure you appreciate.'

They'd been together a long time and had a strange relationship, not quite friends because of their difference in status, but far more than merely employer and servant. They were both aware of where to draw the line.

They didn't chat after that but drove on as dawn began to lighten the sky behind them, though darkness still mantled the countryside ahead.

# *Chapter Twenty-Four*

Patrick didn't say much as they walked back to Pear Tree Lane, but Gregory could see that he was watchful about their surroundings. As was Gregory. It was almost a disappointment when they didn't encounter anything suspicious.

At the cottage, Patrick held out a silver coin and thanked his companion.

Gregory would have preferred to refuse it, but money was short so he accepted the florin and mumbled a thank you. He wasn't in a position to turn down two shillings for such an easy job.

His companion held out one arm to stop him going away.

'Look, I may not be around for a while. Could you keep an eye on this house for me? I'll pay you to come round and—'

'Yes, I'll keep an eye on it, and on Mrs Bella next door too, if Mr T is away. I ent getting a lot of work at the moment so it's not as if I've anything else to do. Nice lady, Mrs T, and so is her husband. Nor you don't need to pay me for keeping an eye on things at your place. I'd do it anyway.'

'You're a good chap.'

'Mmm. Will you be coming back here again?'

'I hope so. I like the feel of Honeyfield – what I've seen of it so far, anyway.'

'You'd fit in well here, sir. Eh, it's a grand place in peacetime. I'd swear even the birds sing more sweetly here than in other places I've been.'

Suddenly embarrassed by his own fanciful words, he muttered farewell, calling his dog to heel. But before they went into the house, he waited by the gate to see that Patrick was safely inside Orchard View. Miss Cotterell threw herself into his arms even before they'd closed the door. A smile at the sight of that lingered on Gregory's face. He could smell weddings in the air.

He ambled down the little street, stopping at the end to look back. Nice little street, this. Shame to think of anyone bringing violence here, wanting to hurt its occupants. Damned shame.

They didn't need or deserve trouble in Honeyfield. Men from the village had given their lives for their country and now that peace had been declared, those who'd survived just wanted to get on with living.

He wished he could have gone to war and done his bit, but his damned eyes always let him down for close work. As a lad he'd been told to wear spectacles, but he'd refused to walk round looking like an owl with the stupid contraption falling off his nose whenever he threw a ball or wrestled with another lad.

His poor eyesight wouldn't stop him helping to build a war memorial to the fallen in his spare time, though. That at least he could do.

He walked on slowly, still thinking about this situation. It came to him suddenly as he reached his gate that the best thing to do would be to catch the villains and give them a sound drubbing, and be done with the problem once and for all. Peace in Britain should mean peace in Honeyfield as well. And who better to make sure of that than those who lived here and knew every inch of the village and the nearby countryside, eh? You didn't have to be able to read spidery little squiggles in a book to do that.

He handed over the money to his wife, asking if she could spare enough for him to buy half a pint of beer. When she handed back sixpence, he couldn't resist kissing her soundly on the lips.

She stared at him in surprise. 'Kissing in the daytime! Aren't you afraid your friends will see you acting soft? What brought that on, anyway?'

He shrugged. 'Just felt like it.' Then he set off for a drink with his friends.

Her voice echoed after him as he opened the front door to leave.

'I know what you're after tonight, Gregory Clarke.'

She didn't sound annoyed about it, though. He could always tell. He chuckled as he closed the door behind him. He'd look forward to pleasuring her later. She was a good lass in bed. She'd been a good mother, too, till their children left home, and they'd both been relieved that their son had come through the war safely.

Gregory frowned. That was another reason for sorting out these villains. He didn't want them hurting people like his son during the years to come.

And what was he doing daydreaming like that? He should be working something out to help end this mess. He'd tell his friends at the pub what was going on and they'd talk about what exactly they could do to put paid to such human vermin.

They'd feel the same as him about protecting their families, he was sure. His friends might be too old to fight for their country, or they might not see well enough to aim a damned gun, but they could deal with troublemakers if they banded together. You didn't need to see all the wrinkles on his face from two yards away to thump a chap who deserved it.

He'd have to spin out his one drink to last all evening. Eh, he missed going to the pub now money was tight. There had been lean pickings round here lately and if that damned Spanish flu came here, it'd find a lot of people who weren't in the best of health to fight it off. Thank goodness you could still catch the odd rabbit or two. You needed meat to keep your muscles strong.

Now, stop daydreaming, Gregory, he told himself again. You and the lads have some villains to catch, then a war memorial to build.

Opening the door of the pub, he walked briskly into its light and warmth.

When Patrick got to the front door, it opened before he could knock and as he stepped over the threshold Georgie flung herself into his arms.

'You took so long! I was worried about you.'

He edged her further inside while still keeping hold of her soft body – just for a minute! – then carefully slid the door bolts into place with one hand.

'Everything all right here?'

'Yes. We've been waiting for you to get back and for it to get dark.'

She hadn't pulled away, so he gave into temptation and kissed her. Ah, she felt so good and—

Rosie called out from the kitchen, 'Tea's ready!'

He stepped reluctantly away from Georgie but his feelings escaped him. 'What a time to try to court a lass!'

'Any time is good for you to court me. After this is over, you won't let anything, even my father, stop you, will you, Patrick?'

'You've worried about him doing that a couple of times. Is he a big chap?'

'No. Tall and thin, and he's nearly sixty now, but he's used to taking command and people always seem to end up doing as he tells them, one way or the other.'

'Well, we'll face that hurdle when we come to it. To hell with them all. You and I are definitely courting.'

She beamed at him and he knew that one thing at least was going well in his world. He put his arm round her shoulders and they walked together towards the kitchen.

Just being beside her made him feel good. She was so special, such a lovely honest woman. He wouldn't be answerable if anyone hurt her.

They were all quiet as they ate their tea, the only sounds being the clink of spoons on the big plates and a soft

'Mmmm, please,' from Martin when he finished his first helping of stew and was offered another by Rosie.

Although all three men tucked into a second helping, neither of the women did.

Patrick pushed his empty plate away with a happy sigh. 'You're a good cook, Rosie. Thank you.'

'I only know how to do a few things, nothing fancy, but I do enjoy cooking, I must admit.'

'When this is over, I'll give you a cook book,' Georgie offered. 'Someone gave it to me once, but I'm not interested in cooking, let alone fiddling around with fancy things. I wasn't interested in the man who gave it to me, either. I haven't even touched it for years, because it reminds me of him, but it's got a lot of recipes in it and you'll have no bad memories tied to it.'

Dennis looked at her in surprise. 'What do you like doing then, if you don't mind me asking, Georgie? I thought all women liked keeping their houses nice and looking after their families.'

Her voice came out sharper than she'd meant it to. 'Aren't they the men's houses too?'

He stared at her blankly, so she didn't pursue the point. A lot of men had the same reaction, couldn't see women anywhere except in the home. Even when she was doing war work, and doing it well, some men had treated her as if she was a different and rather inferior species. And most women who'd taken over men's jobs had still been paid less than them for doing the same work, hadn't they? That seemed so unfair.

She realised Patrick was repeating the question his friend had asked.

'What do you like doing, Georgie?'

She turned to him as she answered, hoping he wouldn't mock her. 'I like to be out of doors much better than fiddling around inside a house: driving cars, walking through the countryside, riding horses, not to hunt – I think chasing foxes is a silly waste of time – just to enjoy the countryside. My father's wife stopped me doing that sort of thing when she decided I was old enough to be married off. She kept me sitting round indoors fiddling with embroidery or practising the piano.'

She chuckled as she added, 'Though you'd have to pay people to listen to a concert if I was involved, so I was never invited to perform, and my embroidery always got into a tangle of threads and crooked stitches. As for her idea of a good husband, it didn't match mine at all.'

'Was life that tedious?'

She smiled as a happier memory suddenly surfaced. 'Mostly. But there were good moments. Time I spent with my twin, particularly. And even *she* couldn't keep me penned up all the time, so I escaped sometimes and went for long walks. Once, the housekeeper had her young nephew to stay and he brought his Meccano set with him. He was more interested in reading books about other countries in the Empire than in building things. He wanted to emigrate to Australia or Canada one day, you see. So I lent him some of our books and he let me play with his toy while he was there. My father's wife would have thrown a fit if she'd found out.'

She saw them staring at her. 'Sorry. You can't be interested in that.'

'Yes, I am,' Patrick said quietly.

Martin leant forward, joining in. 'I've seen them

Meccano sets in shop windows, but never touched one. Well, they cost a lot – toys for rich children, they are. Might be interesting to fiddle around with, though. I like building things too, especially walls. Stone walls.'

She didn't think he even realised that his big, rough hands had shaped placing a stone on an imaginary wall in the air to illustrate his point. Some men were like that. Not good with words, but good with their hands.

She tried to lighten the mood. 'When this war is over, I'll buy one of the biggest Meccano sets there is and we'll all have a little holiday at Westcott House. Those who want to can play with the Meccano, or just laze around and eat some good, hearty meals without having to rush off anywhere or struggle to stay safe.'

Rosie stood up. 'That'd be lovely – a holiday, I mean. I don't want to build things, but I'd love to lie around all day like a lady and read a book from start to finish without being interrupted. But what I'm going to do now is wash the dishes and scour out that saucepan. Just eat the last couple of spoonfuls for me, Martin, there's a good lad. It'd be a shame to waste it.'

He scraped every scrap off the pan while he was at it, and Georgie exchanged amused glances with Rosie. That man certainly liked his food.

Rosie took the empty pan off him. 'Don't scrape a hole in the bottom.'

Georgie had noticed her put a kettle over the kitchen range before they began eating and now she poured the hot water into a bowl. Rosie was so well organised with details. 'I'll dry the dishes for you. And the men can sweep up the crumbs and tidy the room.'

They looked a little surprised at being asked to do housework, but did as she'd told them when Patrick set an example.

Rosie winked at her. 'Thanks. I know there won't be anyone left to see the clean dishes once we leave, or the tidy room, but I can't bear to leave the place dirty.'

By the time they'd finished clearing up and set their bags and bundles ready near the back door, dusk had veiled the garden outside in ever-darkening shadows.

'Time to leave,' Patrick said. 'The moon isn't due to rise yet, thank goodness, so if we're careful, no one will see us go. I'll light a candle and leave it upstairs and we'll take another candle stub into the front room before we open the back door, so that the house still looks occupied. Two minutes, everyone.'

Just before the first three set off, he said, 'If you hear or see anyone, don't make a shushing noise. That sound carries a long way on a still night. Just grab hold of the nearest person and squeeze hard, then stand absolutely still.'

Dennis, Rosie and Martin left first, with Patrick standing just outside the kitchen door, flattened against the wall in the dark shadow cast by the eaves, in case anyone attacked and help was needed.

It was good to have someone like Patrick guarding your back, Dennis thought as he led the other two in single file towards the back of the garden, with Rosie walking between the men. He and Patrick had checked out the best route earlier.

Every one of his senses was on high alert, but he hoped

they would make it without problems. He didn't want Rosie getting hurt.

By the time they got to the mainly leafless bushes along the back wall, his eyes had grown more accustomed to the dimness. He turned to the right. It was only a few steps to the ruined fence that had once separated the two properties.

When he looked over his shoulder, he saw Patrick go back into the house, presumably to fetch Georgie.

Dennis was about to send his two companions across the Tesworths' back garden to their summer house when he saw a man come round the side of the house they'd just left. Thank goodness the others were still next to him. He grabbed their shoulders and gave them a quick squeeze. They stood still immediately.

Then he could only wait, straining his eyes to see what happened. He hoped Patrick didn't come out again or there'd be trouble.

From the angle of his head, the intruder was looking up at the lighted window of the bedroom with the candle in it. After a few moments, he turned and went back the way he'd come. Wanted them to be asleep before they struck, Dennis guessed.

He waited a few moments but the man didn't return, so he tapped Martin and Rosie on the shoulders and gave them a little push.

The two of them moved through a gap in the ruined fence and across the back of the grounds next door, leaving him to wait and listen. Everything was quiet, thank goodness. He prayed it'd stay that way and let the other two get away before the intruder returned. He didn't want anything to happen to Rosie, let alone Patrick or Georgi

A light was showing in a window on the far side of Mr T's house, which was helping Martin and Rosie pick their way across the rear garden. The wooden summer house was painted white, but it was only a shadowy grey mass in this dimness.

Dennis could see his two friends a little more clearly now, dark silhouettes against the pale summer house. Then they vanished through the black oblong of its doorway and all was still again.

From where he stood, he couldn't tell whether they were safe inside it. Their enemies could have set a trap. No, surely not? He had to assume that his friends were safe – there had been no sound since they went inside – but he'd still take great care how he entered the place when his turn came.

He waited for Patrick and Georgie to come out and join him, his eyes scanning and re-scanning his surroundings.

What was taking them so long? What if the intruder came back again and brought others with him?

'Time to get ready,' Patrick told Georgie when he'd come inside after seeing the others reach the back fence.

He opened the door a fraction, then closed it again with great care and whispered, 'I heard something moving just outside here. It's not Dennis, I'm sure. Stay where you are and don't make a sound.' He went to peep out of a corner of the kitchen window. He was, he hoped, hidden behind a couple of large bottles on the windowsill.

There! He hadn't been wrong. A man came into view, moving very slowly indeed, staring up at the lit bedroom.

… several long seconds, he stood motionless, then turned …nd went back the way he'd come.

Their enemies must be planning to do something tonight.

Once the stranger had vanished round the front of the house, Patrick waited a minute or so, then took a chance and opened the door again. He pulled Georgie out and locked it, then led her to the back fence, all the time listening and watching carefully. To his relief she too knew how to move quietly.

They then found Dennis waiting as planned. He pressed one finger against his lips, leant closer and mouthed the words, 'Intruder, wait.'

Patrick nodded and they stayed where they were for a little longer to check that the man hadn't heard them leave the house.

After a while Dennis jerked his head in the direction of the summer house and Patrick nodded, waving one hand to indicate that the other two should go first. He stayed where he was, watching them and the house he'd just left alternately.

It seemed a very long time until his friends vanished into the summer house. Only then did he follow them, pausing on the way across the garden to listen very hard before continuing.

You couldn't be too careful when lives were at stake. Especially Georgie's life.

Inside the summer house it was dark and Patrick was glad when Mr Tesworth flashed a torch round briefly as if to show them their surroundings. When he moved to lock the door they'd come in by, Patrick grabbed his hand to stop him. 'Does that key work quietly? They may still be out there in our garden.'

'Martin told me about them. They didn't waste much time, did they? Luckily I oiled the lock earlier.'

Mr T turned the key and though it made a clicking sound, it was very faint and it seemed unlikely that it could be heard above the usual night noises.

'We should leave straight away.'

'What about your wife?'

'I have a fellow I trust staying with Bella and neighbours who'll come running if she calls for help. I'll come home to her once I'm sure you're all safe. My friend came in the back way before it got dark and said he saw no one loitering in the street.'

'Is he armed?'

'They both are. How many did you see?'

'Only one man, but I'm sure he didn't come alone. He seemed too confident for that. I think the lighted candle upstairs put him off going inside, but I'd guess they're planning something for later tonight, after we're supposed to be asleep.'

'Then we'd better get you away from here as quickly as possible, eh?' Tez moved to the rear wall and shone his torch quickly to show them the hidden door before unlocking it and reaching out to move some strands of ivy aside.

A man was standing outside. 'This is Cole,' Tez whispered and beckoned to them.

They left the summer house one by one, Patrick last of all, then he heard the sound of a key being turned in the lock. Having two locked doors between them and the attackers made him feel a little easier, because the perimeter all of the orchard was higher than his head, so a person would have to climb up on something even to see over it.

Cole led the way to the right, walking close to the wall and turning his head occasionally to make sure they were still following him.

They must have gone about a quarter of a mile before he held up one hand and stopped next to another big wooden door in the wall, putting a finger on his lips to indicate they should continue to be quiet. He produced a key and when they were all inside the garden on the other side, he locked the gate again.

Another man came across to join them, accompanied by a dog. It was tall but thinner than Gregory's Rex. It came to sniff them one by one and its master said 'Friend!' each time, as Gregory had done with Rex. Well-trained animals, both of them.

Not until that was done did Cole beckon again and lead the way towards the big house at the other end of the large garden.

They entered the house by a back door into what seemed to be the servants' quarters. These were bigger than the whole house they'd just left. Patrick had seen places like this, or sometimes only the ruins of them, in France.

He felt a great deal better about Georgie's safety now they were indoors again.

He wondered when their pursuers would try to break into the house they'd left. He'd have loved to see their faces when they found no one there.

'This is Doohey,' Cole told them once they were all indoors. 'He and his dog Jago come to help out here sometimes when there's trouble. He'll be staying around tonight to help keep you safe.'

A woman came to join them.

'And this is my wife Sal, who works here at Honeyfield House.'

'We've got rooms ready, but it's a bit early to go to bed, so I've got the kettle simmering. Would you like a cup of cocoa and a piece of cake?'

The men all made approving noises.

Rosie chuckled. 'They're stomachs on wheels, this lot are, Sal. They never turn down food. I don't know how they fit everything in. I wouldn't mind a cup of cocoa, though.'

'Where are the other women?' Cole asked his wife.

'Sitting in the library, chatting. I'll take them a jug of cocoa in but I won't introduce you to them until the morning.' She went across to the huge kitchen range and moved a large copper kettle on to the hotter part. 'Soon be ready.'

'The chaps in the village are planning to give them sods a good trouncing,' Cole announced gleefully. 'And I'd be happy to help if I wasn't needed here.'

It was rather an anticlimax to have got here without trouble, Patrick thought. Surely they couldn't have got away as easily as this?

He had a feeling that their troubles hadn't ended yet, because their pursuers had never been far behind them. It was the sort of feeling he'd had at times during the war. He always paid heed to it, always. It had saved his life once or twice.

These people must know a lot about Georgie. How?

Was it that toffee-nosed captain who'd blabbed? Or was it someone else?

And was her father safe? Did he know the villains were after his daughter? Or was he out of the picture permanently?

# *Chapter Twenty-Five*

Cotterell and Mathers timed their arrival in Swindon for the early morning. They stopped to buy breakfast from a small workmen's café on a side street and waited impatiently for the bacon and eggs to arrive.

'Ah, good. Here it is. I never think well on an empty stomach.' Cotterell picked up his knife and fork.

'I never say no to a meal. I went hungry too often as a child.'

After a few mouthfuls, Cotterell said, 'We'll go to Simpton Street once we've finished. I've been there before, so I'll tell you the way.'

'Won't they be at work by then?'

'The men will but the women will probably be at home. It's too early for them to have gone shopping yet. Women are usually easier to deal with.'

They knocked on the door of Number 17 and a young woman opened it.

'I was a friend of Mary Jane Baxter, who once lived here. My name is Cotterell. Ah, I see you recognise it. I was wondering if my daughter came here recently to look for her mother's family?'

'I'm too busy to talk.' The woman tried to close the door on them.

Cotterell held it open with one foot. 'I'm not going to hurt you, madam, but my daughter is in danger and I need to reach her as quickly as possible. I know she wanted to find out about her mother so if you've seen her or know anything, I beg you to tell me.'

A sturdy young man came along the hall from the rear of the house. He must have been listening because he said quietly, 'Better let them come in, Helen, love.'

She stepped back and opened a door halfway along the hall, gesturing to them to follow her inside.

'Thank you. I'm Gerald Cotterell and this is Mathers, who helps me. And you are?'

'Wally Grant. My mother was Mary Jane's older sister. And this is my wife, Helen.'

'I'm pleased to meet you both.'

The front room was full of stiff furniture and didn't look as if it was ever used, but Cotterell went over to the sofa when Wally indicated he should sit there. He waited for Mrs Grant to sit down before following suit.

'I don't know what you think we can do,' his host said.

He studied the young man, then nodded as if he liked what he saw. 'What I tell you mustn't go any further. This is a matter of national security and could affect the coming peace talks.'

He sat waiting while his host looked at him in shock and

studied him all over again, as if expecting to see something different in his face.

'My mother didn't want to have anything to do with you, Mr Cotterell, but I heard from another family member that you truly loved my aunt.'

'Yes. I was extremely upset when Mary Jane died. I'd have married her if I hadn't been married already. I persuaded my wife to bring up the twins who cost your aunt her life, and pretend they were hers. I wanted to avoid the stigma of bastardy for them. You know what people can be like about that.'

Wally nodded.

'But I've many times wished I hadn't done it. I knew already that my wife wasn't a good mother, though I didn't realise how unkind she'd be to Georgie until it was too late. But even then I had to think of my country's needs as well as my own.'

'Your son was killed in the war, I believe.'

Cotterell inclined his head, pressing his lips tightly together and looking down for a few moments.

The young man took a deep breath and said, 'As it happens, I don't approve of pretending my aunt Mary Jane didn't exist and I wish I'd been here to meet my cousin when she turned up.'

'Georgie did come here, then?'

It was the young woman who answered. 'Yes. On Wednesday. And she seemed a decent sort. But Wally's mother was ill and I didn't want to upset her.'

'I hope your mother has recovered now,' Cotterell said politely.

'She died. Spanish influenza.' Wally turned to his wife. 'Get that piece of paper, love.'

She went out and brought back a slightly crumpled page torn from a writing pad. 'This is where your daughter said to send word if Wally wanted to contact her.'

'I was going to do that, but my mother died that same evening and we had to bury her quite quickly. They're rushing the funerals through with no thought to how the families feel.'

'I'm sorry for your loss.'

'Yes. I am too. She was a good mother. I haven't even gone back to work yet because my father's been ill as well. It looks as if he'll recover, though. I would have gone back to work if the war had still been on, but as peace has been declared, things are not as urgent and I was able to take a few days' leave.'

'Your daughter seemed upset by what I told her about the family,' the young woman volunteered.

'Yes. She would be. Georgie wanted very much to meet her mother's side of the family, to have some relatives. I have very few on my side, you see.'

'We'll do something about that now,' Wally said. 'And we can do it openly, since my mother isn't here to protest. I loved her dearly but she could hold a grudge better than anyone I've ever met.' He fell silent and made a furtive swipe at a tear.

Cotterell studied the piece of paper. 'Honeyfield. I'd hoped you would have given her shelter here. Honeyfield won't be safe enough. I pray we get to her in time, because these traitors won't hesitate to kill her if their mission fails.'

'What?' Wally gaped at him. 'Someone wants to *kill* her?'

'I'm not exaggerating.'

'Then I'm coming with you.'

'Why?'

'To make up for us turning her away.'

For a few slow moments Cotterell frowned at him, then shrugged. 'As long as you'll obey my orders.'

Wally nodded at once.

His wife looked at him anxiously but didn't try to persuade him not to go.

'We'll use Westcott as our base – it's my country house – and drive across to Honeyfield after dark.' Cotterell turned to Mrs Grant. 'Is there anyone round here with a telephone in case we need to contact you?'

She shook her head. 'No. Only posh people have telephones. I trust my Wally. He's got a good head on his shoulders and he doesn't take risks.'

'I know how to defend myself, too,' Wally added. 'I don't seek out fights, but sometimes you can't avoid them.'

'Good to know.'

They were on their way within minutes.

This time Cotterell got behind the wheel. 'I'll drive.'

'Won't your enemies be watching out for you at Westcott, sir?' Mathers asked. 'If you were in the back, you could slide down out of sight.'

'We won't be going to the house itself, or even through the village, but to my head gardener's cottage, via a slightly different approach to the rear of my property. The cottage stands on its own and I can trust Spalding absolutely.'

'And this car? Someone's bound to notice it,' Mathers persisted.

'There's a big shed. I keep some guns and other items there in case there's trouble when I'm away on one of my

.ttle jobs. I had to leave London in a bit of a hurry this time, didn't have time to arm myself properly, so I left my London driver behind and told him to take the bureau car back, then I came straight here.'

Mathers waited for him to go on and when he didn't, prompted, 'Don't you think you should tell us who the traitor at the bureau is now, sir?'

'Well, the problem is I'm not sure whether we have one traitor or two. I'm certain about Butterly now, and fairly certain Jordan is all right. But I'm not risking working with him till I'm completely certain. So we'll hide at Spalding's house till it's dark and then make our way to Honeyfield.'

'But what about Miss Georgie in the meantime?'

'We have to trust whoever is with her to keep her safe. And *she* is no fool, believe me. But if these people catch me, both our lives will be in even greater danger because I won't betray my country, whatever they threaten. I'll use some of my spare clothes from here tonight and you can play the master and sit in the back of the car, Mathers.'

'Yes, sir.'

'You mean we have to hang around all day?' Wally burst out. 'Couldn't *I* do something? No one knows me.'

'I'm afraid not. But I do appreciate you coming because we don't know how many of them we'll be facing. You not only look like a very strong young fellow but I'm certain you're not a traitor.'

'Of course I'm not.'

'I'm sure you'll be patient.'

A slight smile twisted the young man's mouth. 'Do I have any choice?'

'No. Sometimes waiting is all one can do.'

Mathers didn't press for any further information. There was no pushing Mr Cotterell into doing something until he felt the time was ripe.

He and Gerald Cotterell were getting a bit long in the tooth for fighting, actually, so he was glad of some help. He liked the look of this young fellow. A strong chap, if Mathers was any judge from his sturdy build, and didn't seem stupid.

When they got to the head gardener's house, they hid the car, then Mr Cotterell said he could do with a nap. Mathers was left to entertain Wally.

The young man frowned as he watched the older man go upstairs. 'Does he often do that? Take naps, I mean.'

'He's been on the run for days and I doubt he's slept well the whole time. Now that I'm with him, he knows I'll keep careful watch while he catches up on his sleep.'

'I don't think anyone could force Mr Cotterell to do something he thought was wrong. I had a teacher like him once. He got exactly that look on his face when he thought something was important. If he gave you an order at times like that, you didn't argue, just did what he wanted quick smart.'

'Exactly.'

'Pity, though. I'd have liked to hear more about my cousin.'

'I've only known Miss Georgie for the past couple of years myself, but that's enough to respect her. She's a good lass.'

After a pause and another searching stare at his young companion, he said, 'I've been with her father for decades and know the family background. I can tell you something about her, and I don't think he'll mind, you being her cousin and wanting to meet her. She'd do anything to get to know her mother's family. She was close to her twin but after he was killed, she was very lonely and sad.'

'I'm not sure it'll bring her closer to my mother's generation, but us younger folk think they were unkind to cut my aunt off so completely. They refused to tell us anything about Mary Jane, but we overheard things and put the details together piece by piece. Such a pity the boy was killed.'

'Yes, very sad. Mr Philip was a fine young man.' Mathers hesitated, then decided in for a penny, in for a pound. 'But history has repeated itself in a way. The young lady he was going to marry was carrying his child. She married Mr Philip's best friend instead to protect the unborn child. That man has been invalided out of the Army and she now has a fine little son, also called Philip. He's nearly two, and big for his age.'

Wally smiled. 'I've got a young son, too. Three, my Robbie is. And we have another child on the way.'

'Congratulations.' Mathers tactfully asked a few questions about Wally's family, then finished giving a bare outline of the difficult time Georgie had had in recent years.

'I'm trusting you not to spread this round the rest of the family without her permission,' he warned in the end.

Wally smiled at him, a smile so like Miss Georgie's that Mathers was startled for a moment.

'No. I won't do that, I promise you.'

After which, Mathers allowed himself to doze in an armchair, Wally found a newspaper to read, and everyone waited for darkness to fall.

* * *

Once the sun had set Gregory went out to check whether any strangers were prowling round the village. This time he took his friend Jack with him. He and his friends had divided up the village and would take it in turns to patrol each area.

They saw the two cars parked on the outskirts of the village near the main road and edged a little closer. A man was standing next to the second car, leaning down to chat to someone in the driving seat.

'How many other fellows do you think there are?' Gregory whispered.

'Could be as many as six or eight, with two cars to drive around in.'

'Mmm. Better make sure the rest of the lads are out and about, then.'

'And tell Constable Browning.'

'We've nothing to tell the police. Let's wait until something happens.'

'No, Greg. I'm not doing anything that might lead to fighting without telling Browning about it first. He's my wife's second cousin, remember, and he'd never forgive me.'

'Oh, very well. You go and tell him and *I* will pass the word to the lads about where these sods are parked. Meet you back by the church gate.'

Only a few seconds later, Gregory heard a muffled yell, then silence. He didn't go to find out what had caused it, because it'd do no good to be caught on his own when he didn't know how many he'd be fighting.

He went to knock on several doors and get everyone out and about before going to investigate what had happened to his friend.

* * *

This time Gregory took the town's best-known poacher with him. Frank was getting on in years but had eluded capture by gamekeepers his whole life long, to the admiration of his friends. He'd taught Gregory some of his tricks. Who better to have by your side when the situation was getting more serious by the minute?

It was a good thing the two of them were more skilled at moving around without being seen than Jack, because damned if there wasn't one of the sods keeping watch a short distance along the road from the cars.

Frank dug an elbow into his companion's ribs and pointed to himself.

Gregory nodded. If Frank wanted to handle this, let him.

He got into a position where he could keep an eye open for anyone else approaching and watched his old mentor in admiration. Frank hugged the shadows and moved as silently as a ghost till he was in a position to tap the stranger on the head and catch him as he fell.

By the time Gregory joined them, the man's hands were trussed behind him and a rag had been stuffed into his mouth.

Frank whispered, 'We'll take him to the police station and let Browning look after him. Can't leave him lying around for them to set free.'

They explained to the constable that the village was under threat and thank goodness he had the sense to believe them because Mr T had warned him there might be trouble. Browning said he would call out a relief constable.

When they left him the two made their way slowly and carefully to Pear Tree Lane, but they didn't see another watcher.

'Something's not right. There ought to have bee another watcher or two round here,' Frank said suddenly. 'You hide in that garden and keep an eye on whether anyone comes into or out of Pear Tree Lane. I want to go and check something.'

It didn't occur to Gregory to argue. Not with Frank. Or to go with him. Not if Frank wanted to do this on his own.

Frank wouldn't get caught.

Gregory hid behind a water butt and kept very still. It was damp and uncomfortable, but he didn't intend to get caught either.

# Chapter Twenty [illegible]

Jordan drove the borrowed car tow[illegible] [illegible], hoping he'd not have trouble [illegible]ding the [illegible] He'd overheard Conrad mention it on the [illegible] than once and had put that [illegible]er pieces [illegible] together like a jigsaw puzzle [illegible] the past [illegible] There was no doubt in his mind that [illegible] the [illegible] likely place for Georgie to [illegible] and [illegible] place Conrad would be heading [illegible]

He'd found Honeyfield [illegible] the [illegible] kept in the cabinets of wide [illegible] drawers [illegible] easy enough to memorise [illegible] And [illegible] was shown on the map, so [illegible] a big p[illegible] roads were notorious for misleading [illegible] to ask directions.

[illegible] time he was lucky. He [illegible] any trouble and found a place [illegible]

# *Chapter Twenty-Six*

Jordan drove the borrowed car towards Honeyfield, hoping he'd not have trouble finding this big old house. He'd overheard Cotterell mention it on the phone more than once and had put that and other pieces of information together like a jigsaw puzzle over the past few weeks. There was no doubt in his mind: that house had to be the most likely place for Georgie to be hiding and was therefore the place Cotterell would be heading for.

He'd found Honeyfield on one of the many detailed maps kept in the cabinets of wide, shallow drawers at the bureau. Easy enough to memorise the location. And the house itself was shown on the map, so it must be a big place. But country roads were notorious for misleading people so he might have to ask directions.

This time he was lucky. He got to Honeyfield without any trouble and found a place to park outside the village under some trees, before heading on foot towards the old manor house. It was dark but he could see well enough to avoid making a noise. He was tired and hungry, but that could wait. He had to find Cotterell.

He was almost caught as he approached the gate and he had to roll into a muddy ditch to escape detection by two men who looked like scruffy poachers and clearly knew their way into the grounds without using the wide main gate.

He let them get ahead and followed them silently to a concealed single-person gate. He'd played tracking games during his childhood with his brothers and cousins, never realising how useful that skill would be in his present life.

On the other side of the narrow gate, he stood still to check that the way was clear, but he couldn't see any sign of the men, so moved forward quietly.

Suddenly he felt a flash of blinding pain in the back of his head.

He regained consciousness in what seemed to be a shed full of garden implements and groaned as movement made his head throb. Or tried to groan but could only make a gurgling sound in his throat. Whoever it was had stuffed some foul-tasting rag in his mouth and fastened it there, damn them. He felt as if he was choking.

A grim-faced man, who must be keeping guard over him, watched him struggle for breath and warned him, 'I can see you're having trouble breathing. Don't try to make any sound when I remove the gag, or you can be sure it'll be your last.'

Jordan kept quiet, gulping in breath. He watched the

man, who kept staring out of the window as if waiting for someone to join him.

The only thing he could do to help himself was use the slow minutes that ticked past to study his surroundings. He couldn't see any way of escaping. The person who'd tied him up knew how to do it and there was nothing sharp within reach to rub through the ropes binding him.

He was furious at himself for getting caught, absolutely furious.

His captor moved to and fro in an attempt to keep warm, beating his hands against his chest and arms. Twice he went outside for a moment or two, each time gagging his captive again. The second time he came in hastily and didn't close the door properly.

Jordan watched all this sourly. He was so cold his extremities were going numb, but he didn't want to choke to death so he kept quiet.

Suddenly the door banged open and another man burst into the shed and attacked Jordan's captor. They struggled for a few moments, sending objects crashing from shelves, but the newcomer was bigger and stronger. When he managed to kick Jordan's captor in the groin, the man tumbled to the ground, yelping and gasping for breath. Before he could pull himself together, the attacker had his hands tied behind his back.

Then the attacker turned to study Jordan, shining a torch at him. 'Who the hell are you?'

'I was just passing by and that man thumped me.'

'Don't lie. People don't "pass by" an isolated place like this. I'm not untying you till you convince me you're not a traitor to our country.'

Jordan didn't know what to say or believe, but this was the only chance he'd have to get free, so he decided to risk it and tell the truth.

Cotterell drove the car with Mathers beside him and Wally in the back. He seemed to know every twist and turn of the side roads and used some very narrow lanes in the last stage of the journey.

'Once I've driven a road, I never forget it,' he commented at one point, as if answering a question. 'We'll leave the car here and walk into Honeyfield from the north. There's a rather useful orchard there which runs behind a few properties. Wally, how good are you at moving quietly round the countryside?'

'Um. I'm not sure. I grew up in a town.'

'Hmm.'

A few moments later he braked suddenly. 'Ah. First sighting of our enemy. I might have known they'd find this spot. We'll leave our car here and go on foot from now on. We're lucky they didn't spot us coming.'

He got out with a nimbleness that belied his years. 'I'll ask you to stay with the car for the time being, Wally. Near the car would be better than inside it, though. We'll come back for you once we've checked that old ruin. It'd make the best hiding place for strangers, indeed the only one if they wish to stay undetected. Mathers, I think you should have your gun ready.'

'I've already taken that precaution, sir.'

The two older men seemed to melt away into the darkness and Wally didn't hear a sound after that.

He found a slight rise in the ground about ten yards

away from the car and lay down behind it, feeling foolish, not to mention cold. What mad impulse had made him volunteer to help look for a cousin he'd never met? He'd die of shame if he let himself be captured like a rat in a trap.

On that thought he felt around him and found a couple of stones which he could hurl if he needed to delay an attacker. He was a good bowler when he got the chance to play cricket.

He wished *he* had a gun. And a warmer overcoat. He clamped his teeth together to stop them chattering.

When he heard the faint sound of footsteps coming towards him, he thought it might be Mr Cotterell and Mathers returning, but soon realised it wasn't. He could only see one person.

Oh hell, he hoped the man didn't see him and wasn't armed.

Cotterell nudged Mathers and leant close to say in a low growl of a voice, 'They don't seem to have a guard outside, so I'll go up to the back of the cottage and see if I can eavesdrop to find out what they're doing. That part of the wall must have fallen in last winter, so I doubt the interior will be soundproof.'

He didn't wait but edged forward. He didn't know why or how, but at times like this all his senses felt sharper, and everything seemed to happen more slowly, as if fate was deliberately giving him time to think out what to do. Or maybe his thoughts had speeded up. Who knew?

He stood very still next to one wall of the cottage and soon spotted a faint light coming from inside the sounder part of the building. There were several chinks between stones where the mortar had fallen out. He listened hard, utterly motionless, then took a cautious couple of steps into what had been the outhouse.

Ah! He could see part of the inside through one of the holes. Not much to see, just two men.

'Ready?' one asked his companion.

'Of course I am. I still think we should have attacked that house in the village while we were there the first time, though. We wasted a good opportunity.'

'Well, if that's the best you can do, don't try to think. I'm in charge and I've done this often enough to know it's easier to catch folk unaware when they're sleeping. We've got orders not to hurt Cotterell's daughter, and to do this without disturbing the neighbours, remember. Apart from any other consideration, that Tesworth chap is a crack shot, I'm told.'

'So am I a crack shot. I'll take care of him if he tries to fire at us.'

'How many times do I have to tell you? We're *not* to shoot anyone except as a last resort. That's why we're trying to do this quietly.'

'By the time we get there, the birds could have flown.'

'You said there was candlelight showing in one bedroom and in the front room downstairs. Does that sound as if they've flown? We saw that chap go into the house and hug her earlier on, didn't we? If he has any sense he'll be bedding her while he's got the opportunity. Strange that a dried-up stick like Cotterell could produce such a pretty daughter.'

Cotterell stiffened in fury for a few moments at how they were talking about Georgie, then forced himself to calm down.

He watched as the men blew out an old-fashioned candle lamp and left the cottage. As they walked towards the village, he rejoined Mathers and reported what he'd overheard.

'They haven't captured her yet then, sir, which is good.'

'Yes. The chap who took her away from London must be good at his job. I'll owe him a lot for that. These fellows think she's still in the house next to the Tesworths. I'd bet they've left it by now. It's what I'd have done, anyway.'

'But where could they go?'

'The big house, maybe. We'll go and get Wally before we go there, though. If it comes to a fight, he'll be useful. He's a strapping young fellow.'

'We don't want to lose them.'

'Don't worry. I know a short cut or two through the village. I used to visit it as a lad, and I've called in here a few times since when I've needed somewhere to lie low.' He chuckled and added, 'I'm on very good terms with the most skilful poacher you'll ever meet.'

When they went back to the car, they saw two men rolling about on the ground, struggling in silence apart from a few grunts. One was Wally.

'Hell fire!' Cotterell muttered. 'We need to stop this before they wake the village.'

They hauled the stranger off him and Cotterell said, 'Keep quiet, you, or I'll knock you unconscious!'

The moon was starting to show, though it wasn't a full one by any means. It was enough, however, for Cotterell to recognise the man and whisper, 'Gregory Clarke, what the hell are you doing out here?'

Their captive froze for a moment, then grinned and got up as they let go of him. 'Mr Cotterell. Nice to see you again, sir. I'm just helping catch one or two villains who're trying to disturb the peace in our village. This one was lying in wait near the car, and if it's your car, he was probably going to attack you.'

Wally was alternately glaring at Gregory and trying to brush the worst of the mud from his clothes.

Cotterell stepped in. 'This one is a young relative of mine and he's helping me out tonight.'

'Ah. Sorry, lad.'

'Tell me exactly what's going on in Honeyfield,' Cotterell said. 'Every single detail.' He listened carefully to the tale of strangers causing trouble and the vague plans put together by Gregory and his friends.

'So my daughter is all right?'

'Yessir. Mr Farrell knows what he's doing. Good chap, he is.'

While he was speaking, Frank appeared out of the darkness, hands held out sideways to show he came in peace.

'This is Frank, sir,' Gregory explained.

'I know Frank.'

Frank touched his hat in a gesture of respect. 'Nice to see you again, Mr Cotterell. But we've caught a fellow over near the gates of Honeyfield House, a gentleman by the way he talks, who says he's working for you, sir.'

'His name?'

'Jordan. He's not feeling so good, I'm afraid. Our chap must have hit the noble captain a bit hard.'

'Tell your friends to save their muscles for our enemies. They can hit *them* as hard as they like.'

'They'll enjoy doing that. Everyone's a bit annoyed at having our peace disturbed.'

'And rightly so. I think we need to go to Pear Tree Lane first and see whether the men I've been watching have managed to catch my daughter.'

Frank chuckled. 'They haven't managed it. She and her friends were staying at the house next to Mr T's, but I saw all five of them leave it earlier. They went through the orchard towards Honeyfield House.'

'You're sure of that?'

'Oh, yes. I make it my business to know what other people are doing when they're out and about after dark. I've kept out of the hands of the law all these years by keeping my eyes open.'

'How many from the village are keeping watch tonight?'

Frank shrugged. 'Good few. Not sure. Ten, maybe more.'

'Right. Then I have a job for you and your friends. Get to the house in Pear Tree Lane and see if you can catch the villains who're about to attack it, thinking my daughter is still there.'

'What shall we do with them?'

'Tie them up, take them to the police station and hold them there. It doesn't matter who they say they are, if they've tried to break into that house or hurt someone you know is decent and honest, they're our enemies. I'll have some people sent down from London to take them away tomorrow, but first I've got to catch the ringleader. I doubt he'll be doing the dirty work tonight but I think he'll have felt obliged to come and oversee things here, given the importance to them of getting hold of me again.'

'Happy to oblige in any way we can, sir. Um, who is the ringleader, in case we bump into him?'

'Not someone you know. His name's Butterly and he's about five foot five tall, almost completely bald and talks very softly. You stick to hunting his minions and leave him to me and my helpers. There are a few villains around, so there will be a reward for anyone who captures one of them. Ten pounds to each man involved in a capture.'

Frank brightened. 'That's well worth fighting for. They won't escape, sir. But I think I'd better come with you and let my friend here spread the word. Otherwise someone might kill you by mistake.'

Cotterell laughed. 'Very well. This is turning into quite a farce.'

Mathers said sharply, 'Farce or not, bullets can still kill you, sir, so please don't take any chances. Frank, I want Mr Cotterell properly protected. What he's doing is important for our country.'

'Yessir.'

Cotterell took over again. 'Thank you, Mathers, but I usually manage to look after myself. Now let's go and find out who they caught up at Honeyfield House, whether it really is Jordan.'

Mathers turned to Wally. 'You're not hurt, are you?'

'Just a few bruises. Nothing to worry about.'

'Good lad.'

Mathers moved forward. 'Shall we walk there or drive, sir?'

'I think we'll drive. It might be safer to ride in a car, and anyway, I'm a bit tired. It's been rather a hectic few days. Butterly must have had quite a few people chasing me. It kept me on my toes.'

As they got into the car, Mathers asked, 'Are you sure the traitor is Major Butterly, sir? He seems such a fusspot, not at all the sort to use force. And his family goes back to the Norman Conquest. They're British to the core.'

'I'm very sure of him. There are bad eggs in every basket, you know, especially if they're paid handsomely. Butterly's family have lost nearly all their money and land. I must say he's been very cunning, had us all fooled for years with his fussy ways. It's Captain Jordan I'm not quite certain about, fairly sure, but you know me: I like to be totally correct before I act.'

'He came to the London house to keep an eye on your daughter.'

'Yes. And he had a chance to capture her then but didn't, so that speaks well for him.'

'He hired the men looking after her, ex-soldiers who'd been invalided out. He chose well. I'd have trusted them too. No, I'd not have thought him a traitor.'

'I don't really, but I'm not taking anything for granted.'

As they were about to set off, they heard a sound and Cotterell said quietly, 'Don't do anything till we see who is coming up the drive.'

## *Chapter Twenty-Seven*

Cole rushed into the kitchen of Honeyfield House. 'There's a car coming up the drive and the person isn't trying to hide his arrival. It's no one from round here or I'd recognise it. We'll take care of it; you go and hide, miss. Just to be safe.'

'Let's see who it is first,' Georgie said. 'Where can I see the car from?'

'The front drawing room, miss. This way.'

Patrick joined them. 'You're still not going anywhere on your own, remember, Georgie?'

'I was with Cole.'

'You're with *me* all the time for the moment.'

Sal watched them leave the kitchen and looked at Rosie. 'Men! They always leave the women out of it if they can, don't they? Let's go and take a peek from the dining room.'

The car drew up and a man jumped out of the front

passenger seat to hold the rear door open and allow an older gentleman to get out.

'I know that man,' Georgie said almost immediately. 'He works with my father. He's all right, I'm sure.'

Patrick studied the two men who'd got out of the car. 'Your father is chasing a traitor. I don't think you should trust anyone.'

'But Major Butterly's been at the bureau for years. He handles all the administration and paperwork, so they must trust him absolutely.'

'Nonetheless, we'll hold back and keep an eye on him.' There was a steely edge to his voice as he added, 'What better position than that from which to betray his country without being suspected?'

'But he—'

Cole said quietly, 'We can invite him in on his own and insist he leave his men outside. Then you can watch every move he makes, Mr Farrell. Just make sure you don't let him persuade you to leave with him, miss, whatever he says.'

'This is ridiculous. I tell you, he's well respected, dines with my father at his club regularly.'

'Humour us,' Patrick said quietly.

'Oh, very well.'

'I'll let him in,' Cole said.

'No, I'll let him in,' Sal said from the doorway. 'It'll look better to have a woman at the door. You go and wait at the back of the hall, Cole. It'd look strange to have you sitting in here with Miss Cotterell.'

'I'm not leaving her,' Patrick said firmly.

'Of course not.'

The door knocker sounded loudly.

She made a shooing motion towards Cole. 'Go on. Get out of sight.'

When she opened the door, she found the man who'd opened the car door for the passenger pointing a gun at her. 'Major Butterly is here to see Miss Cotterell. Take us to her. If you want to stay alive, you'll not move an inch from now on without my say-so, woman. And you'll keep your mouth shut. Not even a squeak.'

The passenger walked calmly up the steps and into the house. 'Well, where is Miss Cotterell?'

Sal didn't hesitate to tell him that. There was such an icy look in the eyes of the one holding the gun that she was certain he'd kill her without hesitation. 'Miss Cotterell is in the drawing room, sir. This way.'

'And remember, if you value your life, no move without my instructions.'

Feeling like a traitor herself, terrified they'd kill her out of hand, Sal led the way into the drawing room. There was no sign of Cole in the hall, thank goodness.

Her husband was their only hope now.

Patrick was standing behind Georgie's chair, trusting in Cole and Sal to check out the visitor. Expecting only the gentleman who'd been driven here, he was first surprised, then dismayed to see two men follow Sal into the room. She was looking terrified, and no wonder, with a gun prominently displayed in the second man's hand.

Bitter self-blame ran through him. He had failed Georgie.

She didn't say a word, but stiffened and waited.

'Stay where you are, both of you,' Major Butterly said. 'Who is this man, Miss Cotterell?'

'He's a soldier who was employed to drive me here. He was about to take his leave of me before returning home.'

'Come, come. We both know that's not true. He's been acting as your bodyguard since you left London. I want to know where he's from. What's your name, fellow?'

'Farrell, sir.'

'Come round and stand where we can see you and do not, if you value Miss Cotterell's life, make any move to resist.'

Patrick moved round to the place indicated, exaggerating his limp.

Butterly watched him with a slight frown. 'Jordan said you'd been injured, but I'm surprised he'd employ someone who walks that badly. Probably out of sentimentality.' He turned back to Georgie, leaving his bodyguard to keep an eye on Patrick and Sal. 'Has your father arrived here yet, Miss Cotterell?'

'My father? He's in London. I haven't seen him or heard from him for days.'

He studied her as she spoke. 'Your words have a ring of truth. But that only means he hasn't told you he's coming here, so I think we'll wait for him. You, woman. Go and sit in that chair in the corner and *do not move from it*.'

Sal did as he ordered, visibly shaking with terror.

'I do not require you to make conversation,' Butterly said. 'If anyone tries to escape, my friend here will shoot to kill. And he's a very good shot. Is that clear?'

They all nodded.

To Patrick's amazement, Butterly picked up a copy

of *The Spectator* from the table and began to read it.

His henchman stayed by the door, still and watchful.

Patrick felt sick to the soul for being so careless. How the hell was he going to get Georgie out of this?

Just before the turn-off to Honeyfield House a man ran out into the road, waving at them to stop.

'I know him. He's all right,' Frank said. 'Hurry up and tell Mr Cotterell whatever it is you stopped us for.'

Mathers let down the window and the man bent towards it.

'You know the car that's driven up to the big house not long ago?'

'Yes. We were just about to go and find out who was in it. Did you see?'

He nodded. 'I have good eyesight at a distance and it's starting to get light. Man with a scar on his cheek got out of the front and opened the back door to a bald fellow wearing posh clothes.'

'Was the old fellow tall or short?'

'Short.'

'What colour was what's left of his hair?'

'Gingerish.'

'I know him. He's the traitor I've been trying to trap.' Cotterell turned to Frank. 'I think you'd better get out of the car here and find your own way to the big house. Have you got a gun? Good. See if you can get inside at the back without being seen and be ready to shoot the bald man or his henchman if they get away from us. Shoot to kill.'

Frank slid quickly out of the car and set off for the trees at a loping run.

'And there's another man as says you'll vouch for him, Mr Cotterell. We got him locked in a shed. Jordan, he says he's called.'

'Ah. I was going to check him out. Can you bring him to me?'

The man beckoned and they brought Jordan out from some outbuildings. His eyes brightened at the sight of Cotterell.

'Sir, Major Butterly's the traitor, not me. And they tell me a car went up to the house a short time ago.'

'Yes. Butterly was in it. They described him to me. He'll be waiting for me there and I was already aware that he was the traitor. What I'm not sure about is whether you're working with him.'

'I'm damned well not!' Jordan hesitated, then said, 'I've been liaising with Torson at the Admiralty, actually, trying to find proof about Butterly. It was thought you had enough on your plate. I'm sorry I couldn't tell you. I was ordered not to.'

'Ah. You even knowing Torson's name speaks well for you.' Cotterell studied him. 'You don't look all that steady on your feet, so you'd better stay with these men until I've sorted things out.'

'Butterly will have you killed, sir.'

'He can try. But there are several other people at the house. It's Georgie I'm most concerned about. Wait for us here.' He looked at the man guarding Jordan. 'This man is definitely not a traitor.'

'If you say so, sir.'

The car drove on and Jordan turned to his companion. 'Look – Mr Cotterell is in grave danger. He might care most about saving his daughter, but our country needs him. We've got to go and help him, stop them killing him.'

Frank came round the side of the shed to join them. 'I was going up to the house, but waited to see what was happening. Let's get right out of sight before we discuss it, then. Have you lot no more sense than to stand there in full view of anyone passing by while you work out what to do? Best we move into the woods.'

Frank led them away from the shed and stopped behind some holly bushes. 'This place is as good as any. Keep your voices low and tell me what you're planning to do, Mr Jordan.'

'Mr Cotterell told me to stay here but I think we should go up to the house because I reckon they're planning to kill him. Before we do that, I need a handgun. They took mine away when they captured me. I'm a pretty decent shot and I may be of use to Cotterell in a crisis.'

Frank gave him a thoughtful look, then felt inside his rather baggy jacket. 'This one do? It's my spare.'

Jordan examined it. 'Good gun. Expensive. How did you get hold of it?'

Frank merely tapped the side of his nose and winked. 'I'll come up to the house with you. We don't know how many of them are still on the loose.' He turned to the other man. 'You stay outside and if the bald man or his scarred friend come out, shoot them on sight. Mr Cotterell says shoot to kill. If you'll follow me, Mr Jordan—'

'It's Captain, actually.'

He ignored that. 'I know a way through the shrubbery that takes us round to the laundry door. It can be jiggled open if you know the trick of it.'

'Wait a minute. What about the women who've taken refuge in the house? They could be used as human shields.'

'They'll have hid. Them as run the place have got a hiding place or two set up, but Sal told me some of the women have their own places too, they're that afraid of being caught by them as have hurt 'em before. You don't have to worry about them, but you do need to keep quiet.'

He led the way, followed by Jordan who proved to be surprisingly good at moving quietly.

When they got near the house, they saw the car still sitting outside the front, with a man standing beside it, looking rather nervous and holding a handgun.

Putting one finger to his lips, Frank took them on a little detour that wound up at a one-storey addition at the rear. He grinned at Jordan, pushed the poorly fitting door a couple of times as if to get the feel of it, then bounced it slightly. He let out a pleased grunt as it jerked out of its big, old-fashioned lock.

When they went inside they found Cole standing there with a couple of scrawny women, all three of them armed with laundry implements. At the sight of Frank they relaxed.

'Have you called the police?' Frank asked.

'Daren't make a noise. And what can Browning do, anyway? He hasn't even got a gun like these sods have. They keep pointing one at my Sal. Thank goodness she's had the sense to keep quiet and do as they ask.'

Jordan asked, 'What's happening?'

'They're holding Miss Georgie, Mr Farrell and my Sal in the drawing room at gunpoint, threatening to kill them if they move. Sounded as if they were waiting for Mr Cotterell. I couldn't hear what they were saying once they shut the drawing room door. I been trying to work out what to do, only I don't want my Sal hurting.'

'We've got guns but we don't want innocent folk getting hurt either,' Jordan said.

Just then they heard the sound of another car approaching.

'It's like Swindon Station here today,' Cole grumbled.

'Is there somewhere I can watch them from?' Jordan asked. 'I need to see who this is.'

'Yessir.'

'Take your boots off first or they'll hear you, however quietly you walk,' one of the women advised. 'Footsteps echo on them floorboards.'

The other men left their shoes and boots in the laundry, but Frank stuffed his into the game pockets on the inside of his overcoat. 'What I don't understand is why they aren't keeping better watch,' he said.

'Their men are scattered round the village. And anyway, Butterly is a senior figure at the bureau. When he kills Cotterell and his daughter, he'll probably blame it on Farrell and kill him too.'

Cole scowled. 'So he'll have to kill my Sal as well to keep it quiet.'

'And he won't hesitate to do that. I need to go and see what they're doing, then work out a way to stop them.'

Cotterell made Wally and Mathers get out of the car a little way up the drive, even though they protested.

'There's a high chance of someone getting killed – probably me,' Cotterell told them. 'You can help out afterwards, because you can be sure I'll take at least one of them with me. I'm gambling that I can at least save my daughter.'

The two men watched him go.

'Brave man,' Wally said.

'You don't know the half of it, lad. You all right to go on?'

Wally nodded. He didn't want to get killed, of course he didn't. But he wanted to help catch these sods. What patriotic Englishman wouldn't stand ready to serve his country?

Mathers tugged him away from the drive. 'Let's see if we can get up to the house without being seen. There's an outside chance we may be able to help him.'

Wally nodded and followed the older man.

At one point they found a little shed with some gardener's tools and Mathers picked out a long-handled fork. 'If all else fails, you can jab them with that.'

Wally nodded. He felt better with a weapon in his hand, though he didn't like the idea of stabbing right into someone's flesh with it.

He wasn't sure about anything at the moment, except that this was a bad situation and he'd do his best.

## *Chapter Twenty-Eight*

It was dawn before Cotterell drove up to the front of the house and parked his car to one side. As he got out, a man appeared from behind the big car, pointing a gun at him.

He spread his hands to show that he was unarmed and walked across to the front door quite openly.

'Keep your hands away from your pockets.'

He raised his voice. 'Nice to see you, Dewton. I was right to leave you in London, wasn't I?'

Dewton spoke even more loudly, sounding vicious. 'Leaving me there only slowed us down a bit. You're a fool to have come here. I always hated working for you, Mr Know-It-All. Stop there.' He opened the front door and gestured to Cotterell to go inside first, calling, 'Visitor for you, Major.'

Cotterell moved forward.

Butterly stood up. 'Thank you, Dewton. Have you searched him?'

'No, sir. Didn't want to do that on my own. He's a tricky sod.'

'He doesn't usually carry a gun, but please check him out.'

Dewton patted Cotterell down, removed a knife from his pocket and shook his head. 'That's all I can find.'

'Stay in the hall for now. Don't close the door to this room, in case we need you. No one else to come in or out of the house.'

'Right you are, sir.'

There was silence in the drawing room, then Butterly smiled. 'I was right. Your daughter is your weakness. No, don't sit down. Stay exactly where you are. You know what we want from you.'

'Yes. My compliance in your betrayal of our country.'

'A country that forgot its Germanic roots and needed teaching a lesson.'

'Your masters didn't manage that lesson, though, did they?'

'That's all water under the bridge for the moment. We need to make the most of a bad situation at this time. As Goldsmith said: *He who fights and runs away, May live to fight another day. But he who is battle slain, Can never rise to fight again.*'

'You always were overfond of quoting poetry, Butterly. This is real life and I think you underestimate your fellow countrymen's loyalty. May I kiss my daughter before you kill us?'

'As long as you keep your hands in full view. If you don't, she will be the first to die.'

Sal gasped and began to sob loudly.

'Shut up, woman.'

Cotterell moved forward, flicking one quick glance at Patrick.

And suddenly all was chaos.

As Cotterell reached his daughter, he flung himself in front of her and a shot from the scarred man at the door hit him in the side.

Patrick snatched up a nearby chair and hurled it across at Butterly, barely in time to stop him shooting Cotterell again.

Sal had shrieked and dived down behind an occasional table, distracting the scarred man from firing a second shot. For lack of anything else to hand she tore off her shoe and threw that across at him. She was accurate enough to spoil his aim, and the bullet meant to kill Patrick only glanced off his arm.

Outside in the hall, Cole had tackled the driver, who yelled, 'I'm on your side, you fool. Get out of my way. Mr Cotterell needs help.'

Jordan was standing in the doorway now and saw Butterly raise his gun arm again.

Wounded as he was, Cotterell was still shielding his daughter with his own body.

Without hesitation, Jordan fired at Butterly.

The bullet hit him in the forehead and he crumpled to the ground.

Patrick was wrestling with the scarred man, trying desperately to keep him from shooting again.

As Butterly fell, clearly dead, the scarred man changed tactics. He still had his gun, but he wasn't trying to use it on Patrick now, but on himself.

Cole went into the room and clubbed the scarred man on the head from behind.

As he fell, the poacher was there to kick the gun out of his hand.

The silence that followed was just as shocking as the burst of noise and explosions had been and no one moved for a few moments.

Jordan didn't lower his gun until he'd gone across and made sure Butterly really was dead.

Frank came to join him. 'Nicely done. You're a good shot, Captain.'

'Thank you.' He turned to where Georgie was cradling Cotterell in her arms. 'Is he dead?'

'No. But he's losing a lot of blood.'

Sal was beside her in an instant. 'Get me some clean kitchen rags and a bowl of water, someone. Here. Let me do this, Georgie. I've nursed a few people in my time. And I need boiled water, not water from the tap.'

Ignoring his own injury, Patrick knelt beside her as Georgie edged away from her father. 'Someone should phone the doctor and police.'

Georgie was pale but in control of herself. 'I'll do it. I saw a telephone in the hall.'

Cole came running from the kitchen carrying clean cloths. 'Rosie's bringing some boiled water.'

When Georgie came back, she paused for a moment in the doorway to take a couple of deep breaths.

Patrick and Sal were still bent over her father so she went quickly across to them. 'How is he?'

'Not dead yet,' her father said in a faint voice.

'His cigarette case kept the bullet away from his heart, but he's lost a lot of blood.'

'You're injured too, Farrell.'

'It's only a flesh wound. You're all right, Georgie? Not hurt at all.'

'No, I'm untouched. Thanks to my father and you.'

Two of the group of men who'd been clearing the villains out of the village came in through the front door and one called, 'What can we do here?'

'We've got things under control,' Jordan said. 'Who's in charge in the village?'

'Mr Tesworth.'

'Tell him to check every single house and garden, make sure the rest of this nasty bunch of thugs have either been caught or chased away.'

'He's doing that already, sir. He sent us to see if you needed help.'

There was the sound of a pony and trap.

'Who's that?'

'The doctor. Old-fashioned chap. Won't buy a car. But good at his work. I'll go out and see to the pony, sir.'

The doctor tut-tutted over the injuries, lifted the blanket covering the corpse and pronounced Butterly dead and shrank back in disgust when the scarred man spat at him and refused to be examined.

'Constable Browning will be here soon,' Frank said soothingly to the doctor.

'Well, it makes a nice change for him not to be looking for you or one of your disreputable friends, doesn't it?' the doctor snapped.

Frank chuckled. 'It does. I'll have to do something to blot my copybook again, or I won't know myself.'

* * *

Georgie went upstairs when they put her father to bed and of course Patrick followed.

She waited outside to let Mathers undress her father, then he came to summon her to the bedside.

'He won't sleep till he's spoken to you, miss. And he wants to see Mr Farrell, too.'

The two exchanged quick glances.

'You're not to let him put you off courting me,' she told Patrick firmly.

'Only you can do that, Georgie love.'

'Well, we'll be all right, then.'

Her father was lying against the pillows, looking pale and tired.

'You ought to be resting, Father. Can I get you anything?'

'Mathers will see to my needs. And I will rest once I've spoken to you. Are my eyes deceiving me or have you two turned into a couple?'

'We have. And nothing you say or do will make me change my mind.'

Patrick put his arm round her shoulders. 'He hasn't said what he wants yet, love.' He looked up to see Cotterell studying them and gave him back an answering stare before asking, 'Are you going to try to keep us apart?'

'No. I lost the woman I loved but I've never forgotten how it felt. If it's clear to me that you two feel the same way about each other, I'll give you my blessing and help you find a job of some sort.'

'No need for that, sir. I've got one in mind already and I'm considering buying a small business. I have some money saved.'

Cotterell stared at him. 'Have you, now?'

'Yes. I'm probably going to buy the car repairs busir you passed on the way into the village. Though I've plar to sell cars as well.'

'Good business to get into. Cars are the coming thing. We'll all have one some day.'

Patrick turned to Georgie, ignoring her father completely. 'I'm sorry I haven't been able to discuss the business with you properly, love. I'll show you round the place tomorrow. There isn't a house with it, so we'll have to find somewhere to live.'

She smiled. 'I've already found a place. I know you don't want to use my money but you'll let me spend it on a house, surely?'

He opened his mouth to protest, then closed it again with one of his wry smiles. 'The house next to the Tesworths?'

'Yes.'

'It needs a lot doing to it so make sure you get it at a good price.'

'We'll bargain for it together. Sadly, they never believe a woman is serious when she tries to knock the price down.'

'You're an unusual woman, love. They might believe you. Still want to work with me as well?'

Her face lit up. 'You know I do. I'm not a housewife at heart.'

'I don't want to marry a placid woman. I love your clever mind and lively attitude to the world.'

Cotterell cleared his throat and they both jumped in shock.

'Sorry to disturb you two lovebirds, but I need to rest.' He was smiling, though.

'Do we have your blessing, Mr Cotterell?' Patrick asked.

…es. I think a happy partnership is a good basis for a …rriage. She'll lead you a dance, mind.'

'I'll do my best to keep up with her.'

'Good. Now call Mathers in to help me and go away. Mind you propose to her properly. It's a bit tiring getting shot. I need to rest.' He slid down in the bed and closed his eyes.

# *Epilogue*

The wedding took place in Honeyfield and the little parish church was full, gentry and villagers cheek by jowl.

Dennis, Rosie and Martin were up at the front, at Georgie's insistence, all wearing new clothes. Rosie was also wearing a simple engagement ring and was wiping away happy tears as she waited for the bride to join the groom.

Patrick stood by the altar, feeling as if his collar was choking him, still amazed to be marrying Georgie.

He clung to one thought. If he didn't make her happy it wouldn't be his fault. He'd lay down his life for her.

His best man, Wally, nudged him with his elbow and Patrick jerked to attention, gazing along the aisle at Georgie, lovely in a simple cream silk dress and small hat with veil, coming towards him on her father's arm.

She was beaming, didn't seem to be at all nervous.

…d suddenly Patrick wasn't nervous either. They had …ng way to go with their new business and home, but …adn't wanted to wait to marry. Already part of the house was reasonably habitable and they'd do up the rest in their own time. The important thing was that they'd do everything together.

'Are you sure?' he whispered as she stopped beside him.

'Of course I am, you fool! What a time to ask me that!' She swatted at him with her bouquet.

The minister looked startled and Patrick was betrayed into a chuckle. Even Cotterell was smiling.

But as he made his responses, emotion choked Patrick's throat. To have all this: Georgie, a business, a home, and friends. So many good friends. He was the luckiest man on earth.

'I now pronounce you man and wife.'

He kissed her, smiling as he pulled away. What more could any man hope for in the peace that had followed the storms of war, but to have a woman like her beside him?

'Kiss me again,' she whispered.

So he did, and hang what anyone else expected of them. They'd make a good life together in their own way.

ANNA JACOBS is the author of over eighty novels and is addicted to storytelling. She grew up in Lancashire, emigrated to Australia in the 1970s and writes stories set in both countries. She loves to return to England regularly to visit her family and soak up the history. She has two grown-up daughters and a grandson, and lives with her husband in a spacious home near the Swan Valley, the earliest wine-growing area in Western Australia. Her house is crammed with thousands of books.

*annajacobs.com*